About the Author

Keith Dixon was born in Yorkshire and grew up in the Midlands. He's been writing since he was thirteen years old in a number of different genres: thriller, espionage, science fiction, literary. He's the author of seven novels in the Sam Dyke Investigations series and two other non-crime works, as well as two collections of blog posts on the craft of writing. When he's not writing he enjoys reading, learning the guitar, watching movies and binge-inhaling great TV series. He's currently spending more time in France than is probably good for him.

THE STRANGE GIRL

KEITH DIXON

A Sam Dyke Investigation

Semiologic Ltd

Copyright

THE STRANGE GIRL

CHAPTER ONE

DESPITE WHAT MOST people think about private investigators, I don't spend all my time waiting in my office for beautiful blonde women with mysterious eyes and long legs to walk in and offer me money to find their missing relatives.

And the first time it happened, it was just my luck she was brought by a cop.

His name was Howard, and I'd had a couple of dealings with him over the years. He was the very embodiment of the word Plod - although he was thin, almost bony, his demeanour was so heavy you felt that if he stood still long enough he'd grow roots.

So when he knocked and poked his head around my office door I wasn't expecting much in the way of entertainment.

He glanced around the empty room and nodded.

'You're in, then.'

'Apparently.'

'Got a job for you.'

Perhaps I should have sat up straight and showed some enthusiasm, but to be honest I don't have a lot of enthusiasm these days. My son, Dan, had traded Bitcoins online for me during the last three months, and I'd done surprisingly well. In fact, the income I'd made in the last three months had outstripped my investigation earnings for the last two years.

Not so good for the motivation.

Now Inspector Howard opened the door wide and stepped back. A young woman walked past him and into my life.

Is that too corny?

Possibly, but that's what it felt like. She was tall and slender, with the kind of walk that placed one foot in front of the other, like a catwalk model on a tightrope—not that kind of splay-footed amble people usually adopt when entering a space they don't know. She moved into the room as though she owned it, looked for a seat and commanded it, placing slender hands on either arm of the chair as she sat. It looked grateful to receive her.

She shook her head to release her hair and it bobbed once and settled. It was long and ebony black, framing a pale, oval face with hazel eyes at its centre. She crossed her legs, but she was seated on the far side of my desk so I couldn't see them. I didn't need to see them to know they'd be great.

I hadn't realised I'd stood up until I found myself sitting down. Howard had also come in by now and moved the other client chair to take his place beside her.

I said to the woman, 'You're not blonde.'

'Is that a problem?'

'We'll find out. I'm Sam Dyke.'

'So I've heard. Inspector Howard told me that while he wouldn't trust you, you'd probably do a good job. He said you'd be persistent. Was he right?'

'Yes. He never trusts me.'

'But are you persistent?'

'I keep trying to be. Every now and then I give up.'

She turned to Howard.

'He thinks he's funny. Will you tell him, or shall I?'

As she turned, I caught a glimpse of her profile. I've seen worse. Straight nose, delicate chin, earlobes like porcelain shells. Long eye-lashes, too, beneath a high and gently-sloping brow. I've already mentioned the black hair, but I'll add the fact that it seemed to fall in natural waves to her shoulders without any help from product or styling.

Howard leaned forward in his chair and placed a hand on my desk.

'This young lady needs your help, Dyke. I've told her you'd do the job. Don't let me down.'

'Or what, you'll never talk to me again? I can live with that.'

He didn't move and kept staring at me, his lips slightly pursed in irritation.

I shifted my gaze to the woman. 'You have the advantage of me. You know my name. I don't know yours.'

'Let me explain the situation first. Then you can tell me whether you want to hear my name.'

'I'm all ears.'

She relaxed into the chair, uncrossing her legs and reaching for her handbag. Howard leaned back and looked out of the window behind me, into Crewe town centre, as though trying to demonstrate that he wasn't going to listen to what she said. Either that or he found shoppers fascinating.

The woman had opened her handbag. She said, 'Can I smoke?'

'I'd prefer it if you didn't. It might set off the fire alarm. I don't like fires.'

She placed the handbag on the floor again, every action precise as though it had been considered for several minutes beforehand.

She said, 'My father is Lorenzo Strano, and he was a policeman. Several years ago he was found guilty of selling steroids and was sent to prison. He served eight years and was released last month.'

She paused and I wondered if she was going to cry. She'd given no sign of emotion but there was an intensity in her expression that led me to think she might just burst into tears.

I said, 'Must have been bad for a policeman in prison.'

'Probably. I wouldn't know. Since he's been released I haven't seen him.'

Howard said, 'That's where you come in.'

The woman glanced sharply at him then turned back to me.

'When my father was sent to prison my mother took me away. I was seventeen and didn't argue. I was angry with her and I was angry with him. Can you understand that?'

'Of course.'

'After that first year I went away to university and I've been away until the last few years. Now I'm back in the area and I'm something I never thought I'd say—I'm a business-woman. I have a good life with good friends and a fancy office.'

I said, 'But the simple version is that you want me to find your dad?'

'Your first deduction, I'm impressed.'

'And what do you want me to do when I find him?'

'I want you to tell me where he is.'

'And what will you do then?'

She stared at me. 'That's up to me, the client, don't you think?'

'Not if you go round to his place with a sawn-off shotgun because he abandoned you and your mother. Not if you set a gang of thugs on him. Do you see my point?'

'Not entirely. This is a financial transaction, isn't it?'

'My point is, what if he doesn't want you to know where he is, possibly for very good reasons of his own?'

She turned to Howard again.

'This isn't going well. Do you have another investigator on your list?'

I said, 'Look, I'll find him for you, if that's what you want. But you have to be prepared for the fact he might not want to be found. You might have a conversation with him and then he vanishes again. Why else do you think he hasn't been in contact?'

Her lips tightened and her hazel eyes found a touch of steel, and the atmosphere in the room gained a little electricity.

She said, 'Not that it's any of your business, but relations between my father and me weren't always good. You have to remember I was seventeen when all this happened. I daresay I blamed him for breaking up the family. And I daresay I didn't hide it.'

'What does your mother think?'

Howard brought his attention back into the room as though a code word had triggered him.

'Maria died a couple of years ago. Anjelica nursed her but the cancer took her in the end.'

A grateful look passed between the young woman and the policeman, as though he'd said something she couldn't. And now I had a name - Anjelica Strano. I liked it, though its owner was turning out to be rather spiky.

I said, 'So now your father's out of prison and you think he's steering clear of you because you weren't getting on. Did it occur to you he might be embarrassed or ashamed? Perhaps he doesn't want you to see him after eight years in a prison environment. Perhaps he's got tattoos or was beaten up. Perhaps he wants to be the one who decides when you actually see each other again.'

'I understand that. But I don't know for certain, do I?' She hesitated briefly. 'I don't want him to think I bear him a grudge.

I've grown up. I've lost my mother … I don't want to lose my father as well.'

There was no doubt it was tempting. I would have liked Anjelica Strano as a client. I would have made sure we had regular client meetings, probably in a more relaxed environment than my uncomfortable office.

But her father was an ex-cop. Which meant that to learn anything, I'd probably be talking to other policemen—something neither they nor I would like. Moreover, it seemed like a fool's errand. If he wanted to talk to his daughter it was his right to choose when and where to do it. There was no reason for me to be mixed up in this, nothing I could use to defend my involvement in the case—if it was even a case.

I said, 'I appreciate your situation, Miss Strano. But I don't think there's anything I can do for you. If I were you, I'd talk to some of his old friends and see if they know where he might have gone.'

Howard interrupted again. 'We've tried that. No one knows anything. That's why we thought we'd use a professional. But we came to you first.'

I ignored the jibe and so did Anjelica. She said, 'Don't you want to know the real reason he was sent to prison?'

'I don't see what difference it will make.'

'He gave up.'

'You mean he admitted it?'

'It was a big trial, lots of pressure. TV and newspapers. He was accused of buying and selling steroids from a man working in a gym. There seemed to be no doubt he was guilty. They found steroids in a suitcase in our house and there were witnesses who saw him talking to his supplier and other witnesses who allegedly bought from him.'

'Sounds open and shut.'

'But my dad offered no defence. For the first time in his life, he had nothing to say. Just took it, day after day in the dock, saying nothing. Didn't defend himself.'

The intensity had returned to her face, sharpening her features, putting a light in the back of her eyes. She'd laid a hand on the desk between us. Her fingers were long and slender and tipped with pink.

I said, 'So why do you think he was silent?'

'Isn't it obvious?'

'Explain it to me.'

'He was either guilty or he was protecting someone.'

'So he put himself in jail? Hard to believe, for a copper. What was his defence team doing?'

'Nothing. They barely questioned the witnesses and seemed bored most of the time.'

'You watched it?'

'A few days. Then I couldn't stand it. He'd given up, so in the end even *I* thought he must be guilty. I was young, I didn't know anything.'

'Why have you changed your mind?'

'Because I'm my father's daughter, and I don't give up. Like you, I'm persistent.'

TWENTY MINUTES LATER I'd agreed to look for Lorenzo Strano. I didn't want to and I didn't need the work. But I couldn't argue with the strength of the young woman's conviction and the fact that Howard agreed with her. He was as cold-hearted as they come, so if he'd seen enough to bring her to me, there was probably something in it.

After we'd arranged terms and she'd given me some photos of her father, they both got up to leave.

I said to her, 'How did you find the Inspector here? Why him?'

'He knew my father and was the only one to send me a Christmas card every year. Sounds silly, but it meant a lot to us. Everyone else acted as though he'd never existed.'

Howard had turned away but I thought I saw some colour in his cheek.

I said, 'That's tough. Coppers usually stick together. It doesn't bode well. If they didn't want to speak to you then, it's not likely they'll want to speak to me now.'

As if in reply, she handed me an index card on which she'd written two names and telephone numbers.

'Talk to them. They knew my dad. They wouldn't talk to the Inspector but then he's still an officer of the court, as they say. They wouldn't talk to me because … well, because they know who I am. They're probably embarrassed.'

'And you think I can bully them into talking.'

'I'm sure you'll find a way.'

I said to Howard, 'What's your opinion? Why do you think he's gone into hiding?'

'I don't have an opinion. You're on your own with this. I've done what I can because I know the family, but I can't do any more.'

I understood. He was probably acting against policy by steering the young woman towards me in the first place. It was harder these days for individual policemen to act independently, whatever their rank. His hands were almost certainly tied.

He looked as though he might add something but instead just nodded at me and led her to the door. Before she left completely she came back into the room, shook my hand and almost as an afterthought gave me a business card.

She said, 'About my name. I don't use Strano any more. There was so much publicity about the case I changed it.'

'So what do I call you now?'

Before answering she walked back to the doorway then turned to look at me from within her cloud of long black hair.

'Strano is Italian for "strange". It was my nickname at school. The Strange girl. You can call me Anjelica Strange.'

CHAPTER TWO

AFTER THEY'D GONE I sat in my chair for a while and stared at the door. Then I stared at the wall, followed by a brief session of staring at the chair in which Anjelica Strange had rested her shapely bottom. Staring seemed to replace thinking for a few minutes, but when I got back to thinking I wondered what I was doing by accepting the case. I didn't need the hassle of dealing with policemen, current or former, and I wondered whether I'd taken the job simply because I was attracted to Anjelica Strange.

It also struck me that her story was familiar to me in ways I didn't quite understand. After I'd thought about it longer I realised that her relationship with her father was similar to my relationship with my son, Dan. When we'd first met he'd been angry because he thought I'd made no attempt to find him and possibly rescue him from his foster home. The fact I had no idea he was even alive didn't reduce his animosity. Anjelica Strange's intensity when talking about her father reminded me of the fire I'd seen in Dan's eyes those first few days—the hurt of being overlooked, of being thought inconsequential. I recognised that look in her eyes, having seen it in his.

In the end I picked up the piece of paper she'd placed on my desk before leaving. She'd mentioned two men who knew her father when he'd been on the Force, and she must have known I'd capitulate because she'd written down their details before even entering my office. Her handwriting was neat and rounded and listed Gareth Leatherby and Arthur White, with mobile phone numbers for each one.

I picked up the phone and dialled the number for Gareth Leatherby and after several rings a quiet voice came on the line.

'Who's this?'

'Is this Gareth Leatherby?'

'You first. Who are you? Who gave you this number?'

I told him my name and explained how I'd come into possession of the number.

He said, 'Anjelica Strange? Strano's kid?'

'Yes.'

'I told her I wouldn't talk to her or that weasel Howard. So take a running jump, pal.'

'Do you know why she wanted to talk to you?'

'Something about her dad. Who are you again?'

'She's asked me to find him. You're the first port of call.'

'Me? You can fuck right off with that. Some kind of private nonce, are you?'

'That's what it says in my Yellow Pages ad—Nonce to the Stars. Where can I meet you?'

'You can't.'

'You haven't hung up yet. You're interested, admit it.'

'Funny man.'

'You're in a pub or a bar, aren't you? I can hear pool in the background.'

He said nothing for a few seconds.

'So that's right—it's about her dad?'

'Came out of prison and she hasn't seen him since. She just wants to know he's okay.'

Another pause.

Then he said, 'The Regina, Shelton. Up past Saint Mary's Church, on the corner, near the Land Rover garage. I'm in on the right. I'll be here another hour.'

'I'll be wearing a carnation in my button-hole.'

'Better not. You wouldn't get through the door.'

IT TOOK ME half an hour to get down the A500 and take the turn-off up into Shelton, a nondescript urban outlier of the greater Stoke-on-Trent conurbation. It was heading towards Monday lunchtime but still quiet on the roads, although that might have been because no one actually wanted to go there.

In the midst of the red-brick commercial wreckage that was the main road through Shelton, St Mary's Church stood like a beacon of Victorian propriety, set back from the road in its own lush green grounds and thrusting upwards as though promising sanctuary from the broken-backed and commonplace existence surrounding it.

But like most people, I suspect, I barely gave the church a glance as I passed the Land Rover garage and found a parking place close to The Regina. It was an old urban pub that had been renovated a few years ago but had quickly returned to its former level of decrepitude, like a dressed-up tramp who prefers his worn-out jacket and string belt to a smart suit.

Its large wooden door was tough enough to withstand a horde of thirsty navvies a hundred years ago, but when I wrestled it open and went inside I saw Leatherby at once. He was wearing L'Air de Cop—the set of his shoulders, the alertness in his eyes, even his conservative dress sense added up to serving or former Police Officer. And of course he was sitting at a table alone, nursing a long dark pint.

I bought a beer from the woman at the bar and slid in opposite Leatherby.

'I forgot my carnation.'

'I could tell you were private straight away. Come in like you own the place.'

He was heavy-set across the chest and had started on a series of chins, but his eyes moved quickly and his complexion was relatively unlined. He was somewhere in his late fifties judging by his thinning hair and the first liver spots on his hands. I thought maybe he'd kept himself fit when younger but had given up when it became too hard.

I said, 'Why'd you agree to a meeting with me when you wouldn't talk to Anjelica or Howard?'

'I must have forgotten. Do that all the time now. Wait till you get older, you'll see—you forget lots of stuff. Important stuff.'

He took a sip from his pint, looking at me carefully over the top of the glass. Cagey. Telling me he wasn't going to give anything away without a fight.

I said, 'When did you know Lorenzo Strano? Did you work together?'

Another sip, taking his time, then he put the glass down and wiped his bottom lip almost delicately before speaking.

'No sweet nothings? No chocolates? If you're going to shag me you could at least act as if you like me. Don't they teach you anything these days?'

I leaned back and crossed my arms, told myself to slow down. I was on his turf and he was in charge because he had the answers to the questions.

I glanced at my watch.

'You've got somewhere to be in twenty minutes. I didn't want to waste your time.'

He nodded, as though he approved of my change of tack.

He said, 'So who's paying you? The girl?'

'She's the client. But you didn't hear that from me.'

'Yeah, I guessed. Mother's dead, if I remember right. Pretty woman. Big eyes, Italian genes in there. Girl must be what, mid-twenties?'

'Around there.'

He put his drink down and leaned back on the bench seat. Behind him an alcove led into a small room where a couple of men with shaved heads were playing pool, the balls clacking together insistently and punctuated by the men's cries of jeering disbelief or open-throated triumph. The rest of the bar was empty except for a young couple having a hissing argument in a far corner. The place smelled of dead beer.

Leatherby said, 'She thinks he didn't do it, right? Daughters and dads. He can't do any wrong. My guess is he's gone off because he's embarrassed. Ashamed. One or the other. He's done the time and just wants to sink into the wallpaper now.'

'So you think he did do it?'

'I didn't say that.'

'You suggested.'

'Did she tell you what happened? I mean, the case?'

'Not in so many words.'

He nodded again. 'We worked in a unit run from Stafford but with an office in Boothen Road.' He glanced up at me, checking I knew Boothen Road was where Stoke Police HQ was situated. 'Right shit-hole it was. We mostly worked fraud, white collar stuff. Never saw an actual villain from one week to the next. They were just names on paper.'

He went on to repeat what Anjelica had told me—that Strano had been caught buying and selling steroids and the case had been notorious because he was a serving policeman.

'We should have known something was going on. He was never interested in keeping fit, but he'd joined a gym a few months previous. Before you know it he's made a contact and he's on the streets selling steroids. Class C drug. Fourteen years maximum for supplying. A couple of solid witnesses to the buy. Suitcase full of the stuff in his wardrobe. No one sticks up for him, not his boss, nobody. It was a first offence and he might even have got off if he hadn't been a copper. Made an example of him.'

'Who was his boss?'

'Passmore. Billy Passmore. He was supposed to be a friend of Strano's. You wouldn't know it, the way he clammed up. Disowned him. Looked the other way. Biblical, it was—Pontius Pilate or whatever, washing his hands.'

He'd lowered his voice and I looked around to see if someone else had come into the bar. There was no change, except the arguing couple had given up hissing and had stopped talking altogether.

I said, 'Why do you think Passmore didn't stand up for him?'

At this point Leatherby became vague. He looked away, shrugged, took a pull on his drink. He felt me staring at him and caught my eye briefly before looking away again. He coughed.

'You'd have to talk to him about that. It's just what I saw.' He knew this wasn't enough, because he added, 'Don't get me wrong—I think Strano was guilty. There was too much evidence.'

He made this point by placing his finger firmly upright on the table, as though pinning the evidence beneath it. I took a sip from my beer, which was warm and flat.

I said, 'Would you have said you knew him, before he did what he did?'

'I worked with the bastard, didn't I? Shared a desk. Same office for five years, us two and half a dozen others. You'd think

I'd know him, wouldn't you? But if you'd have asked me, I would have said I knew fuck all.'

'So were you surprised when he was caught dealing?'

'Not so's you'd notice. You have to understand: he was always a bit up himself, believed his own publicity. Didn't really have any friends. Never mingled, just went home to the missus. So we never knew what he was up to when he was off work. He was tight with Passmore, though. Had dinner round his place and so on, when Passmore was still married. Poor bugger, his wife ran off with a funeral director. That was worth a laugh. Not sure he saw it that way, mind you.'

We both thought about women for a moment.

Then I said, 'Why do you think he did it?'

'What, sell drugs? How the hell do I know? Perhaps he was bored. Perhaps he needed the money. His girl was coming up to university age, perhaps he wanted to give her a going-away present.'

'Did he ever flash the cash? New car? Fancy suits?'

He snorted. 'He was always the best-dressed of any of us. Italian taste. Good-looking bloke, too, jet black hair even into his forties. His wife worked in an office somewhere, so they did all right. If he did make any money he kept it quiet. Perhaps it's in another suitcase somewhere. Maybe he picked it up after he was released. Perhaps he's on the Costa del Sol as we speak.'

'Didn't you think it strange that he just started dealing, out of nowhere? Didn't anybody ask him why?'

'He wouldn't see any of us when he was inside. A couple of my mates tried to see him but he refused. Just his defence brief and I suppose his wife and kid. I don't know what he said to them. Didn't the daughter say anything to you?'

I hesitated. 'I'll get to that.'

'You didn't ask, did you?' He laughed humourlessly. 'Take it from me, it's a family that doesn't give much away. You won't get to know them. And I doubt you'll find him. If he wants to be gone, he'll be gone.'

I was getting near the end of my drink and my patience. Leatherby had the usual embittered cop's self-justification high on his agenda.

I said, 'So you worked with him for five years and never saw any signs of dishonesty before, though you didn't actually like him. Why didn't you stand up in court and tell them he was an honest burgher?'

'"Honest burgher?" Fuck me, read a book, have we? I didn't say anything because I wasn't asked. His defence was crap and more or less rolled over. And he wasn't much better, just sat there in the dock and said nothing. I thought he was guilty then and I think it now, but he didn't put up much of a fight. We all saw it in his face. We thought he'd done it and been caught and there was nothing we could do, even if we'd liked the bastard and wanted to.'

'So much for cops sticking by each other.'

At last this got to him. He leaned forward and poked a nicotine-stained finger at me.

'Listen, I've got no brief for the job now. They dumped me when I was surplus to requirements. Down-sized when I had good years left in me. But Strano brought it on himself. He didn't want to know us, acted as though he was better than nine-tenths of the people he mixed with. Except the boss, then he laid back and let himself be fucked. So he got what he asked for. But he didn't complain and we turned over and got on with it. There were some changes made to the unit, reorganisations, Passmore moved upwards to the starry heavens and a year later

Strano was forgotten. That's it. I've said everything I'm going to say, so don't let the door bang your arse on the way out.'

I stood up and dropped a ten-pound note on the table.

'Have the next one on me. And the couple after that. Don't drown in your own shit.'

He picked up the note, turned it over, then without looking at me tore it in half and let it drop to the floor. I walked out.

Outside I breathed in deeply and the air felt clean and light, as though my lungs were finally able to filter out the heavy coating of self-pity and misery that seeped from Leatherby's pores.

But I was beginning to see a problem with this job: if Strano had no friends amongst the people he worked with, who else was left?

CHAPTER THREE

GOLF CLUBS IN Cheshire are like casinos in Las Vegas—unavoidable, and full of people with an exaggerated faith in their ability.

The following morning I drove up a long pebbled drive to the front entrance of Jenner's Park golf course, a secluded and selective establishment south of Wilmslow. It was more than a golf club—it was a complete leisure environment, as I'm sure the brochure made clear. I passed under a redbrick gatehouse, drove by the tennis courts and the covered swimming pool and found a parking slot around the back of the faux nineteenth century clubhouse. When I climbed out of my Mondeo I smelled the tang of conifers and heard the thwack of ball against racket. We were well into autumn and the air was cooler each day, but out here in the Cheshire countryside they had an arrangement with a compliant deity to ensure it was never too cold or too windy. I took off my leather jacket to appear more like One of Us when I went inside.

My understanding of golf clubhouses was that somewhere there was a bar and the rest of the space was filled with lockers and maybe showers. But that was obviously old-school thinking, because this place was like an upscale hotel—reception, conference rooms, two restaurants. It might have started as a golf club but it had ambitions beyond itself.

Arthur White had told me to meet him in the Nicklaus Room, so I did. A solid wooden bar curved from the entrance door for about a hundred yards—probably a solid wedge shot—and the floor space stretched away filled with comfy low leather chairs and sofas, heavy aluminium and glass tables scattered between them. A wide picture window at the far end gave a close-up view of the eighteenth hole, two duffers in primary-coloured pullovers just finishing off and shaking hands.

Arthur White was sitting by himself furiously thumbing his phone with both hands. He'd described himself perfectly—to a tee, you might say. He had straight white hair cut short, a round pink face and wore a tight-fitting suit and tie. Sweating slightly, he looked like a car salesman desperate for the first sale of the month.

He glanced up at me but carried on typing, finally flinging the phone down on to the padded sofa.

'Dyke?'

'That's me. Have I come at a bad time?'

'What, that?' He gestured towards the phone. 'Bloody wife. You wouldn't think we were divorced two years ago. She has more say over what I do now than she did before. Don't get married. And if you do, never get divorced. Are you married?'

I shook my head. 'Not now.'

'Good man.' He pointed to the chair next to him. 'Don't stand there like a lemon. Can I get you something to drink? Roger knows me, he'll bring us a couple of G and T's, if you like.'

I sat down. 'Not for me. You go ahead.'

He sat upright on his seat and raised an imperious arm, showing a stained pit beneath it. His hand made some kind of masonic gesture and then he gave the thumbs-up to Roger behind the bar, who presumably had understood the code.

White brought his focus back to me and looked me over as though he hadn't been paying attention before.

He said, 'I didn't mention it when you phoned because it didn't occur to me. But you do realise I didn't know Strano professionally, don't you?'

'I was told you worked in the police at the same time. Wasn't that true?'

'Oh it's true enough, but I never worked *with* him. We were barely ever in the same building together. I worked from Stafford. I was an SIO—Senior Investigative Officer. Big cases. I was never really sure what he did, to be honest. Kept it to himself.'

'So how *did* you know him?'

'Photography. We were in a photography club together, sponsored by HQ. Upskilling, I suppose they'd call it. A man from what used to be the Polytechnic came over and gave courses and Strano and me used to talk. Nice guy.'

Something had been nagging at me about White and I suddenly realised what it was: his accent. This was Cheshire Central, with membership of the golf club probably running to several thousand pounds a year. But White had the distinctive burr of the native Stokie. Without being snobbish, I wouldn't have thought this environment was his natural home. He must have saved up a lot of his pennies. Or twisted somebody's arm.

I said, 'So what did you think when he got sent down? Were you surprised?'

He looked around and leaned forward on the leather sofa, which squeaked a complaint. His eyes peered up at me from his pink, polished cheeks and oozed sincerity.

'I tell you now, the reason I agreed to talk to you today was because he was fitted up. I didn't believe he was guilty then and I don't believe it now.' He sat back, still staring at me as if to convince me by sheer force of eye-contact. 'He was no saint, but I never saw anything nasty in him. I'm a good judge of character, me. I didn't get to be an SIO without looking into the souls of a lot of bad people. It wasn't in him.'

'Did you talk to anyone about it? Raise any doubts?'

'I had a few words with my boss, but there was nothing we could do. I'd have stood up in court for him but was never asked. I tried to see him but he wasn't taking visitors. I haven't seen him since.'

Roger arrived at that point with White's gin and tonic and a little plastic stirrer to move the slice of lime about. The best places serve lime with their gin. When Roger had gone, White picked it up eagerly and drank about a third in one go. You would have thought he hadn't taken in liquids for a week.

Looking at me carefully, he said, 'He must be about ready to come out now. Why are you involved? What kind of investigation is it?'

I'd been sparing with the details when talking to him on the phone, but he didn't seem to need them. He'd been surprisingly quick to agree to a meeting.

I said, 'He's been out a month, actually. No one's seen him. People just want to know he's okay. He hasn't been in touch with you?'

'Me? Why me? I only met him once a month for about a year. Not exactly one of his best mates.'

'So why do you think your name came up as one of his friends? Someone I should talk to about where he might be?'

He took another sip of his drink. Everyone I talked to lately seemed to be drinking. Perhaps it was my charming presence.

He said, 'I guess he knew I was on his side. I didn't get to see him, but I did write to him, at least in the beginning. He never wrote back so I gave up. Perhaps it meant something to him that a fellow officer still believed in him.'

'Very touching.'

'Call it what you want. You should know something about me, Mr Private Investigator. I've been a loyal member of the police force for nearly forty years. I never made it to the pinnacle because … well, not everybody can. The point of a pyramid is that there's a point at the top. You can't all stand on it. So I might be doing desk work now and have more free time on my hands than I want. But I know the job and I knew a good man when I saw him.'

I let him cool down for a moment, then said, 'What do you know about Billy Passmore?'

He frowned and swirled the ice cubes in his glass.

'Funny you should mention that name.'

'Why's that?'

'He's a bit in the news, isn't he? Going to be heading up some new anti-corruption unit, taking in all of the various forces from the Midlands northwards. Big wallah.'

'Is he up to the job?'

He lifted his head quickly, his white hair flashing under the chandeliers.

'You didn't hear otherwise from me.'

'But.'

'You know that old saying about the fox and the hen-house — you wouldn't put one in charge of the other.'

'You're saying he's corrupt himself?'

White put his glass on the table and looked around. The two duffers from the eighteenth hole had brought their bright pullovers into the bar and were ordering loudly from Roger. At the bottom end of the room a man in a dark suit was making some kind of computer presentation to a smartly-dressed woman; I realised his droning voice had formed the backdrop to the conversation between White and myself. I heard a vacuum cleaner somewhere. It was still only ten o'clock and White was on his way to being drunk. Perhaps the gin and tonic hadn't been his first.

He suddenly reached out and grabbed my wrist.

'No one knows we had this conversation, right? I could make your life really dismal otherwise.'

'Do I look like I'm taking notes?'

He let go of my wrist.

'There were always rumours about Passmore but nothing was ever said out loud. Maybe that's the definition of a rumour.'

'What kind of rumours?'

'Nothing specific. A vague rumour. Even foggy. Misty.'

'Arthur, if you've got something to say, say it.'

He glanced around again then picked up his glass and stared forlornly at its emptiness. I thought he might pull out the slice of lime and suck it for the remnants of alcohol it contained.

He said, 'He had a problem. Some said it was behavioural, but that covered a multitude of whatsits. Others said it was a tendency to addictions. He used to smoke a lot, apparently. And he did some weird things. Wear the same tie every day for a month, then change it for another. Take his car to the car wash every night. Stuff like that.'

'Sounds anal but harmless.'

'You'd think so, wouldn't you? But when you're a senior copper these things have ramifications. They impact on people. They take note.'

I was confused now. Leatherby had said Strano was definitely guilty and had known what he was doing. White was telling me Strano was a good guy and his boss was the odd one. I wouldn't say either Leatherby or White were objective witnesses, though, which meant the case had become more complicated.

As always.

CHAPTER FOUR

AFTER I LEFT White starting his next G and T, I drove back to my office in Crewe. Some more heat had come into the air and there were shoppers parading around with almost an air of late-summer abandon in their short-sleeved shirts and thin summer dresses.

My office is over an empty furniture store, left in darkness a few years ago by the Croatian guy who found it too expensive to import and sell East European furniture, especially when most of the stuff his competitors were selling was brought in from China. He went back to Croatia muttering about foreign imports, which was pretty rich, actually.

I spent the afternoon on paperwork and a little bit of online research about Strano. There was a lot in the archives of the local newspapers, though not so much nationally. Strano was positioned as a rogue policeman with a previously unblemished record. There were quotations that seemed polished enough to come directly from the police press office rather than the various senior officers to whom they were attributed, and a couple of photographs of a dignified but sad Strano walking into the courthouse building where he was being tried. He was a broad man with a lush mop of black hair and thick eyebrows, and I saw where Anjelica Strange got her looks from.

In the end I didn't learn much more from the Internet than I'd learned from the people I'd already spoken to, so at five o'clock I shut up the office, walked out into the warm air and drove home.

My house is still technically in Crewe, but sits on the edge of the countryside that lies close to the main route heading past the train station on the way out to Nantwich and Chester. You turn off a back road on to a track between tall trees and negotiate a bend in the track before you see the house itself, a redbrick building that someone told me was probably built as a vicar's lodge judging by its shape and size, though part of the lower floor was subsequently turned into a garage with a sunken pit and large doors to one side. I'd redesigned this section so there was a gym where the garage had been, with large picture windows above it that angled around the building to look out over the fields behind.

I always liked my first sight of the house as I turned the bend in the track, so I didn't want it to be spoiled by the sight of a big black vehicle parked on the clearing in front of the downstairs windows. It was one of those creepy long wheel-base monsters that look as though they've been extended at the rear like a beetle with an extra jointed carapace. It was probably American. The windows at the back were tinted, but I didn't have to wonder about who was inside because as I pulled up both rear doors opened and a couple of giants got out and stood upright, squinting in the sunlight as though they'd been kept in the dark and fed growth hormone. One was blonde and elongated, like a Swedish swimmer. The other was swarthy around the jaw and had the large features of a Cro-Magnon cave-dweller.

They came around their monster car and leaned with their backs against it, folding their arms. When I climbed out of the

Mondeo I felt like Gulliver in reverse. I tried to stand tall but it was wasted effort.

The dark one spoke in a voice with the bass turned way up. 'You Sam Dyke?'

'Who wants to know?'

'I do. Me and him.' He jerked a thumb towards his fair colleague, who nodded sagely, then added, 'Don't bother asking us in for tea. We're delivering a message.'

'Looks like the Post Office must be over-staffed.'

'We hear you're looking for Larry Strano. Don't bother. He's all right. He doesn't want to be found. In fact, he wants to be left alone. Ain't that right, Terry?'

Terry unfolded his long arms and pointed a finger at me as though he didn't want to lose the competition to be the most intimidating thug.

He said, 'That's right. Left alone.'

'Oh come on, boys. You'll have to do better than that.'

The first thug frowned dramatically. 'You ain't listening, are you? We was told you'd try to resist our charms. You don't want to see our charms.'

'How can I resist them unless I see them?'

This confused both of them and they glanced at each other before standing upright and lowering their arms.

I said, 'Look, boys, I just want to know where this is coming from. How do I know Mr Strano is really okay? You might have used your charms on him for all I know. He might be in the boot of your car.'

They both glanced at the boot of their car, as though surprised to find it had one.

The first thug said, 'He's not in the boot of the car. I don't know where he is. He has friends looking after his interests, that's all you need to know.'

I took a shot in the dark, which admittedly was a risky thing to do when confronted by two cave-men.

I said, 'How did Leatherby know where to find me?'

Give him his due, Cro-Magnon Thug did his best to cover up his look of surprise—he fought his eyebrows into submission and barely widened his eyes at all. It was his friend Terry who gave the game away with his startled sideways glance.

Cro-Magnon Thug said, 'Who's Leatherby?' but his heart wasn't in it. Now working too hard on his air of innocence, he said, 'I don't know anyone called Leatherby.'

I said, 'Ex-cop, bitter smell to him. Very smooth skin, if you notice that kind of thing.'

He decided not to follow my line on this. 'Our boss is a man with connections. You don't want to get on his wrong side. Larry Strano has got friends now, and they're looking after him. So leave him alone.'

'What if I say no?'

Frighteningly, both of them smiled at the same time, as though this was a word they'd been waiting to hear.

'You don't wanna say no.'

'I might, just to see you get your charms out.'

Cro-Magnon Thug elbowed Terry in the ribs and pointed at me, the smile still pulling at his lips, which were thick and pink.

'I got him going with that, dint I? You and me have got charms, Terry. Shall we use our charms?'

Terry didn't say anything but took a quick step forward and whipped a heavy fist into my gut. Although I'd been prepared for it, he still moved faster than he had any right to for a man of his size. That'll teach me to make assumptions.

The air whoomped out of me and I doubled over, readying myself for a chop on the back of my head.

But nothing came. Terry had stepped back, job done.

I staggered back to lean against my own car, and when I looked up they were both standing with their arms folded again, watching me closely as though interested in how I'd react. I reacted by trying to breathe.

Eventually I wheezed, 'Your charms are irresistible, Terry. Though I can't speak for your mate.'

This amused the pair of them and they punched each other on the arms joshingly for a while, until I was able to stand upright again.

Cro-Magnon Thug said, 'That's what we in the trade call fair warning. Right? You've been fair-warned. Forget you ever heard about Larry Strano. He's off your whatchamacallit ... radar.'

They stood still for another few seconds, as if waiting for another wisecrack, then moved to open the rear doors of the black car again and vanished inside. I imagined them leaning back in their seats and switching themselves off, waiting to be turned on and pointed towards the next target. The car, whose driver I still hadn't seen, came to life with a roar and reversed swiftly, then leaped forward and swept out of my driveway leaving a cloud of both real and metaphorical dust behind it.

STILL DOUBLED OVER, I went inside and sat down. I'd only talked to Arthur White that morning, so it must have been Leatherby who had passed on the word yesterday ... but to whom? The two mechanical giants weren't at the top of any hierarchy to which they belonged—in fact they'd said as much—so what was Leatherby doing by talking about me to someone else? And who was the man with 'connections'?

Anyone who knows me knows the worst thing you can do to put me off a job is to make it a challenge. I found my phone and the information Anjelica Strange had left and rang her.

She answered promptly, sounding as though she needed to be elsewhere. After I described what had happened she thought for a moment but then said she had no idea who the big men might be, and why Leatherby might have set them on my trail.

She said, 'And they just turned up at your house? And told you to stop looking for my dad?'

'They were rather forceful. Not exactly a polite request.'

'So what are you going to do? You're not giving up, are you? Howard said you're like a dog with a bone.'

'He likes a good cliché. No, I'm not giving up. I just thought you ought to know some unsavoury people might be involved. Whatever your dad's up to, I doubt he's turned to religion.'

'Funnily enough, he was a Catholic. He didn't go on a Sunday but he was quite strict with me. Swearing and boys and stuff. That was one reason we fought.'

'You were an attractive seventeen-year-old girl.'

'Don't get pervy on me.'

We stopped talking for a moment.

Then she added, 'So you reckon Leatherby told someone.'

'What do you know about him?'

'Nothing. Inspector Howard found his name by digging, trying to find out who worked with my dad before he was sent down. Apparently there was nobody else around. Everyone's moved on. And Arthur White's name was in a file somewhere. He'd registered some sort of official notification that he thought my dad was being treated badly. Howard and I thought he might be a good person to talk to.'

'He still believes your dad was set up, but no one would listen to him then and he seems to have stopped thinking about it.'

'I don't even care about all that now. I just want to know my dad's okay, perhaps talk to him to check him out. You've worried me with these thugs you've told me about. I hope he's not doing anything stupid.'

I didn't tell her the same thought was on my mind. Prison might not have punished Lorenzo Strano at all—simply introduced him to a different brand of crime and criminality.

CHAPTER FIVE

I WARMED UP the remains of a casserole I'd made on Sunday and ate it while watching the news. War, drones, invasions and bad weather. The world was going to hell in a handcart. All I could do was make a living and keep my head down.

Afterwards I found my phone again and called Dickie Baines, an ex-colleague from my stretch working for the government. He was a big man who'd managed to roll with the punches whenever the current government rearranged its agencies. He was my only contact left with any juice these days.

He said, 'Still pushing the rock uphill with your nose?'

'Still defrauding Her Majesty's Government by accepting a salary?'

We grinned down the phone line at each other.

He said, 'So what do you want? You never call, you never write … except when you want something.'

I outlined the case briefly without naming Lorenzo Strano or his daughter. I then told him I'd been paid a visit by two big men who didn't want an argument.

He laughed. 'You've got a licence plate, haven't you?'

'Might have.'

'You know, I was talking to my boss about you the other day. You remember Dave Nisbett?'

'Jesus, he's your boss now?'

'They either had to sack him or promote him. Guess which way they went. Anyway, we were laughing about that time you bluffed your way into that warehouse. Do you remember?'

I remembered all too well. I'd told a white lie to the owner of a warehouse we suspected of holding half a million illegal cigarettes. He'd let me in when he really didn't have to, and we found the goods. He'd eventually been sent down for a couple of years, but I was hauled over the coals for short-cutting The Process and a mark was made on my record. Together with all the other marks, it helped undermine my position later, when things became seriously dark and difficult. Impetuosity has not always been my friend.

Dickie went on, 'Anyway, the guy who owned the warehouse—'

'Tommy Warnes.'

'—that's right, Big Nose Tommy Warnes, he's just been done for importing Uzis. Can you believe it? He must have been nuts to try it, with his record. Sign of the times, Sam, sign of the times.'

'I watch the news.'

'Bet you're glad you're out of it. We're in a war and no one talks about it. Guns, drugs, white slavery, girls. It's like the fucking eighteenth century all over again.'

I didn't like the sound of this. Dickie had always kept a sense of proportion about what he did but this had the feel of a right-wing rant about to kick off.

I said, 'So if I were to give you a number, do you have access to the right sort of computer? All the right codes and everything to do a friend a favour?'

'All right, all right, ignore what's happening around you, Sam. I get the idea. You're in private practice now and don't need to see the big picture.'

'Just in a bit of a rush.'

'You always were a user. All right, give it to me.'

I read out the licence plate number of the black monster car from the pad I'd scrawled it on.

He said, 'You at home?'

'Use my mobile. I'm going out as soon as we finish.'

'Right. Another damsel in distress to rescue.'

'Don't get bitter, Dickie. It's bad for the stomach.'

He swore colourfully at me and then hung up. I put the handset back on its charger and felt a surge of regret. I hoped Dickie Baines wasn't being discouraged and corrupted by the world he inhabited—and I'd managed to escape through sheer good luck and bad planning.

JUST AS IT was beginning to grow dark I went out to my car and drove round to Dan's house, out on the far edge of Crewe near Leighton Hospital. We'd seen more of each other in the last three months than in all his previous twenty odd years, largely because he'd begun to act as a kind of business manager for me. Since he'd persuaded me to trade in Bitcoins online we'd both done well from it. So well it was now his full-time job and could almost replace mine, if I didn't get so bored staring at a computer screen all day.

I picked up a couple of cans of beer from shop at the petrol station and knocked on his door about eight o'clock.

He opened up, saw the beer, and grinned. 'That's the kind of dad I like. Come in and let's start recycling the profits.'

When I first met him he was an average teenager but with even worse habits. Since then he'd cleaned up—his hair was short, he dressed in dark blue jeans and polo shirts and was more often shaved than not. If anything, I tended to be scruffier than him. From time to time I recognised his mother's genes in the way he looked at people from under his eyelashes, but I was beginning to see more of myself in his no-nonsense approach to conversation and willingness to get down to business rather than endlessly discuss it.

But we sat in his living room and talked for a while anyway. He'd painted the walls white and bought some large prints of American cities from Ikea. With its simple style and bland furnishing, the whole house was rather like a modernist art gallery.

He told me how things were progressing with his business and I told him about Lorenzo Strano and his daughter, and about the people I'd spoken to. I left out the two thugs—I didn't want him to worry about his old man.

He said, 'Have you done your research yet?'

'Some, but I thought you might have more sources than me.'

He stood up and fetched a laptop, then sat on the sofa again. I took a couple of pulls on my beer and watched him get to work.

After five minutes he said, 'I've found a couple of police usenet newsgroups where they were having a go at him.' He looked up and saw me staring at him blankly. 'Newsgroups are like old versions of internet forums. You can post messages and stuff. They call it 'news' but it's just anything you want to say.'

I dimly remembered people talking about them when I worked for Customs & Excise, but I'd never used one myself.

'What do you mean by having a go at him?'

'They reckoned he was guilty and brought the police into disrepute, that kind of thing.'

'Is there anyone standing up for him?'

'Well I'm only looking at a small section here … but no, they're piling in. I get the idea they wouldn't have minded if he was just using the steroids—lots of police are body-builders and body-builders use. But selling them was stupid.'

'Okay, thanks. Anything else?'

He worked away for a few minutes then pursed his lips.

'Have you come across William Passmore?'

'They call him Billy.'

'He was Strano's boss at the time. No one likes him, it seems. Bit of a slave-driver, stickler for rules and regulations.'

'What's he up to now?'

Dan looked up at me, fingers poised on the keyboard.

'Why now?'

'Just interested. Strano went down, I think Passmore went up. Is there anything about him at the moment?'

More typing and use of the laptop's touchpad. Some reading and a bit of lip-pursing.

Then he said, 'Good timing, Dad.'

'Yeah?'

'He's about to become head of a new anti-corruption unit based in Stafford with an office in Stoke. He's the coming man, according to the Police Gazette.'

'I thought only coppers could read that.'

He winked at me. 'It's all online now—which means I can read it. Don't tell anyone.'

Arthur White had mentioned Passmore's appointment to head up the anti-corruption unit but it was good to hear the information corroborated from an official source.

'Does it say anything else about him or the job?'

Dan read a bit further. 'Says his brief is to focus on the relationship between organised crime and corruption of individual officers. Says corruption within the police is actually low compared to other countries but there are areas of concern, such as misuse of IT systems, perverting the course of justice, the growth of crime syndicates and their impact on individual policemen and women.'

I said, 'Sounds like a big job.'

'What are you thinking?'

'I'm sure Mr Passmore is an honest and upright pillar of society.'

'But … '

'But nothing. You have a suspicious mind for one so tender in years.'

He grinned again. 'I wonder where I got it from.'

Before I could reply, my phone rang. I stood up and walked into Dan's kitchen to answer. It was Dickie Baines.

He said, 'Interesting people you know. I should follow you around, meet some fascinating characters.'

'Who were they?'

'Who? Those big wannabes? I have no idea.'

'You're toying with me, aren't you?'

'It's fun. The car they were driving comes back to someone called Jack Jenkins.'

'Who is … ?'

'Another interesting person, I'm sure. But we have nothing. All I know is that he's the owner of a new casino in Hanley. That's an oxymoron, isn't it? Gambling and the high-life in the middle of the Potteries. I can barely restrain my excitement.'

'So he's a good guy?'

'God's sake, Sam, he runs a gambling emporium. Do the math, as our American cousins say.'

CHAPTER SIX

I SOMETIMES THINK in this job I should give up planning and just walk out the door to see what happens next.

A case in point was the following morning.

I intended to drive to my office and make a few calls, see what I could find out about Jack Jenkins and his new casino.

So I opened my front door ready to breathe in the clean semi-country air … and there was another car on my drive. I'd been in the kitchen and hadn't heard it crunching over the gravel. It was a nondescript Japanese something—an old beige Nissan or Datsun with rust patches creeping up like rising damp at the bottom of the doors. The kind of car students were driving twenty years ago.

I stepped out and approached the car and the driver opened his door and stood up.

Lorenzo Strano turned and faced me. He looked older than the photos his daughter had given me, which was only natural. But he looked older than he should have done for his age—seamed in the face, grey at the temples, bulky around the chest, seemingly much older than his forty-seven years. I guess a prison atmosphere will do that to you, together with the stress.

He came around the front of the car and stood almost hesitantly with his arms hanging at his sides. There was a tightness in his demeanour as if he was uncertain what he was supposed to do. We stared at each other for a few seconds, listening to the calls of some starlings in the trees.

Then he nodded at me and said, 'I'm Larry Strano. Are you Mr Dyke?'

'Yes—what are you doing here?'

'Can we go inside?'

I turned and led him back into the house. He looked around nervously as though he thought someone was going to leap out of one of the rooms.

I offered him coffee but he refused. In the end we wound up in my kitchen, sitting either side of the square wooden table and surrounded by the cloying smell of bleach I'd tipped down the sink that morning to clean it out.

He wore a buttoned-down pink shirt and the knot of a florid red tie bulged at his adam's apple. His suit was charcoal grey. He folded his hands together on the table and looked past me, out through the windows to the garden.

'Nice place. Like a bit of countryside.'

'What do you want, Mr Strano? Why are you here?'

His eyes came back to mine.

'You ever spent any time behind bars, Mr Dyke? Got drunk one night, perhaps, had to sleep it off?'

'I was arrested once on suspicion of murdering my ex-wife. Will that do?'

His expression didn't change and I wondered at first whether he'd heard me. Then I realised he was on a mission and wasn't actually listening to what I might say. He had a message and he was going to deliver it.

He said, 'No fun, is it, being behind bars? Not exactly Newgate Prison these days, but when your liberty goes, it hurts. Can't go where you want, have to do things you don't like, mix with people you'd cross the street to avoid in different circumstances. Especially me, given my previous line of work.'

'Didn't they keep you separate?'

'A bit, at first. Then they kind of forgot and I was just another number. Back into general population. Cons never forget, though. They always know who you are and what you've done. Like fucking Wikipedia in jail—everyone knows everything.'

'I get it—you had a hard time. Why are you telling me this?'

'I don't want to go back, do I? I'd had enough after three months. Doing eight years was murder.'

I'd half-expected him to speak with an Italian accent, given his name, but in fact it was vaguely London in intonation. Perhaps one of the working-class areas in the Home Counties.

I said, 'So why are you avoiding people now?'

'Who, Anjie? Why do you think? What have I got to offer her? Sod all.'

'She's worried about you. But you knew that.'

'Did I? Did I know anything? You weren't there when I was sent down. She stopped coming to court before the sentencing. She didn't write. We'd fought over stuff anyway—what do you expect? She was a seventeen-year-old girl. You got kids?'

'The point is, what do I tell Anjelica? She wants to see you, check you over.'

'Look at my nails and teeth like a horse doctor? Not gonna happen.' He laid his hand flat on the tabletop, as though laying the idea completely to rest. He'd gained more confidence and his voice had grown stronger. 'I'll tell you, but I don't want you telling her anything except I'm okay.'

'So why tell me?'

Now he tapped the top of the table, then raised a finger to point at me.

'I know your type. Can't keep your nose out. I'll tell you so's you know what's what and that I mean what I say. Right?'

I nodded. He went on.

'I'd been inside for about five years when a guy came up to me. Said he recognised me from round and about. He said he was friends with a man he called Jenkins. I remembered him from school. He was kind of in our gang. He was big though, and you know what it's like for fat kids. He had a difficult time. So here I was, still a Category C prisoner in Buckley Hall up in Rochdale, and this guy's telling me he knew a man who I was at school with in Princes Risborough, two hundred miles away. Weird.'

'This is Jack Jenkins, right?'

He looked at me sharply. 'How do you know him?'

'He sent two extras from The Matrix to talk to me yesterday.'

'They use his name?'

'I'm not a complete dummy. I worked it out. Did you know they'd been here?'

He looked past me and I knew he was going to lie.

'He shouldn't have done that. I've got nothing to hide.'

'Well he thinks you do. Back to your story … what happened in the clink?'

'I don't know what the deal was, but word got back to Jenkins and the next thing I knew I was being "taken care of". Know what I mean? Given a better room. The screws weren't quite so hard on me. Little things.'

'And when you came out he was there waiting for you with open arms? Christ, that's a bit of a fairy-tale, isn't it?'

His eyes grew hard in his lined face.

'Listen, I don't give a shit what you think. When I came out I had nothing. Maria had died, Anjelica didn't want to know me, so I thought, and I certainly didn't have a job to go back to, and no pension either. He offered me work at the casino. I'm away from Anjelica, got my own little place. I just have to look scary at the casino now and then, and other gigs from time to time.'

'What's that mean?'

'Jenkins runs a security service on the side. Special events, VIPs, things like that. I go up to Manchester, occasionally down to London. All legit. It's run as a separate company, even has an MP on the board of directors. Some big clients.'

I couldn't find it in me to blame him. His work prospects must have been limited. If it wasn't working for Jack Jenkins in security, it would have been someone else. Or set up his own company. But with a CV like his, it wasn't likely customers would be beating down the door.

He stood up.

'That's where I am. I'm okay and I'm doing a decent job, keeping out of everyone's hair. You can tell Anjelica I'm all right and she doesn't need to see me. Tell her what you like— I'm embarrassed or ashamed or whatever. But she shouldn't worry about me.'

I stood up to face him. 'One thing.'

'What's that?'

'Why did Jack Jenkins send two goons here yesterday to threaten me? Why is he being so protective of you? Has he got a crush on you or something?'

'I can't answer that. Maybe he's loyal, unlike some of the shits I had to deal with when I went down.'

'You mean Billy Passmore?'

He looked startled but quickly covered it.

'Passmore? What the fuck's he got to do with anything?'

'He didn't exactly stand up to be counted when you went down for eight years.'

Strano did up the buttons on his jacket, which slid over his chest and kept its shape perfectly. Beautiful tailoring. Old habits.

'That's between me and him. You can certainly leave him out of the frame. Can I go now?'

'You can do what you want. I didn't ask you to turn up on my doorstep and fill my ears with honey.'

'What does that mean?'

I shrugged. 'I don't know. I have a poetic turn of phrase sometimes.'

He stared at me for a moment, then turned and left, shutting the front door quietly behind him. This time I heard his old car's engine rattle into life and drive off. Quiet settled in the house like a heavy blanket.

He'd pretended not to know what I meant, but we both knew exactly what I'd said.

CHAPTER SEVEN

I DID GO to my office eventually, but I didn't stay there long. It was hot and stuffy and I wanted a reason to go out, so I phoned Anjelica Strange as soon as I arrived. She'd given me an office number, a house landline number and a mobile number. I rang the last of these, thinking it would be more direct. I was right. She picked up on the second ring.

I told her my name.

Without preamble she said, 'Have you found him?'

'Can I talk to you face to face?'

'A simple yes or no would do. You're scaring me.'

'Yes, we've talked. He's okay, but I need to speak to you about it.'

'What did he say? What's he doing? Where is he?'

'That's what I want to talk to you about. Can I come see you?'

'What, here?'

'I have no idea where you are.'

'Look at the card I gave you. Not the office address, the other one. You'll have to find your own way here, I haven't got time to talk you through it, I'm on a deadline.'

She hung up and I looked at her business card again. There was an office address in central Manchester and one in Blythe Bridge, a village the other side of Stoke. I presumed she worked from home a lot and needed to make the address public. I locked the door and headed for my car.

BLYTHE BRIDGE IS an odd mix of low-riding bungalows, slightly up-market semi-detached houses and discreet, super-secret, set-way-back-from-the-road demi-mansions. You drive out of Stoke on the dual carriageway towards Derby, hang a left at a large island and shortly you're driving down the main street. If you blink you're likely to be out the other side again. I'd never been able to work out who lived here—it was too far to commute to the Toyota factory at Derby and too upscale, in the main, for the pottery workers in Stoke ... when there had been actual pottery workers. Perhaps it was teachers and academics from the various colleges and schools scattered around the local area.

I don't know why I was surprised, but I was: Anjelica Strange's house was one of the larger houses on the main road, concealed by a high laurel hedge that had completely swallowed the wooden fence it had originally stood behind. A white plank gateway was open when I arrived and a pebbled drive swept up to the house and then left, down a slight incline to a double garage, in front of which a Porsche Boxter and a BMW Z4 squatted facing me and looking like bugs competing in an Ugly competition.

I parked my Mondeo—which suddenly seemed extremely handsome—in front of them and crunched over the pebbles to the front door. My finger on the doorbell sounded a buzzer about a quarter of a mile away, further back in the house, and eventually Anjelica Strange answered it. She was wearing less formal clothes than the morning she'd swept into my office like an Italian princess, but her blue sweatpants and tight black tee-shirt still did a good job. I admired her ability to get into clothes that tight.

She said, 'Come in, please,' and left the door open for me to follow her back into the dark hallway and then through into a light sitting-room, both of us clacking over the parquet floor as though we were wearing clogs. She might have been wearing them for all I knew. But I bet they would have been the finest Italian clogs from Milan.

The sitting room was as big as the floor surface of the downstairs of my house, and featured wall-width French windows that led out to a paved patio, with fancy iron furniture scattered around it, and beyond it a long green lawn edged with borders of colourful and lush plants. A hammock hung from a big oak tree about a hundred yards down the garden.

I brought my attention back to the room and found Anjelica using her patented Intense Stare on me again.

'Yes, that's the garden. No, I don't look after it, I have a man comes once a week.'

'I was wondering how you afford the house. Knowing you have staff just increases the mystery.'

'I run my own public relations company.'

'Interesting, for someone who was keen on staying out of the public eye.'

'I turned it around, used the experience and the contacts for my own benefit. I hire good people and get out of their way.'

'Can we sit down?'

'If you must, but I can't be all day. I've got a meeting this afternoon that I've already put back an hour.'

She gestured to a long cream sofa and I lowered myself into a small section of one of its giant cushions. She took a couple of strides and sat on a matching chair on the other side of the room. I wondered if we'd need to text each other to communicate.

I said, 'Your father came to see me this morning. He just appeared on my doorstep. He's looking older but he seems well. If he lost weight in prison he's put it back on again.'

I paused, expecting some questions. She said nothing but eventually lowered her head to stare at the deep-pile carpet between her feet. I had the sense again that she might burst into tears, despite the hard account she gave of herself.

I went on, 'He said he appreciates the fact you were looking for him, but he can't see you right now. If you want the truth, I think he's still ashamed of what he did. He's embarrassed to be the person he is. Obviously I didn't know him before, but he doesn't strike me as one of life's hard-cases.'

She looked up quickly.

'What do you mean by that?'

I spread out my hands. 'He spoke quietly. He was respectful of me. He showed concern for how you felt. I think he'll get in touch when he thinks he can and not before.'

'Where's he living?'

Now we were entering tricky territory. I didn't want to give too much away.

'I don't know where he's living but he's working in Stoke. Security work, suits his background. He's worried about finding any other kind of job, given his history.'

She nodded.

'I thought it would be something like that. He has to work — he always liked work. And he lost his pension.'

I looked around the room, at the expensive wooden sideboard, the modern art on the walls, the comfortable sofas and chairs we were sitting on ... but I said nothing. She hadn't suggested she might help him financially but maybe that was something lurking in the back of her mind.

She said, 'Did he talk about what it was like? In prison?'

'Not a lot. Apparently it started hard but got easier.' I didn't want to mention Jack Jenkins and the protection he'd offered her father. It implied he might be caught up in a life she wouldn't approve of.

She said, 'So he didn't want to see me. Did you tell him why I was looking for him?'

'I said you wanted to know he was okay, that's all. I thought you'd be the best person to say any personal stuff.'

She sighed. 'I suppose you're right. Well that's that. How did he seem to you? Was he happy?'

'He wasn't unhappy. He seemed settled, as if he was getting his bearings again. Trying to work out what to do next.'

She took this in carefully and then appeared to come to a decision. She said, 'This has all happened quicker than I thought. When we couldn't find him I thought he'd gone underground and we wouldn't find him for ages. What were those two men like?'

'Leatherby and White? Let's say they have different views.'

'How so?'

'Leatherby's taken the victim route for himself and is using it to beat everyone else with. He thinks we all owe him something but I don't believe even he knows what it is. He thinks your dad was guilty because he didn't defend himself. And because he felt betrayed, I think.'

'What does that mean? Betrayed by who?'

'He worked with your dad for five years and didn't see any of this coming. I think he believes your dad cheated him in some way.'

She grunted and for the first time a smile pulled at her lips. It lightened the atmosphere in the room considerably.

She said, 'Lots of people said that to me, in so many words. They didn't see it coming. They wouldn't have believed it of my dad, not Lorenzo Strano … They used to mention it as if I was supposed to take comfort from it. But what they were really saying was my dad had betrayed them the same way he'd betrayed me and my mum, so they knew what we were going through. As if.'

'People have different ways of showing sympathy.'

'If you say so. What about the other one, White?'

I thought back to the Nicklaus Room in the golf club, to Arthur White's ruddy face as he opened his slit of a mouth to pour another G and T down it. The attitudes of Leatherby and White towards Strano had been so different it was as though there was some information missing that was necessary to clear things up. This sense of incompletion had been nagging at me ever since I'd driven away from the clubhouse.

I said, 'Arthur White didn't know your dad well. They were in a photography club together, so he only knew him socially. But he respected him. He didn't think he was guilty, in fact. He thought it was a set-up.'

Anjelica Strange sat up straight and folded her arms as if to ward off an unexpected idea.

'Well that's nonsense, obviously.'

'Why do you say that? Did you think he was guilty? Didn't you believe your own dad could be innocent? Didn't you want him to be?'

Her eyes took on a little fire. 'Don't you dare say that to me. Of course I wanted him to be innocent. I didn't want him to go to prison and leave my mother and me by ourselves, with no support and no money. That's a stupid thing to say.'

'Perhaps you're right. But I gather there were some alternative theories that were never really pursued.'

'Such as what? Aliens took over my dad's brain through mind-control and made him sell drugs?'

'White mentioned Billy Passmore, your dad's boss at the time.'

Now she stood up and looked down at me. Scorn was written all over her features.

'Well that's another theory we can shoot down in flames straight away. Billy Passmore was the only one who was good to us, my mother and me. He came and saw us and while I know he thought Dad was guilty, he helped us as best he could. Got the police press office to do things for us, write statements for the papers and so on. Looked after us.'

'Then why didn't he stand up in court and defend him? Why was there a whispering campaign about Passmore amongst the people who worked for him?'

'You'll have to ask him that, won't you? As far as we were concerned he had nothing to do with whether Dad was guilty or not, and he couldn't really say anything other than what he did, given his position. He said Dad had never given any hint he might be engaging in criminal activity. What else could he have said?'

'Doesn't sound like much of a cheerleader to have on your side.'

She paused as though she was gathering herself.

Then she said, 'I think you'd better go. Send me an invoice. You've found my dad and delivered a message. You don't need to start opening inquiries into Billy Passmore.' She stopped, then walked to the window and looked out at the garden. 'What you don't know is that he became like a second father to me when Dad went to jail. He helped me set up this business and put me in touch with some good people and good clients.'

'Perhaps he felt guilty for not saying anything in court.'

She turned to me. 'Perhaps he felt cheated, too. Perhaps he felt Dad had let him down but it wasn't my fault, nor my mum's. Perhaps he wanted to help.'

We stared at each other for a moment, then I stood up. I couldn't bear the look in her eyes. I wanted to shake her hand, or touch her in some way, give her some kind of physical comfort. She looked like someone who had never known a hug.

I said, 'You'll get my invoice at the end of the month. A couple of days' work and some petrol expenses.'

'All right. I'd be grateful if you'd leave now.'

She wasn't looking at me and in fact had turned away completely. Her figure in the tee-shirt was outlined against the light from the French windows. She was tall and slim and somehow tragic.

It seemed she wasn't going to say anything else, so I left the room and walked out of the house.

I reversed my car in the drive, turned and went out on to the main road, then pulled in by the side and killed the engine. There was so much going on between this bunch of people that I couldn't see myself leaving it alone. I try to view my work as a service rendered and paid for, but sometimes the people involved create such patterns of disquiet and concern and mystery in my head it's hard to let them go. That people should be allowed to screw up their own lives is something I haven't yet come to terms with.

I picked up my phone and made a call.

CHAPTER EIGHT

SHE'D CHOSEN A pub in Knutsford, which was about halfway between where we each lived. Knutsford always gave me the sense its overhanging buildings on its narrow roads were about to topple over, but once I went through the gnarled wooden doors of the pub the space inside opened up and was modern and well-lit. No roundheads or cavaliers in sight, no matter what the heavy roof beams and quartered windows might have promised.

I bought a pint and found a seat in a corner where I could stare at the people at the bar before they started staring at me. It was only just five o'clock but the place was already filling. Perhaps there wasn't much else to do in Knutsford, once you'd finished admiring the architecture.

I thought about my meeting with Anjelica Strange earlier in the day. I'd handled it with the sensitivity of a rhino in a greetings card shop. I hadn't thought about how the message from her father might affect her—essentially, he was saying he didn't want to see her. She might have already guessed that because of his actions since he'd left prison, but to hear me say the words was the kind of confirmation that was brutally unwelcome.

I hadn't taken that into account. I'd stayed calm and rational and completely unfeeling. Good job. No wonder she more or less threw me out on my ear.

I also started to revisit my thinking about the attitudes of Leatherby and White. One was definitively anti-Strano and one was positively pro. But if Leatherby thought Strano had been guilty all along, why did he contact Jack Jenkins and kick off a confrontation between me and the two giant thugs that was intended to protect him? Why was Leatherby in bed with Jenkins?

A shadow fell on my table and I looked up. Belinda McFee stood there, grinning.

She said, 'This is a first: you paying for a drink. How are they hanging?'

'According to gravity. Do you want a drink?'

'I'll get it.'

She turned on her heels and fought her way to the bar. Belinda was a private detective based in south Manchester who like me worked alone, disliking the restrictions and formality of corporate investigation groups. She was not yet thirty and had been working in the field for less than a year. She was athletic and resourceful and kept her femininity hidden behind modest trousers and jackets. However, she had long brown hair that she never pulled back into a pony-tail or constrained in any way, as though wanting you to know that in fact she was an attractive woman and was just dressing down for work reasons.

She came back with a suspiciously clear glass.

I said, 'Vodka?'

'Tonic water. I'm a month into a two month dry-spell. Reboots the liver, I'm told.'

'Was that a problem?'

'Come on, Sam. You know what it's like pulling an all-nighter outside someone's house. A little relaxant always went down well.'

'It would put me to sleep.'

'That's because you're an old man. Now, what did you want?'

I explained the case so far, telling her everything that had happened from Anjelica Strange's first visit to my meeting with her earlier that day, and including the intervention from Jenkins' men.

'It all sounds a bit low-key for you, except for the meeting with the big guys.'

'I thought it would be straightforward and in the end it was, but not because of anything I did. I just interviewed two men and then the cave-men came to me, followed shortly after by Strano himself.'

'So the case is closed. What do you need me for?'

I glanced around at the men and women in the bar. If I'd have gone up to any of them and said what I was about to say to Belinda, they would have thought me crazy. I was hoping she was experienced enough by now to know I wasn't.

I said, 'Something doesn't feel right.'

I waited for her to laugh, but she didn't. She was an attractive woman with a very direct gaze and it was unnerving to have her stare at me for a full minute without saying anything. I would have liked to look away, but that would have been cowardly. So I took a draw on my beer instead, finding its foam terrifically interesting for a little while.

Eventually she said, 'I've only been quiet because I'm trying to work out what's going on for you. Last time we worked together I gave you a real telling-off for your white knight syndrome. I don't think you've learned anything in the meantime, have you?'

I shrugged tiredly. 'I can't help it if my clients seem to be young women these days. It wasn't always like that.'

'I think they sniff you out.'

'Okay, okay, I get the point. You think I'm feeling sorry for Anjelica Strange and want to help her.'

'Tell me I'm wrong.'

'Perhaps not entirely. But you must admit, everything that's happened so far is weird. The threats, then the magical appearance by Strano himself, the fact two people who knew him had completely different views on whether he was guilty or not. And where do Jack Jenkins and this Passmore character fit in?'

'Why are you so interested in Passmore? He sounds like he's just a cop doing his job and keeping out of trouble. No difference there.'

I'd finished my drink and I had nothing to play with now. I leaned back in the hard wooden chair and held up my hands.

'If you don't want to help, that's okay. I thought you might like a couple of days' easy money.'

'Doing what?'

'I don't trust the fact that Jack Jenkins cosied up to Strano when he was in prison. First, if he's a legitimate businessman running a casino, how come he had enough influence to make Strano's life easier in jail? Secondly, what does he have to gain from it? I don't believe he was overcome with fellow-feeling and kindness when he heard Strano was in the clink. Those are the basic questions I'm working with.'

'So what do you want me to do?'

'I'll pay you for a couple of days to sit on Jenkins. Find out where he lives and where his casino is and just watch him. See where he goes and who he talks to. Find out what kind of operation the casino is. I looked it up earlier and it's called The Lucky Strike. How's that for cheesy?'

She'd been listening to me with a professional attention, eyes narrowed, frowning slightly. Now she leaned back in her chair and finished her drink, placing the glass on the table.

'I'll do it because you asked me to, and last time we worked together I think we did some good. You don't need to pay me.'

'I can afford it.'

'You'll do the same for me some time. But I want you to know I'm not buying in to the whole damsel-rescue thing. Unlike you I don't need to believe my clients are the good guys.'

'They're called scruples.'

'That's bullshit, Sam. You're just dressing up your personal preferences with a moral justification. You can't escape the white knight riding away inside you. It'll be your undoing one day.'

'I don't need another telling-off, Belinda. If you'll do the work, that's great. I appreciate the favour. How I want to think about it and how you want to think about it can be different. I know you won't take any money, but see it as a financial transaction anyway. No feelings involved for you. Just keep me informed about what's going on. I'd do it myself but those goons knew me and they've probably got pictures of me now from the Net and plastered them everywhere.'

A few months ago Belinda and I had been involved in a case that had caused a splash not just in the local papers, but throughout the UK. My face was spread all over Google Images, if you cared to look.

'You still got the same phone number and email?'

'Yes.'

'I'll get back and do some research, start tomorrow morning.' She stood up. 'And don't listen to me. I don't mean to tell you off. Your heart's in the right place. But you can be too much of a soft touch.'

I smiled at her. 'Oh, bugger off. I'll speak to you soon.'

She gave a little wave and then worked her way through the pub and left. I contemplated having another drink but thought it wouldn't be wise, so left just in time to see her pink Volvo pulling away from the kerb fifty yards down the road.

CHAPTER NINE

THE FOLLOWING EVENING I decided to take a look at The Lucky Strike. I'd checked it out online, where a fancy panoramic photograph gave me a good idea of what to expect, but there was nothing like a personal visit.

It was beginning to grow dark as I drove east towards Alsager and eventually turned on to the A500, the link road that joined the five towns of the Potteries to the M6 motorway. The road cut an arc through industrial zones that were slowly dying as the economy fell apart. Since Stoke's pottery manufacturers had largely sold out to Colombia and China, nothing had arrived to take their place. People still worked and shopped, but I had no idea what they did to earn a living unless it was work in the same shops their husbands and wives bought from. It was as if the place was slowly eating itself.

Twenty minutes later I was pulling into the car park of The Lucky Strike, one of three relatively new casinos that had opened up within a quarter of a mile of each other on the western approach to Hanley, an area that the city council seemed intent on developing by encouraging gambling and supermarket shopping. The casino was a large square building painted a dull grey and lacking windows—the intention being, as in Las Vegas, to mask the fact that outside of the artificial lighting of the casino, real daylight was coming and going as the world turned. I'd seen online that it was open from midday till six the following morning, at which point I guessed the restaurants re-stocked and an army of cleaners moved in to mop up the spilt bar snacks and forlorn hopes left on the floor by the transient clientele.

Half a dozen broad cantilevered steps supported by metal risers led up to the massive glass doors of the entrance foyer. Inside the lighting was pink and purple, suggesting a kind of sophistication known only to sheiks and maharajahs in the palaces of the East. The doors winked as a group of girls in tight dresses went inside, talking at high speed.

At the top of the steps stood two large men crammed into monkey suits and dress shirts, and despite their best efforts still managing to look like wrestlers at a society wedding. One of them was the more paleolithic of the two thugs who'd been to see me a couple of days before. His eyebrows not only met above his nose, they entwined and performed a sinuous dance. As I went to pass through the doors he placed a large coarse hand on my chest.

'I knew you wouldn't listen. Saw it on your face. Your funeral.'

'Shouldn't you be off somewhere with your friend, polishing each other's dicks?'

He took his hand away, his face a mask of proud condescension, as though he knew what was coming and I didn't, more fool me.

'Don't spit on the floor or grope the waitresses. I'll be here when you come out.'

I moved past him and followed signs to the main gaming room. It bloomed open before me, a huge space in gold and glass, carpeted richly and festooned with modernist chandeliers that hung over the roulette tables which were scattered freely about the room. To my immediate right a bank of hip-high futuristic gaming machines were clacking away for their focused users, all men, all sitting and watching the play of lights like committed air-traffic controllers; and over to the left were arched entrances to poker tables with blue baize tops and largely uninhabited at this early hour.

Above each roulette table there stood a spindly white unit like a lamp-stand supporting a spy-camera that pointed directly downwards. It was difficult to tell whether any of the cameras actually worked, but they would certainly be intimidating if you were thinking of cheating the House.

At the far end of the massive room a couple of steps led up through a large free-standing door frame—evidently a sensor like the ones you find in airports, presumably to prevent players taking chips from the gaming room—and gave access to the bar and restaurants. I could see couples sitting at tables and a few solo members loitering on stools at the bar, counting their losses and presumably drowning a host of sorrows.

The noise from the machinery and the crowd was oppressive, like a circle of hell transported into middle England. The customers seemed to be mostly in their twenties and thirties and were up for a good time even though the night was young.

I wasn't sure what to do, so I ambled over to one of the tables and watched blackjack for a while. The croupier was professional and quick and won more than he lost. The people facing him seemed more excited to find themselves in an actual casino than worried about losing money.

A voice spoke close by me, and when I turned it was a young woman carrying a tray. Her tanned shoulders were bare because she was wearing a spangly bustier that fitted tightly to her waist and pushed her breasts up. Her hair was also pushed up and piled on the top of her head somewhat like a volcano and held in place by a black bow at the front. Her smile was broad and friendly and made me think I already knew her — which wasn't true. I realised she'd asked whether I'd like something to drink. I asked for a beer and she hurried away.

Five minutes later I saw her coming back, carrying four other drinks on her tray in addition to mine. She looked to be in her early twenties, with a pale freckled face and a lightness in her step. She dropped off the other four drinks en route, then handed me mine carefully and looked up at me.

'First one on the house, sir. Enjoy your evening.'

Half an hour later, when I was at a roulette table and beginning to get the lie of the land, she appeared again and asked the same question. I ordered another beer and watched her beetle away and then return. I had a note ready for her and she gave me some change — though not as much as I might have expected. She stopped for a moment and looked around, as though searching out her next mark.

I said, 'You must have a strong right arm.'

She smiled at me. 'Sorry, sir?'

'Carrying that tray all night. Builds up the muscles.'

'I have a break every two hours. It's not too bad.'

I had a thought. 'Are you allowed to talk to customers?'

'It's compulsory. Couldn't do my job if I didn't.'

'Good point. How long have you worked here?'

She brought her attention back to my face. 'A couple of months. Why?'

'You must know the people here quite well — Jack Jenkins, for instance.'

Her smile stayed bright but a worry registered in her eyes.

'I don't talk to Mr Jenkins much. He's busy. Excuse me, I have to go.'

'I'll have another beer.'

'You haven't finished that one.'

'I will have done by the time you bring the next.'

She hesitated, then moved away to the bar. I found an empty table while she was gone and put my half-full glass on it. When she returned I was waiting with more money.

She said, 'I hope you've got a driver to take you home. You're necking these faster than my granny.'

'I like competing with the older woman. I can learn from their experience.'

She shook her head, but she was smiling.

'What do you do when you're not drinking?'

'Me? International playboy, of course.'

'Not another one. This place is full of them. So, really?'

I saw no reason to lie. 'People pay me to find out things.'

'What, like Columbo?'

'Now you're showing your age. He was a police detective. I'm more of a private one.'

Now she was fully focused on me. 'Interesting.'

'So tell me … you've worked here a while—what's it like?'

'What do you mean?'

'The people, the job. What do you tell people?'

'It's a job. The guys who work here ... they're guys. Same as everywhere. You shouldn't ask me questions like that.'

'Why not? I've bought a drink. I'm entitled.'

'I can't talk about that stuff. They don't like it.'

Then her face went through a couple of quick transformations: she stared at me intently as though thinking; then she frowned and looked behind her and, briefly, upwards, perhaps towards one of the ever-present cameras.

Then she said in quiet voice, 'Have you got a business card?'

I nodded, taken by surprise by the change in her manner. I wondered where this was going.

But I took a card from my wallet and laid it on the table. She was reaching for it when another figure arrived behind her. I'd seen him approaching but hadn't taken any notice, which was bizarre, because he was huge. He was both tall and wide, as though he'd been blown up by the insertion of a valve into one of his bloated ankles. He wore, of all things, a shell-suit, one of those plasticated, logo-spattered two-piece jobs that demonstrate a complete lack of both taste and self-awareness. It was blue and white, giving him the appearance of a child's football enlarged to grotesque size.

The girl sensed his presence and turned. This seemed to make him smile and his arm came out to fall like a heavy weight across her shoulders.

He said, 'Hannah, how are you doing, girl? I hope you're not bothering our customers.'

His voice was high and rather precise, as though he were adopting a formal tone for my benefit. His accent reminded me of Strano's, which was no surprise seeing they'd been brought up in the same area down south. He was smiling but there was no merriment in his round face.

The woman turned to him and her demeanour shifted again, became more servile. This girl should have been on stage.

'Hi, JJ. The gentlemen was just asking about the drinks we serve.'

I said, 'I don't like German beers so I was checking what else you've got.'

Jack Jenkins looked from one of us to the other and decided he'd play the game.

'To be honest, I don't like the German shit either. But to be honest again, you have to stock what the punters want, don't you? Hannah, girl, whyn't you go along and look to the guys at that table?' A stubby hand pointed to where four men were gesturing towards her. 'They look like they're running dry.'

She turned back to me and leaned on the table to pick up my empty glass and place it on her tray.

She said, 'Have a good evening, sir.'

When she moved away, my card was gone.

Jenkins watched her walk towards the men at the other table and glanced down at me.

'Gonzo told me you were here. What can I do you for? I haven't seen you place a bet or use a machine yet. Still learning the ropes?'

'His name is Gonzo? Isn't that a character from the Muppets?'

'I gave him that nickname. I like to name the people who work for me. Gonzo also happens to characterise a particular form of journalism that's rather wild and crazy. Like the man himself.'

He'd dropped the prissy, formal accent and had upgraded his vocabulary. Interesting.

He said, 'They told me they didn't think you'd taken the message on board. They said you didn't seem intimidated.'

'Is that why you asked Strano to visit me in person?'

He looked at me speculatively.

'Not as dumb as you look, then. Tell me, Mr Dyke, what's all this about? I employ Lorenzo because I knew him when we were kids together. He was kind to me when he didn't have to be. He was one of the good guys. I happened to be in a position where I could help him, which I did. It's not exactly a sacrifice—he does a good job and knows his stuff. If I can do a favour for someone, isn't that to be applauded? Why the interest from you?'

'I'm a cynic. I don't believe people do things out of charity, unless they happen to be actual church employees or religiously inclined. Are you a devotee of a particular church?'

He smiled without a hint of humour, his cheeks creasing but his eyes remaining deadpan, the small, mean eyes of a castrated pig.

'Now you're being ironic and disingenuous. You know the business I'm in and the kind of business-related decisions I have to commit myself to. What will it take to get you to give up this forlorn pursuit and leave Lorenzo alone?'

'I don't like the fact Leatherby thought he should tell you about our meeting. I don't like the fact you sent Gonzo and Terry to my house. I don't like the fact you persuaded Strano to visit me to try to call me off. Finally, I don't like the fact you've intimidated that girl. There's a lot about you and your behaviour I don't like.'

'I'm truly sorry about that. And for the record, I have no idea what you're talking about.'

There's a certain kind of person whose attitude wraps steel wire around my insides and tightens it until I grow short of breath. Their sense of superiority and self-belief warps the atmosphere around them so they not only inhale their own publicity, but think everyone else should, too.

I said, 'I don't know anything about you or your operation, except it's completely without class. I'm sorry our paths have crossed because it's going to be difficult for one of us to get out of this relationship unharmed.'

He leaned back on his stubby legs and laughed up at the ceiling. I saw the dark insides of his fillings. I wondered whether he was playing to his cameras for the sake of future proceedings.

He lowered his head, the laughter vanishing as quickly as it came. Taking a step forward, he loomed over me, an enormous eclipse that cut out the garish lights of the casino.

'Lorenzo Strano is a valued employee to whom I pay no more attention than anyone else in my employ. Bear that in mind. Have a good night on the tables. I'm sure you'll have good luck.'

He leaned back until he was upright and the light came back into my universe. He cocked his right hand at me as though pointing a pistol and firing it, then walked away, moving from side to side to make space for his gigantic thighs to rub past each other without catching fire.

CONTRARY TO WHAT he'd promised, Gonzo wasn't on duty when I left. Two different men stood aside to let me walk down the steps, one of them even giving me a polite, 'Goodnight, sir.'

As I pulled out of the car park to head home I spotted a familiar car in the street opposite. I pulled up parallel to it long enough to point down the road and do the finger-walking gesture. She nodded and as I drove away I saw her climb out of the Volvo in my rear-view mirror.

A hundred yards further along there was another entrance into a separate section of the retail park. There was a McDonalds still open and I turned into their car park and waited.

A few moments later Belinda appeared and I climbed out of my own car and headed her off, steering her towards the entrance to the restaurant.

I said, 'I'm starving. Share a bag of fries with me.'

'You know how to charm a girl. I'll buy the ketchup.'

'Ketchup's free.'

'Really?'

I paid for our fries and we sat facing each other in the garish light, cardboard boxes of yellow fries between us. A group of adolescent boys were using McDonalds' wifi to follow a football match on a tablet and whooped from time to time as the play ebbed and flowed. We were the only other customers.

I said, 'Can you see enough from where you're parked?'

'There's the front entrance and an entrance around the side where most of the staff go in and out. I can see both from where I am. Lot of staff. They seem to do six hour shifts.'

'Have you seen Jenkins?'

'He blotted out the sun earlier today. I couldn't miss him. His doctor must give him hell.'

'He talks like a professor so he probably gives as good as he gets. I can't imagine him listening to anyone.'

'You've had words already? That's good going for you.'

I doffed a metaphorical cap, using a french fry as a stand-in.

'I was talking to a member of staff and he interrupted. I didn't like his attitude and I let him know it. He knew who I was so he's done his research. He didn't seem to mind I identified his cave-men. He's so arrogant he probably feels armour-plated.'

'So what am I looking for now?'

'I stuck a needle under his saddle, see if he bucks. I'm thinking he won't be able to resist trying something. So watch where he goes, who he talks to. And stay on your guard.'

She pushed her box of fries away as though the three she'd sampled were enough. I pulled the box towards me.

She said, 'Do you really think he'll do something? After meeting you once? I know you're a pain, but really … ?'

'He thinks he's lord of all he surveys. He's got a licence for the casino and he'll see that as a licence to print money. I might not impact on his radar at all, but on the other hand, if he's a control freak he'll want to know what I'm up to.'

'He's got a lot to lose. He won't want to antagonise the police or the council.'

'Trust me, he's a villain. He won't be able to help himself. He'll like the idea he can put one over on me, beat me in some way. That's where the arrogance of crooks always lets them down. They get bored and they start to believe the way everyone treats them is only what they deserve. Someone like me comes along and doesn't bow down, it niggles at them. Read the memoirs, they all say they want to lead a quiet life, no bother from the cops, just a steady stream of illegal income. If you read a bit deeper, what they really want is respect—though they don't want to do anything to deserve it.'

Laughter lit the back of Belinda's eyes. 'That's the most I've ever heard you say in one take. He really got your goat, didn't he?'

'I rise above that kind of petty behaviour. Are you sure you don't want these fries?'

'No, I better get back to the car. Otherwise my boss will think I'm shirking.'

'Bosses, eh? Capitalist swines, the lot of them.'

She stood up and the boys from the other table forgot the football and watched. I couldn't blame them. Her leather jacket and tight trousers did something to male hormones.

She said, 'I'll keep in touch. Check your emails and texts.'

Then she walked out of the McDonalds with half a dozen pairs of eyes following each step and every sway.

Including mine.

CHAPTER TEN

THE AIR WAS cool after the heat of the McDonalds and she pulled her jacket collar up around her neck. In the middle distance she could hear the roar of the M6 motorway, winding its way south to Birmingham and north towards the Lake District, splitting the divide between Liverpool and Manchester, the great rivals.

She had always liked urban life and even now relished the smell of diesel and the roar of a big-cylinder engine. Having driven lorries for the army in Germany she'd nurtured an affinity for transport, almost to the point of being geeky in her appreciation of smooth-running mechanisms.

Perhaps it was because she'd momentarily tuned out of the present that she was taken by surprise. The first hint she had of something amiss was an overpowering smell of male deodorant that was surprisingly close. In normal circumstances she was adept at street-fighting, having taken lessons from a military expert, but the arms that came around her from behind were too quick and too strong, and as she was bundled into the back of a darkened van she decided not to fight for the time being but to keep her senses alert. If she fought it was likely she'd be rendered unconscious, and from the feel of the man who'd gathered her in, even her best moves might not be enough to deter him unless she were in full daylight and facing front.

So she let herself go limp and settled down on to the cold corrugated floor of the van even as its engine started up and the rear doors were closed with a cushioned slam. Within a few seconds the passenger door banged shut and the vehicle drove off. It had taken less than ten seconds.

THE VAN DROVE for twenty minutes and she couldn't tell its overall direction. It turned both left and right, hit long straight stretches but never really accelerated, and then would spend several minutes idling as though stuck at traffic lights.

She found a blanket that smelled of petrol and folded it to make a soft seat, propping herself up against the wheel arch. She groped around in the dark but there were no tools or ropes or anything she might use. The space was without windows and was completely black except for a couple of pinpricks where the side panels of the van had rusted through. She was cut off from the driver by a thick wooden partition that she guessed was removable if you had the right tools.

She didn't.

Eventually the vehicle stopped and the rear door opened just long enough to let another, smaller man climb inside. There wasn't enough light to see beyond him but from the sense of the acoustics she thought she was in a large warehouse or loading bay of some kind. It was still dark in the van and when the man spoke it startled her.

'Close your eyes, duck. We're not going to hurt you. I've got to put a blindfold on.'

'Fuck off and die.'

'Ah, there's no doubt I will, eventually. But I stay in the van until you put this on.'

A length of material brushed against her face and she reached up to swat it away.

The voice said, 'Ah, come on, you know you want to.'

It brushed against her face again and this time she took it.

'Good girl, now put it on and we'll be getting somewhere.'

'It's on.'

'Let me feel.'

A small pair of hands found the side of her head and adjusted the elasticated blindfold until it was secure over her eyes.

'Good, now we can go.'

She heard the doors open and sensed light through the blindfold, though she couldn't see anything. A hand found hers and pulled her forward, then she was guided first on to a box that had been placed just outside the rear doors, then to take another step on to the ground.

Here the air smelled faintly antiseptic, like the corridors of a hospital, as she was pulled forward and an arm linked in hers. She sensed a man of about her own height walking beside her and leading her firmly forward.

'Don't worry, duck, I won't walk you into a wall. Now keep those blinkers on till I say take 'em off.'

He led her across what felt like a large expanse of concrete, then through a door and along a corridor. Here the acoustics gave her a sense of a cramped area devoid of life.

Another door was opened and she was pulled inside and told to halt. Abruptly, the blindfold was pulled down from her face and allowed to lie around her neck. The man who'd led her inside had already stepped back and she heard the door close behind him as he left.

She was in a mid-sized office that was carpeted in functional grey carpet tiles and lit by two overhead fluorescent bars. Facing her was a wide wooden desk and to either side, lining the walls, which were windowless, were low black leatherette chairs with aluminium arms. All of the chairs were taken by big men in dark suits who were looking at her appraisingly. She was used to that from her time in the Army so she wasn't distressed. It was like an undertakers' convention; she guessed they were bouncers from the casino. The air was rank with maleness—some of it testosterone, some of it sickly-sweet deodorant worn, presumably, to mask the overpowering male smell generated between them and in whose daily funk they had to work. The man who had picked her up and deposited her in the van was probably amongst them.

What was more worrying was the sight of Jack Jenkins sitting on the far side of the desk, his blue and white shellsuit giving him the appearance of someone managing a gym rather than overseeing a sophisticated gambling operation. He must have been tagging along in another vehicle.

She wondered where they'd brought her—she hadn't been aware of another building owned by Jenkins, but then she hadn't been following him for long.

Jenkins was sitting sideways at his desk, presumably because he couldn't get his massive thighs beneath it. He was smoking a thin cigar between his stubby fingers, his flat eyes showing neither warmth nor humanity as they squinted through the cigar smoke. He waved the cigar towards her and encompassed the room.

He said, 'All is revealed! You've been on a magical mystery tour, haven't you? Did you worry you were going to end up in a lorry going to Pakistan? A bit of white slavery? I've got some contacts if you're interested.'

She looked at him, trying to keep her face free of expression. She wasn't going to give him the satisfaction of antagonising her. He could play his games but she wasn't about to join in.

A grim smile creased his round face and he leaned forward so his elbows were resting on his desk. It was bare except for a green wire in-tray and an iPad. She saw how his brown hair was combed forward to hide the pink skull that was starting to show through like the hide of a dog succumbing to mange.

He said, 'Who the fuck do you think you are, spying on me all day? Stuck outside there in your prissy pink Volvo like Lady Penelope.'

Again she said nothing and tried to relax her stance. She now knew there were two men on her right hand side and three on her left. The two to her right were smaller than the others, but that wasn't saying much—they were still a foot taller than she was. The three on her left were big and muscular, and she thought two of them were probably the two who had confronted Sam Dyke a few days ago—one was dark-haired and had large, primitive features, the other was pale and thinner. The third man was younger and was grinning and glancing continually towards Jenkins like the idiot brother just waiting to pull the wings off a wasp. He had skin like sandpaper and a squint in his left eye. His hair was cut short and she could see an anchor tattooed on his skull. She hoped it had hurt.

Jenkins said, 'Listen, Belinda McFee, you come into this room as a known quantity. I've done my research on you, consulted my personal Googlers. I understand in circumstances like these, confronted with the prospect of pain and probably humiliation, someone in your position has to maintain a stoical and possibly comical front. You're trying to earn respect from a bunch of people who, in actual fact, couldn't give a shit about you. But I understand and respect that. You wouldn't be doing your job if you simply gave me the information I want.'

'I don't know what you're talking about, despite your glib use of language.'

'There! Good! You've joined in the conversation. This is the attempt now to postpone the moment when pain will be endured. I appreciate your work there. Good job.'

'The only pain I anticipate is having to listen to you talk for the next twelve hours.'

A couple of the men stirred in their seats and Belinda wondered if she'd pressed a button. It was likely this bunch wouldn't be too enamoured of Jenkins' verbal diarrhoea, especially if most of it went zooming over their heads.

Apparently it had struck home with Jenkins, too. He pushed his seat back and stood up, stubbing out his cigar on a thin ashtray. He wasn't looking at her as he came around the desk, which she took as a bad sign.

He said, 'All right, let's cut to the quick. I know who you are and you know who I am. We're both professionals, though of course I can't speak for the ragged crew lining the walls here. So, Belinda, what is it you're doing by sitting watching my little club?'

He had come close and towered over her, his mouth smelling of dark tobacco and alcohol, his breath wheezy, his face sheened like an apple drawn from a bucket of water and left to dry in the sun. She realised two of the men had also stood up and now one on either side of her gripped her arms. She felt her mouth go dry even while she looked up at the three faces surrounding her.

She said, 'You know I've always loved you, Jack. Why do you treat me so bad?'

He smiled again, then leaned down and took her left hand in his giant paw. He stroked it briefly, then seized her little finger and snapped it back till it broke.

CHAPTER ELEVEN

I WAS BARELY awake the next morning when my phone rang. The sun was shining and birds were singing and for a moment I thought I'd lost a few months and Spring was busting out all over.

A woman's voice said, 'Hi, sorry if I got you up. It's Hannah Hall, from The Lucky Strike.'

I had to think hard for a couple of seconds before remembering the girl who'd brought my drinks and taken my card the night before.

I glanced at my clock and said, 'Let me guess, you've just got off your shift.'

'Wow, a private detective with psychic powers. Actually, no, my shift finished at midnight. I just woke up. So anyway, can we meet? I'll buy you coffee.'

'Name it.'

'You know the mall in Talke? That's about as out of the way as I can think of. Do they still have the coffee shop upstairs?'

'Far as I know. Ten o'clock okay?'

'Aren't you interested in what I want to talk about?'

'Hey, it's a free cup of coffee. I'll talk about whatever you want. Throw in a biscuit and I'll do impressions.'

THE MALL AT Talke is one of those retail outlets where they sell last year's clothes, remaindered books and cooking gear that for some reason has gone out of style and is now worth half what it was twelve months ago.

I parked and rode the escalator up to the Italian coffee shop, nestled amongst the girders and utility pipes that had been left exposed as part of its futuristic design.

Hannah Hall was already waiting for me and glanced around as I took the chair facing her. She was wearing black trousers and a baggy sweater underneath a shiny zip-up top. In The Lucky Strike her hair had been piled on her head and her make-up had been so defined I could hardly see her features. Now she seemed to be wearing no make-up and her brown hair fell on to her shoulders and part-way down her back. She seemed younger, too, maybe in her early twenties, with an open, pretty face characterised by wide, almond-shaped eyes that contained some intelligence.

I sat facing her and she said, 'Don't you want a drink?'

'Perhaps in a minute. I'm curious now.'

'Did you tell anyone you were coming here?'

'Only my three hundred Facebook friends. Why?'

'Don't joke. I didn't choose this place because of the coffee. I don't want anyone to know we've met.'

'I'll be as serious as you like, just tell me what's going on.'

She took a sip from her paper-cup and set it down delicately on the table as though its exact position might influence what I might think of her.

She said, 'When you came into the casino last night, were you working?'

'Can't a chap have a night off? Lose a little of his own money?'

'I told you, this is serious.'

'I can't talk about my work or my clients. Ask me another question.'

'I don't care who you might be working for. It's what you were doing there that's the problem.'

'In what way?'

She paused. 'Have you ever heard of Gloria Steinem?'

'The American feminist?'

'Very good.'

'Don't look so shocked. I can read and do joined-up writing and everything.'

'Sorry.'

'What about her?'

'Early in her career she got a job as a bunny at a Playboy club so she could write about the experience. It made her name as a writer.'

She stopped speaking and looked down. The coffee shop wasn't so much a shop as a large open space that accommodated stands selling baked potatoes and other fast food. The floor was tiled and there were no soft furnishings anywhere, so that people's voices and the scraping of chairs and footsteps echoed and were magnified. Below us, dozens of shoppers strolled idly through the mall, their voices and the high-pitched yells of their children rising upwards towards us in an indistinguishable cacophony.

I said, 'What are you telling me?'

'Can't the great detective work it out?'

'You're a writer?'

'Bingo. First year out of a journalism degree. At the Sentinel. Just part-time at the moment.'

'Births, marriages and deaths.'

'No, more of the online side. But I want to do more writing and less website layout.'

'So you're moonlighting at the club in order to expose it? That's a dangerous game. I wouldn't advise it.'

Her face lost some of its softness.

'I didn't come to you for advice. I don't need advice from some hardcase who thinks he's James Bond and talks like Wallace and Gromit.'

'Very harsh. I might need that coffee now to mask my tears. And besides, Gromit doesn't talk.'

'So are you going to tell me what you were doing there?'

I leaned forward and put my elbows on the table.

'I don't know why I should tell you anything. I don't know who you are or why you're here. And my business and my clients are exactly that—my business. What do you want?'

She put the lid on her coffee mug and tapped it down till it clicked closed.

'What I want is for you to not screw up what I'm doing. I don't know who you're working for, and in fact I don't know anything about private investigators at all. Except in films and TV. But I've spent a month working there and getting to know people and keeping my eyes and ears open.'

I leaned back and tried to appear relaxed. The thought of this young woman getting caught up with Jack Jenkins and his dealings was frightening. I'd only met him once, and according to Dickie Baines he wasn't on any official radars—but having met the man I knew his clothes wouldn't wash clean. He carried malevolence around with him like the smell from his rubber shoes.

I said, 'If I tell you what I'm doing, what will you do? What difference will it make?'

In reply, she leaned down and pulled a paperback-sized tablet from her bag, placing it on the table and opening its cover so it switched on.

She said, 'Do you use Evernote?'

'You'd have to ask my son. I don't think so.'

'I write stuff on this and when I'm connected through wifi it syncs to the cloud.'

'Your notes?'

She didn't reply because she was looking down at the device and opening an app. She tapped twice on the screen and then read what was there. Finally she looked up at me.

'It's hard watching what's going on and serving customers at the same time. You need eyes in the back of your head. But if you know what to look for, and people don't think you're a threat, it's amazing what you can learn.'

'Say more.'

She glanced down at the tablet. 'I won't give you all the detail because it's boring. But Jumbo has meetings with all sorts of people, and telephone conversations and even faxes, believe it or not.'

'Jumbo is Jenkins?'

'They call him Jumbo Jack if he's not there. When we call him JJ he thinks it stands for Jack Jenkins but it doesn't.'

'What else?'

She took a deep breath. 'I think the casino's a front. I'm not sure what for, but there are all sorts of strange goings on.'

'Such as?'

'For example, you'd think Saturday would be one of its busiest times, wouldn't you? Saturday afternoon, people can be bored and come in to do a little betting. Have a drink and watch the big TV. The other two local casinos are open then. But every Saturday The Strike is closed until six for normal punters. Instead there's another bunch of people who get privileged access, round the side. None of the waiting-on staff are used so there's no food or drinks being served unless JJ and the zombies do it themselves, which I doubt.'

'So what's going on?'

'Whatever it is, it's not legal. I've tried to hang around outside as though I'm waiting for my shift to start, but those big guys come out, close the doors and tell us to move. They clear the car park. I've managed to see cars arriving afterwards, but you don't get to see who's going in or coming out. When us plebs arrive at six everything's exactly as it should be, ready to go.'

'Don't they lose business to the other casinos? That's a big chunk of time on a Saturday. Customers will get pissed off and go elsewhere.'

'You'd think. But JJ lets them have a Happy Hour from six till seven—every drink free, whatever sort. That brings them back in. And to be honest, six o'clock is when the real action starts. Before then it's people with nothing better to do.'

I tried to work out what this activity might mean but I didn't have enough information.

Hannah went on, 'The only other clue I've got is that there are some new people around, just in the last two weeks.'

'What new people?'

'About twenty of them, young men.'

'What do they do?'

'That's it. They don't do anything. They're just hanging around, watching us work, watching the customers spend money. They sit at a table and drink and talk and laugh, then they go out for a bit, then they come back and drink some more.'

'What do they say?'

'I have no idea. They're Asian—Singapore or Hong Kong or Malaysia. They look at all the women as if they've never seen one before.'

'Do they talk to JJ?'

She gave a short laugh. 'I think they not only talk to him, they give him orders. He's twice as big as them but he's nervous around them, very placating, a big oily grin all over his face.'

'What do the other people at the casino think? You must have talked to them.'

'Not really. You don't have much spare time. And those gorillas in black suits walk around everywhere, sticking their noses in the kitchens, standing by the bar when you're fetching drinks. Staff turnover is high because most people can't take it for long.'

We sat quietly for a moment and watched a group of four girls below us in the main stretch of the mall. They were laughing and pushing each other and their shrieks and laughs came to us as if from a different world. Hannah was probably only half a dozen years older than them but she suddenly seemed much older.

I said, 'So what's your theory?'

'I don't know. If you do some research you find all sorts of stuff around gambling and organised crime in Asia, Singapore, the Philippines: gambling syndicates fixing games, triads being involved and all sorts. But it's hard to think it's going on in Stoke. Where's the money?'

'As you said, it could all be a front for something else.'

She put her tablet back in her bag.

'Your turn. What's your interest in the place?'

I wondered how much I could tell her. I had a duty of privacy towards Anjelica Strange that I didn't want to breach.

I said, 'My client is looking for someone. That someone has a connection to The Lucky Strike. I was there last night to check it out. That's as much as I can say.'

'Is that all? Not exactly a fair swap.'

'I have a client, you don't. It's not fair to her to go blabbing about her business.'

'So it's nothing to do with Jumbo Jack or whatever illegal stuff might be going on behind the scenes?'

'I didn't think so before, though I'm not certain now. You're right to think there's something odd going on. Casinos are so regulated they have to tread carefully. They're under constant scrutiny.'

She must have seen something in my face.

'But you've thought of something, haven't you?'

I wiggled my eyebrows.

'You don't get to do bad stuff and get away with it unless you've got an umbrella of some kind. If there's illegal activity going on, either it's not been spotted yet or it has and it's being sanctioned by someone.'

'You mean someone's looking after JJ? So he can do what he wants and get away with it?'

'That's a possibility.' I paused for a moment, thinking. 'Have you got a card?'

'No, I don't want you contacting me. I'm not carrying anything that can connect me to anyone.'

'What about your tablet and its notes?'

'Password protected.'

'Okay, so what if I have to get in touch?'

'Facebook friend me and send a private message. I check that most days. Look up my name, I'm the only Hannah Hall in the Stoke area. I'll friend you back.'

I stood up and she followed suit.

I said, 'I think you'd be best served if you quit this job and went and worked in Toys 'R' Us. The clientele aren't quite so difficult to deal with.'

She ignored my attempt at lightening the mood.

She said, 'What are you going to do now?'

'Well Gromit and I are going to see if we can find some Wensleydale down in the Food Court. Care to join us?'

She shook her head dismissively and walked off, smaller and frailer than I remembered her in the casino, when she was all gussied up and trying to look older and more confident and more like a denizen of an adult world she barely understood.

WHEN I REACHED my car I sat in the driving seat for a while and thought. This case seemed, like Spring, to be busting out all over. What had seemed a straightforward missing persons job had opened up into something much nastier. Of course none of it was any of my business. I'd found Lawrence Strano, talked to him and talked to Anjelica. All I had to do now was send in my invoice and go back to counting my Bitcoins.

But I knew that while this would have been a responsible course of action, it wasn't one I was likely to take in a million of your earth years.

Besides, I'd already pointed Belinda at Jumbo Jack Jenkins and asked her to find out where he went and who he saw, and I wouldn't have done that unless somewhere in the back of my scheming mind I was anticipating another strange turn of events. What Hannah Hall had told me about JJ and the influx of Asian 'customers' was intriguing and worrying in equal measure.

Of course what I should have done was call Inspector Howard and told him everything I knew.

But I had no evidence, no suggestion a crime had been committed, nothing on which to even base a request for a search warrant. It was gossip, rumour and speculation, all of which might have been fine as the editorial policy of a right-wing newspaper but wouldn't suffice to get Howard an audience with a judge.

After I'd done some more thinking I found my phone and called Dan. As was his habit nowadays, he answered on the first ring.

'Dad, you're up early.'

I glanced at my watch. It was almost eleven o'clock. Cheeky beggar.

I said, 'Do you still own one of those information terminals that help you probe other people's lives?'

'The laptop is at your disposal. What do you need?'

I gave him JJ's name and asked him to see what he could find out, if anything.

I said, 'There may not be much. He seems to have kept his nose clean.'

'I have sources not known to the common man.'

'Contacts in the NSA?'

'I couldn't tell you, otherwise I'd have to kill you.'

'It might be a relief from dealing with offspring who constantly try to outsmart you.'

'When the game's so easy, it's rude not to try.'

'See you later.'

'Not unless I see you first. See how easy it is?'

CHAPTER TWELVE

I WAS BEGINNING to believe my drive was being mistaken for a car park. When I turned the bend in the track, yet another large car was parked outside the front door. It was a dark blue SUV and it was empty.

After I'd parked and walked to my front door, I realised why it was empty—the passengers had broken into my house. Seeing they'd left their car out front I didn't think they were trying to hide or were likely to be dangerous, so I went inside cautiously.

Inside my living room I found Jack Jenkins sitting on my sofa as though he owned it. Standing to one side were Gonzo and Terry, and between them was Belinda. She was wearing the same clothes she'd been wearing the night before and she looked terrible, her hair lank, her face pinched and drained of colour. The men held her by the upper arm and she wasn't struggling. I noticed a couple of the fingers of her left hand seemed to be at odd angles. A heat began to build in my belly and I told myself to calm down and be sensible.

Jack Jenkins, JJ, Jumbo Jack … all three of them were housed in the one surfeit of flesh that was squeezing life from the cushions on my expensive leather sofa.

He said, 'Took your bloody time. I don't understand you, Dyke. Leaving a wonderful house like this unlocked so anyone can walk in. It's a good job my men spotted it and alerted me to the danger. You don't know who could have wandered in otherwise.'

'If you've come here to talk, JJ, then do it. Stop playing games that only entertain your half-witted camp-followers.'

Gonzo and Terry looked at each other as if asking whether I'd called them camp. But they were too occupied with Belinda to do anything about it.

I said to Belinda, 'Are you all right? What's happened to your fingers?'

JJ butted in before she could reply.

'Unfortunate accident when we got here. Caught her hand in the sliding door of the van. Couldn't be helped.'

I turned to him. 'Do me the service of shutting your fucking mouth for one second. Belinda, what happened?'

'Usual bully tactics to get me to talk.'

JJ interrupted again. 'She did well, your girl. Two fingers down and she was still game, still putting up a fight. Only when she saw the five big men standing around, looking her over, getting ready for a bit of fun and games … well, you get the picture. I don't have to use illustrative language for a man of your refinement, do I?'

Belinda said, her voice cracking slightly, 'They're animals, Sam. Literally. They shit where they sleep and prey on creatures smaller than themselves.'

The heat in my belly was reaching a temperature where it was likely to combust. I walked to Gonzo, grabbed his arm and pried Belinda's wrist from his grasp. I looked at Terry and he saw something in my face and released her other hand. She almost fell away from them and on to my chest. I backed away with her. She buried her face in my shirt briefly then drew a large sigh and turned to face JJ and his men.

JJ was struggling to his feet, massive and ungainly and almost falling back on to the sofa again when he briefly lost his balance.

He said, 'You didn't listen the first time Gonzo and Terry came here with my conciliatory offer. Someone had to be punished. Miss McFee did keep her mouth shut about you, but it was wasted effort. I already knew she was working with you. She says she doesn't know who your client is, but I have to be honest with you and say I don't believe that. We all know it's Lorenzo Strano's daughter. For some bizarre reason she seems to have hired you to stick your proboscis into my business. So, Mr Detective, what is it you want to know? Why are Lorenzo's activities so important they've led to the suffering endured so nobly by this poor girl?'

I walked up to him and looked him up and down.

'If you think I'm going to say anything to you after what you've done, you're a bigger fool than you look. Now get out of this house before I call the cops.'

'Oh, those are daring words, Mr Dyke. Very brave. What you don't know about me is I'm very loyal. When I took on Lorenzo I considered it to be a matter of honour, if you like. He became part of my family—not in that awful mafioso-type way, but someone I took under my wing. And once there, I'm going to do everything in my power to ensure he's safe and untroubled by people like yourself who seem intent on bringing up his past. How can you expect him to move on with his life if you keep reminding him of the one mistake he made? That's extremely ungenerous of you.'

'I don't see you moving towards the car yet. I do see lots of hot air, though.'

JJ looked at his two mountainous goons with disbelief on his face, then he took half a step closer to me.

'You really are most intractable, aren't you? Don't you believe that as an employer I have the best interests of my employees at heart?'

I nearly laughed in his face. I turned and glanced at Gonzo and Terry, who had both folded their arms to look more threatening.

'I don't believe you have the interests of anyone but yourself at heart. Fancy language doesn't disguise a one-track mind. You're about as transparent a crook as I've ever met, and I've met a few. The only mystery is how you've managed to evade getting slung in the nick so far.'

His expression didn't change but I thought I'd got through to him. His eyes flickered towards his two men but he thought better of whatever he was going to say and instead edged past me to head for the door.

He said, 'I can't be responsible for what you believe. However, I can be responsible for the outcomes that might develop if you carry on investigating me or any of my employees. Do I make myself understood?'

'The door's over there. Don't trip on the step on your way out.'

He stared at me, his face registering thoughts he didn't put into words. Then he turned and I watched his broad back as it drifted away from me like a receding sail, tacking this way and that as his legs rolled to accommodate each other. His men waited till he was out of the room, then unfolded their arms and followed him. Gonzo stopped briefly and made a gesture towards Belinda as though he was going to punch her, and she flinched. He laughed and nudged Terry in the arm and they walked away, almost whistling in their blithe misunderstanding of the impact of their actions.

IN THE CAR on the way to the hospital Belinda was quiet. She was still in pain and her face was drained and taut, as though she'd seen something she'd never expected to see in broad daylight.

I said, 'You don't have to tell me about it unless you want to.'

'Nothing to tell. They caught me by surprise, which was my own fault.'

'They're big men.'

She glanced at me. 'So, what … I couldn't have taken them?'

'Not what I meant.' I concentrated on the road. 'I meant they're brutal. If you'd have resisted they would have hurt you more.'

'But I would have had my say.'

'Is that what bothers you? You didn't get the opportunity to fight?'

'Just drop it, Sam. I'm tired and hungry. I'm not talking straight.'

We'd come out of the other side of Crewe centre and were on the long road that led directly to the hospital. The houses and shops set back from the road seemed banal and ridiculous in relation to the conversation we'd just had with Jack Jenkins.

I said, 'Did they—'

'No. I talked. Okay?'

'I understand, don't worry about it.'

She was looking out of the passenger window. 'I think we should dissolve this partnership.'

'Is that what it is?'

'Obviously I can't be trusted when things get tough. You should find another man to work with, if that's what you need.'

'They broke your fingers, Belinda. Don't give yourself a hard time about that. It sounds like Jenkins knew who you were anyway.' Something occurred to me. 'Didn't he say he already knew you were working with me?'

'What of it?'

'Who told him? How did he find that out?'

She turned to look at me. 'Putting two and two together. You being an investigator, me sitting and watching them. An easy conclusion.'

'But that's not what he said. He said he *already knew* you were working with me, before he took you prisoner. So how did he find out before he even brought you in?'

She was silent and we both thought for a while, watching houses go by.

Then she said, 'My licence plate. He must know someone who could run plates.'

'And who do we know who has the ability to run licence plates to find the owner?'

Neither of us needed to answer that. We said nothing as we drew closer to the hospital, the Friday afternoon traffic thickening around us.

Eventually she said, 'I can't report this to the police.'

'I know.'

'It's assault but I have no witnesses. And he'll have men who'll swear blind he was water-skiing or bowling at the time.'

'Although of course he couldn't stand too near to the bowling balls.'

She took my drift and grinned.

'For fear of someone sticking their fingers up his nose and trying to roll him down the lane.'

'See, we do make a good partnership after all.' I turned into the Emergency Admissions car park. 'Now grit your teeth and prepare yourself for a bit more pain.'

'Nothing could be as bad as that joke.'

CHAPTER THIRTEEN

THE HOSPITAL SET Belinda's fingers and gave her painkillers. I'd phoned Dan while I was waiting and asked him to phone a cab, so when Belinda finally emerged with a cast on her left hand we trooped out to my car and drove back to the casino. Belinda's car was still on the street where it had been left overnight, and Dan got into the driver's seat and with me driving with Belinda we set off in convoy towards her house in south Manchester, the night dark and increasingly chill around us.

Once there we made her a cup of tea and then finally tiredness overcame her and Dan and I left to drive home. We didn't say much for most of the journey, both of us thinking about JJ's casual cruelty and the mindset it must take to behave like an animal with no awareness of other people's pain.

Eventually Dan said, 'She's tough, that one.'

'I don't think she's finished with Jenkins yet.'

'She can't do anything with her hand in that state. She could barely switch on the kettle.'

'You didn't see the look in her eye. JJ's in for some trouble.'

He shifted in his seat. 'I think she'd be better off not getting involved with him.'

I glanced sideways at him. 'You found something?'

'No, I didn't. And that's the point.'

'Too clean?'

'For someone who's managed to get a gaming licence, he's amazingly vanilla. Married and divorced twice. Never had any problems with the police—which in itself doesn't mean anything, but from what we've seen of him so far he doesn't seem like a shrinking violet. You would have thought he'd had some run-ins with the police at some point.'

'So what are you thinking?'

'Well either he gets other people to do the rough stuff and stays in the background, which we know isn't true, or someone's walking behind him picking up his droppings.'

'Which would only be someone pretty high-up. And why would they do that?'

'Given the environment he works in, I'll bet money is involved somewhere.'

'I'd bet on that too.'

SATURDAY MORNING IN Stoke meant columns of cars heading like lemmings up the hill towards the Potteries Centre—the mall in central Hanley—or turning off to head into the Festival Park retail zone to visit PC World and Toys 'R' Us and Morrisons supermarket.

The air temperature was continuing its decline towards winter as I parked a little way from The Lucky Strike, pulled a watch cap over my head and stuck my hands into the pockets of my North Face fleece. I'd changed my trousers and shoes and hoped I might present a different outline to the one JJ and his men would recognise.

I ambled around the corner of a giant sofa store and found a position where I could see the casino. There were a dozen cars in the furniture outlet's car-park but there wasn't much traffic in and out. A couple pushing a baby stroller hurried by, ignoring me.

It was 11:30 and under the moody skies the grey facing of the casino, together with its square design, made it look like an enormous concrete slab. There were a couple of pipes in its roof through which white steam exited spasmodically. I also noticed about half a dozen aerials and electronic configurations on the roof, about as complex as the bridge of a destroyer. I wondered how many of them were recent additions.

At five to midday a couple of the big bouncers came out of the tall glass entrance doors and scouted the car park. I'd noticed the wooden barrier pole had been lowered earlier, so any punters who didn't know about the afternoon closure and turned up on the off-chance wouldn't have been able to enter anyway.

Seemingly satisfied, the bouncers went back inside and a moment later a different one came out—Terry, the fair-haired one. He half-walked, half-trotted to the entrance pole and put a key into a box next to it, then stood back and waited. Within a couple of minutes two long black cars turned the corner of the retail park and Terry pressed a button and the pole lifted. The cars passed beneath, Terry pressed the button again and the pole came down. The cars purred through the car park and down a narrow access road that led to the side of the casino. They pulled up and half a dozen small men got out of the two cars and hurried inside, their heads down. The cars glided to the end of the road then performed some awkward manoeuvres before returning towards me, now facing outwards. I imagined the chauffeurs inside lying back and lighting a smoke.

I retreated out of sight of the casino and wondered what it meant and what I should do next. The constant hum of traffic around the park was getting on my nerves and I thought maybe I should go home and stare out of my windows at the countryside. That usually calmed me down.

To my right, a small blue Citroen pulled into a lined parking slot and Lorenzo Strano got out. He reached inside the back door and pulled out a rollbag, then stood up and pulled down his suit jacket and brushed his lapels. Always dapper. He closed the driver's door and pressed the fob to lock it, then headed away at an angle to me towards the casino. I guessed he was supposed to be on the current shift.

I moved across to intercept him and called out his name. He stopped and looked at me, frowning. Then he realised who the strange figure with the hat pulled over his brow was and raised and dropped his arms in frustration.

'Is this how you get your jollies, Dyke? Following people around and pissing them off?'

'It's not what you think, Mr Strano. I was here before you. But while you're here I should tell you some things.'

He glanced towards the casino as though fearful it was watching him.

'You can't tell me anything. It's a casino. It's nice and bright and shiny and it pays my rent and the loan for my expensive car.'

'Yesterday Jack Jenkins kidnapped a friend of mine and subjected her to torture. He broke two of her fingers so she'd tell him my name. The fact that he already knew my name didn't seem to figure into his thinking. He did it for kicks. If that's part of any moral universe you want to belong to, then prison has had a worse effect on you than I thought possible.'

'Don't hold me responsible for what other people do. I've had enough of that in my life and it's not going to happen any more.'

'What do you mean?'

'You're right, prison does change the way you look at things. It all becomes very black and white. The things you thought were important seem pathetic, and what you used to believe had no impact on the way you behaved suddenly becomes very relevant.'

'I'm not following you.'

'Let me try to simplify it. Have you ever had a dog you mistreated and yet it still followed you around? You could kick it and beat it and refuse to give it food, but it still looks up at you with big eyes and follows in your footsteps as if you can do no wrong.'

'You'll have to explain that.'

'Just think what it's like to be the dog. You might have some idea of what life has been like for me in the last ten years.'

He turned to move away when our attention was caught by another figure hurrying towards us across the car park. I'd been vaguely aware of a sports car shuttling closer and taking a space but I hadn't given it any attention, hadn't realised it was a Porsche Boxter.

Anjelica Strano wore a woollen jacket with a high collar and tight jeans tucked into ankle-length black boots. Her hair had been blown about as she'd crossed the concrete and her face was red-cheeked, her eyes lustrous. She looked glorious.

But her mood was dark.

She walked up to her father and stared at him, then raised a hand and struck him on the cheek. He didn't flinch and he didn't turn away.

He said, 'Anjelica—'

'Don't say anything. Just listen. I hired this man to find you, and he did. The fact he's now having clandestine meetings with you makes me wonder exactly who I've been dealing with and what I've been paying for. But never mind that. I wanted to tell you that you don't have the right to take yourself away from me. Not after eight years. You owe me time, and I don't want to hear any excuses.' She paused. 'Now I've said that, I think I might have changed my mind. I don't think I want anything to do with you or—' she turned to me— 'you either.'

'Let me explain—'

'No explanations. I followed you this morning because my life so far has taught me not to trust anyone, particularly men. When we spoke last time I saw in your face you weren't going to give up on this. That damned persistence you're so proud of. I knew you'd try to see him again because you don't like to lose, do you?'

'It's a trait I'm trying to overcome.'

'Well it's too late. I look forward to receiving your invoice. And father, nice knowing you.'

She turned on her heels and strode towards her Porsche. Her father and I both watched her.

He said, 'This is going really well for you, isn't it?'

I said nothing but thought to myself the case was probably now well and truly closed.

CHAPTER FOURTEEN

HE HAD ALWAYS been a fastidious dresser and had ensured that every house he'd owned had been equipped with built-in wardrobes and full-length mirrors. His wife had put it down to a form of OCD, a particular need for order and sequence that was useful in some circumstances, but most of the time was simply an irritation to those around him.

Thoughts of his wife came more rarely these days, especially as he didn't see her that often. Only when, as now, he was fixing a knot in a tie, or perhaps ironing a shirt, did their life together come back into his consciousness. Life as a senior police officer was difficult without a partner to be seen in tow at the increasing number of official events and dinners he attended. Although some of his closer acquaintances knew they'd separated, it was something he didn't mention if he could help it. It wasn't only the fact of the separation that hurt, it was the nature of the split that was so debilitating—Sara had 'run off with' a funeral director. Not a high-flying CEO or a well-known actor or even a landscape gardener … but someone who wore black all day long and drove a car at a top speed of twenty miles an hour. What could he tell himself about that? Her life lacked excitement so she'd sought it elsewhere?

It hardly seemed to fit.

He sighed and put those thoughts out of his mind. He finished with the tie, smoothing it down carefully, then picked out a dark blue jacket—Cardin, if he remembered correctly—and slipped it on. He pulled down his shirt cuffs below the level of the sleeves and thought he looked all right. Still trim, his hair peppering slightly but as thick as it was when he was twenty-five, his skin smooth and well-shaved. He'd read recently that smoking tended to produce more wrinkles and he was glad he'd never learned the habit.

He went downstairs and checked everything was turned off and unplugged from the wall. Another of the routines he supposed his ex-wife hated. She didn't understand how careful you had to be with electricity. Circuits became overloaded, fuses failed to work … the next thing you knew, three children had been burned in a bedroom fire. He never left his house without unplugging the television and the kettle, just to be on the safe side.

One last look in the mirror by the door to check his hair was still lying flat and then he left.

Outside, his Citroen C5 gleamed in a watery sunshine. It was still early and he'd read that later in the day it was likely to rain. He expected to be back home before then, though.

He hesitated, wondering whether to go back inside for his umbrella, but decided the hell with it and climbed into the car and reversed out of his drive. What was the point of living if you didn't take a chance now and then?

AS HE APPROACHED Hanley he felt his usual anger start to burn in his stomach. It wasn't anger directed outwardly, it was anger at himself and his own weakness. All his life he'd been careful, neat and forward-looking. So how had he managed to put himself in a position where he owed two hundred and thirty thousand pounds? If he thought about it rationally he knew exactly how it had come about—starting small, then losing progressively bigger amounts as he tried to win back the money he'd lost. The classic loser's progress. He knew gambling was a mug's game but there was something about the prospect of winning, of fate turning those cards up in your favour instead of to the benefit of the unsmiling brute facing you …

Now he was steeped so far in shit he couldn't lift his feet out of it. Any wrong move and he'd face not just shame, but punishment on a nuclear scale, from any number of providers.

Thankfully, his position and role had afforded him a good deal of opportunity as well as protection. There were custodians guarding the guards, but he'd managed so far to keep a clean sheet. So during the last few years he'd been able to wrest back some of the control he'd lost to the syndicate's minions. When first asked to lose a few reports, to ignore what Strano was telling him, it was easy enough. Things were simpler then and he was his own boss. Strano never knew what was going on until it was too late for him to do anything, and then he had found himself in a position he couldn't fight. It was tricky for a while but in the end, faced with little option, Strano had played ball and bitten the bullet. Working at the casino was a fair reward for the bother he must have endured in jail.

Now, Passmore thought, it was time to make the final play. Although he still owed the money, he had an organisation and a structure he could work with. The bunch of oriental ninjas he was in bed with were definitely a threat, and he hated the fact they were currently swarming all over The Lucky Strike in preparation for the Big Event, but he had Jenkins and his team in line and he had a plan to pay back what he owed and get out from underneath without losing face.

After all, that was the most important outcome for the ninjas, wasn't it?

THE SECURITY POLE was open because the Saturday night revellers had left only an hour or so beforehand. Passmore drove through the entrance and up the access road until he was parked outside the side entrance. He glanced around before he got out but could see no one. The threat of rain had abated and the clouds were lifting on the horizon as daybreak grew stronger.

One of the goons welcomed him and closed the door behind him. Passmore stood for a moment in the large open space that led via several corridors to the kitchens, the administrative offices and, once you'd passed through a couple of fire doors, into the main gaming areas. He could feel the magnetic pull of the tables even though they were closed down and he was there on business. He thought of it as a drug he hadn't conquered, yet, and as such it wasn't exactly his fault the lure still attracted him. He felt his mouth go dry and his right hand trembled slightly; he jammed it into his trouser pocket so it didn't give any signals.

Eventually he nodded to the goon, a large man with prominent features, as though they'd been hewn from rock by a sculptor with little talent, and followed him towards Jack Jenkins' office. The concrete floor and the high ceiling reminded him of an aircraft hangar he'd visited as a child, taken to the Gaydon airshow by parents who spent most of the time bickering.

They passed through more doors until they came to Jenkins' office. Its door was open and the goon knocked with a delicate knuckle. Passmore was amused by the effort Jenkins put into being the boss, as though he too wasn't bought and sold by the

Asian syndicate which held paper on all of them and governed their lives with an iron grip.

Unwilling to let Jenkins assume any kind of superiority, he pushed open the door and walked straight in without waiting for a reply. Jenkins, in his habitual shell suit, was bent behind his desk, struggling to close a drawer. His massive shoulders and backside bloomed into the space like the curve of an enormous beach ball.

Passmore said, 'Hard at work, are we? A bit of do-it-yourself carpentry?'

Jenkins stood up, his round face purple with exertion, his hair dishevelled.

He said, 'Your idea to get here this fucking early. Take me as you find me, which happened to be closing a drawer that suddenly has ideas above its station.'

'Can we talk?'

Jenkins knew this was the instruction to clear the room. He nodded at the goon and moments later the office door closed behind them. Passmore looked around and found a chair to his liking, dragging it into the centre of the room so he could face Jenkins directly. He sat on it and crossed his legs and folded his arms, waiting for Jenkins to organise himself and sit down. The light in the room came from drab fluorescents which cast dismal shadows and showed up the coarseness of Jenkins' skin now that his moisturiser had worn off.

Passmore said, 'Your message said you had something to tell me. Speak.'

'Someone's sniffing around Larry Strano.'

'Who? And more importantly, why?'

'Some dickhead called Dyke. Private Investigator. We think he was hired by Strano's daughter to find him.'

Passmore felt his spine straightening in the chair.

'Anjelica? Has she been here?'

'Not as far as I know. Dyke has, though. And we had that woman McFee in for a little chat. Turned out she was connected—'

'You mustn't let Anjelica Strano into this building or let her see her father. Is that clear?'

Jenkins frowned. 'He's her dad. I can stop her coming in, but if he wants to go see her, he can. I can't stop him.'

Passmore felt his anger burning at his innards again.

'Strano won't make a move towards her, I can promise you that. But you must ensure she doesn't come here.'

'Why are you so concerned about her?'

'There's no reason for her to be involved in any of this. Do you hear me?'

Jenkins shrugged, his massive shoulders rising and falling inside his shell suit.

'I've got a lot on my mind, if you hadn't noticed. I've got nearly fifty people working here, I can't keep my eyes on all of them.'

'I don't care about your management style. I don't care about your working practices. You've got a nerve if you think you're going to get any sympathy from me, given the time and effort I laid out to make sure you got this place.'

Jenkins raised a stubby finger and pointed at Passmore. 'I don't want your sympathy. I just want a rational response. Strano's one man. You insisted I took him on and I'm not going to shoulder the responsibility of nannying him. He's your orphan, you can look after him.'

'You really are a weasel, aren't you? If it wasn't for me you wouldn't be sitting there struggling to shut a drawer. And if it wasn't for *him*, I wouldn't be sitting here laughing at you and wondering who your couturier was. Get your priorities right, you arse-face, or both of us will be rinsed down the plug-hole when Phar decides he doesn't like us any more.'

Jenkins sat down, evidently steaming but knowing Passmore was right.

After a moment he said, '"Arse-face" is a bit unfair. It's a good insult but it doesn't mean much. Doesn't create much of a mental image.'

'I'll work on my similes and metaphors. Tell me more about Belinda McFee. I'd like to think my abusing the vehicle database brought some kind of reward.'

As Jenkins outlined what he'd done with McFee, Passmore felt a great weariness settling over him. Torturing a young woman was not what he'd had in mind as an endgame when he started playing poker. He could barely bring himself to look at Jenkins as he explained his visit to Dyke and described what had been said between them.

The room fell quiet and Passmore realised that Jenkins had finished.

He said, 'And in your expert opinion, will Dyke back off at this juncture? Now you've injured his partner and invaded his home? Did he seem like the kind of character to be dissuaded from his chosen path by a demonstration of brute force and ignorance?'

'You had to be there. I didn't have any choice. Your words—this is a game of high stakes now. What was I supposed to do, let him crawl all over us? You have to get off your high horse and realise you're in this game shit-deep, the same as the rest of us. This thing you've got set up is riskier than any game of poker with any Triad boss.'

Passmore felt himself beginning to sweat at the thought of Phar's involvement in their plans. This wasn't what he'd intended either. The idea was to set it up using local talent, people Passmore knew, not to involve ninjas shipped over in bulk from whichever Asian hell-hole they came from. Phar had been in residence for three weeks now after running with his tail between his legs from Las Vegas, the FBI no more than a day behind him. He'd landed at London and headed north immediately, into the obscurity of a gated mansion in south Cheshire, twenty minutes from the casino. And twenty minutes from Passmore and Jenkins, two men who owed him. He'd demanded Jenkins set up a wire-room in the casino so he could come in and gamble—if that's what you called betting on fixed games—every Saturday afternoon. And he'd arranged it so that his men had flown in to different airports around the country and were scattered in hotel rooms and rented flats within the same radius.

There was no doubt he saw Passmore's Event as a big score. It was relatively minor in terms of the monetary value of the prize, but for sheer nerve and shock value, it would make news headlines all over the country and maybe worldwide. Yes it would pay off Passmore's debt, but it would also be a coup. A gambling man to his bones, Phar liked that.

Passmore's sweat pooled in the small of his back and ran down to his seat.

He said, 'Can you keep it together for two weeks? Do I have to look over your shoulder every day?'

'You know, it's funny how you come in here and act as though I'm the problem. I'm beginning to think you're so aggressive just to divert attention from your own fear.'

'The only thing I'm afraid of is you'll screw it up. Kidnap Princess Kate just so she can't spill imaginary beans. Phone in to a television station and threaten a newsreader if she mentions Stoke again. Can I remind you it was you who asked me to come in today? I've got much more important things to be doing on a Sunday morning.'

'Communication is the secret of good teamwork, Billy. If we can't communicate with each other, how are we going to know each other's deepest feelings? How can we ever put things right between us?'

Passmore stood up.

'I've forgotten more about teamwork than you'll ever know. That's all they ever talk about on fucking police leadership courses these days. If you want to work as a team with Phar and his ninjas, go to it. I'll sit and watch, thanks very much. I'll see myself out. Keep those steroid-filled penguins out of my way.'

Jenkins spread his hands, a sly grin pulling at his lips.

'Can't I interest you in a little flutter? A few minutes on one of the machines? Number Three's up for a jackpot soon, I'm told.'

Passmore knew what Jenkins was doing, baiting him, playing to his weakness, but he refused to bite.

'Don't call me again unless you have to. Text the second phone number I gave you. Next time we meet somewhere else, this is too exposed.'

'I could set up a baccarat table for you, if you like … '

Passmore turned and left the room, knowing his ears and the back of his neck were blushing.

ON THE DRIVE back he was consumed with guilt and rage in equal measure. He felt guilty that he was putting himself and others in a difficult situation; and rage at himself and at the people he was forced to work with to achieve his ends.

He barely saw the Sunday traffic streaming past him towards the retail parks and malls of Hanley, each car filled, he supposed, with grinning families eager to spend money on foreign electronic goods. He wanted to be clear of it all, void of responsibility, even of power. Power was no good if you didn't enjoy wielding it, and he'd never taken much pleasure in telling people what to do or where they'd fallen short in exercising their duties. It didn't seem appropriate for someone like him, with all his faults, to be criticising and assessing people who were doing their best. He knew what it was like to be out on the streets, facing all that shit, when inside you were possibly craven or fearful or unsure of your own authority over others. Of course he'd known coppers who were in the force precisely because of that, because they wanted to demonstrate their perceived superiority and being in the police was the only way they could do it legitimately.

But that wasn't him.

For him, it had started as a way of putting things right. As a child in Kent he'd always seen injustice starkly, as an imbalance in the way the world operated. He'd been a cub scout, then a prefect at school. Always looking for a uniform or a designation that would enable him to act with authority, to say, This is wrong and must stop. He thought of it as his moral core, almost biblical in its strength, though he wouldn't dare to bring that level of authority to his actions in the here and now.

He pulled up outside Sara's house and pressed his horn once. The curtains twitched and a moment later the front door opened.

Seeing his daughter again always forced a catch into his breathing. Barely thirteen, she was slim and limber and still child-like in her enthusiasm for life. When he and Sara had separated, the wrench from Bella was the hardest thing to bear. Not to be in the same house as her energy, her smile, her smell. Although he had good visiting privileges, his work schedule meant he couldn't use them all, so this regular Sunday morning outing meant much more to him. It was a fixed point.

She came out of the door running, her skirt flapping around her knees. Each week she seemed older, slightly more lanky, her hair a fraction longer. Soon she would be taller than her mother and catching up on him. Becoming more adult than child, perhaps.

He had unlatched the door and now she yanked it wide open and leaped inside.

'Hi, Dad. You're early.'

'Couldn't wait to get here, sweetheart.'

He drove off and listened to her jabber away in his ear, still half-thinking about what Jenkins had said in that other world. A world he couldn't believe he inhabited. A world Bella could never be allowed to see.

Despite himself, he thought he understood how Larry Strano would find it hard to refuse the call of his daughter. She was another girl who brought life into a room, with her beauty and intelligence. He had tried to help her when he could, showing willing to Strano's wife and daughter like a good boss should. It had been difficult to face them sometimes, given his role in Strano's imprisonment, but he thought he'd persuaded them he was on the straight and narrow.

As they drew closer to their destination, his mind was drawn again to Jenkins and his men and the ninjas. He didn't know when he'd started calling them that, especially as they weren't even Japanese. He had an irrational prejudice that because they were from Singapore and Malaysia they'd be expert in martial arts, like Bruce Lee. But it was more likely they were mathematics wizards who could compute the odds on any fall of any pair of dice at the drop of a hat.

He just hoped they knew how to behave in a civilized British institution long enough to let the Event unfold.

Bella said, 'There's a space, Daddy.'

She was pointing and he saw the gap in the line of cars she was referring to. He drove past it half a car's length, then reversed back into it. He had barely turned off the engine before Bella had opened the door and was outside waiting impatiently.

He turned the mirror and inspected his hair and the hang of his tie. Nothing to worry about there. Then he climbed out of the car and extended his hand. Bella ran to him and took it, her small fist feeling cool and tender in his own.

They walked a few yards down the street, then turned in through the arch over the pathway and, a few yards after that, passed through the wide church doors into the cool darkness within.

CHAPTER FIFTEEN

I DIDN'T KNOW why I was driving to Dan's house in the middle of the afternoon. I had a cover story—something about watching a football match over a beer—but he knew I didn't like football much so it was bound to make him suspicious.

I'd spent the morning reading the Sunday paper and walking around the house, looking for something to do. The clash with Anjelica Strange the day before had set me on edge. Partly it was because I felt I'd been privy to a family ritual that should have been kept private. And partly it was because I didn't like leaving a job unfinished. The thought of Jenkins carrying on his blithe way, like a gigantic whaling ship gobbling up smaller creatures en route, made me sick to my stomach. His treatment of Belinda deserved repayment of some kind, but I was struggling to come up with any ideas short of telling Dickie Baines what I'd found out and letting government agencies take the weight.

Dan acted as though he was expecting me, opening the door, nodding once and then heading back inside. I noticed how he seemed to be thickening around the chest these days, gaining more solidity as he grew into himself and asserted his personality.

I waved the four cans I held in my hand, feeling like a zookeeper tempting a wild beast to come back to his cage with a tidbit. It was rather pathetic and a blatant attempt at currying favour and it didn't fool Dan for a moment. He stopped and looked at me, then at the beer, then at me again.

'What's going on?'

'The match, you know. I thought you might like a break.'

'From what? My hard labour in the fields? I've only been up two hours.'

I glanced at my watch automatically. It was 2:30. He was on a different timescale, staying up for most of the night to trade in Bitcoins.

'I thought you might like to spend time with your old dad. Unless you've got a girl-friend I don't know about.'

Some while ago he'd been involved with an American girl who'd been kidnapped by a Liverpudlian thug. Eventually she and her family had gone back to the States and I hadn't seen him with a girl since. I didn't know whether he was still grieving or just couldn't be bothered.

He said, 'The hours I keep, any sort of friend is out of the question. Are you going to sit down or what?'

I sat down on the sofa as requested, still holding the cans in my hand. Now I felt like an intruder. I didn't know what kind of welcome I'd expected — I hadn't really thought it through. In my head I supposed he'd be glad to see me and greet me with open arms and perhaps a piece of cake.

I said, 'Sorry, this seemed like a good idea when I started out. I forgot you're awake all night. Like shift work.'

'I was about to make a cup of tea. Do you want one?'

'Okay. Too early for beer anyway.'

He took the cans from my hand and took them with him into the kitchen. I heard the fridge door open and close as he put them away for later.

I hunted down the television remote control and found the channel that was going to show the football match. Talking heads discussing what might happen, laughing at their own incompetence. I turned it off again and sat staring into space until Dan came back with two cups.

He said, 'Don't fancy it?'

'They say it'll be a no-score draw. I couldn't take the excitement.'

He sat facing me. He was wearing a short-sleeved black tee-shirt with a faded image of The Stranglers printed on it. He wasn't even born when they were in their heyday. I wasn't very old myself. I became aware of the oddness of the situation between us, a father and son who worked together from time to time but barely knew each other. Perhaps it was my dealings with the Strano father-and-daughter duo, but ideas about family and heritage had begun to swirl through my head in the last forty-eight hours. I didn't know what any of it meant, but it was awkward to think about.

I said, 'My dad used to do shift-work, down the mine. Before I was born, when there was plenty of work there.'

'I read *The Road to Wigan Pier* last month. Tough job down a mine. Was he tall, like Orwell?'

'Who, Dad? Not particularly. Stocky. Had white hair quite early but kept it all his life. Thick. He was like a Welshman.'

'What's your mum like?'

'She was pretty when she was young. There was a photo used to stand on the mantelpiece of them on their wedding day. Thin as rakes, the pair of them. Married in the sixties, but you wouldn't know it from their hair and clothes. Very traditional.

There's a photo of them somewhere going off on their honeymoon in a pastel green Ford Zephyr. I think they went to Filey.'

'Where's Filey?'

'The east coast. Always windy. There used to be a Butlins camp up there but I don't know if it still exists. I don't know if any Butlins camps exist any more.'

We sipped from our tea like an old married couple.

He said, 'What's happening with that Strange woman?'

I told him about my meeting the day before with Strano and his daughter and how it had ended.

He said, 'So that's really it, then? I had a nice call from Belinda yesterday, thanking me for taking her home.'

'How is she? I should have called myself.'

'Yes, you should, seeing as she was injured in the line of duty. She's all right. Bored. Wants to know if there's anything she can do.'

'I'll call her later.'

We sipped from our tea again while we waited for one of us to think of the next topic of conversation.

Dan said, 'Had you ever thought of taking me to see my grandmother?'

The tea-induced quiet became chilly. We hadn't talked about this before, but we both knew it was dangerous territory. My mother lived alone in the house she'd shared with my father for over forty years. I telephoned her most weekends but hadn't been to see her in months. The time had slipped away from me. As far as Dan was concerned, I'm sure he believed I was keeping him away from his grandmother.

And I wasn't sure he was wrong.

Not having seen him grow up, neither I nor my mother had a typical relationship with him. I felt this as a lack, an absence of

… something. Not exactly warmth—I wasn't cool towards him, or dismissive, or any kind of feeling you would characterise as negative.

He was just someone I happened to know now. I hadn't known he'd been born because my wife had run off to London saying she'd had a miscarriage and didn't want to know me any more. So it wasn't as though I was aware of his existence for eighteen years and felt his absence during that time. Instead there had been nothing, no fatherly feelings at all.

Now he said, 'Don't you ever wonder what it's been like for me? I had lots of families while I was growing up but none of them was real. And I had no grandparents, no actual grandparents. Now grand-dad's dead and I've never met my grandmother. It's like you're hiding me from her.'

'That's not true. There just hasn't been time.'

'You're supposed to make time. That's what being a family means.'

'I don't even feel we *are* a family.'

This was going horribly wrong. I hadn't intended for that sentence to come out as harshly as it seemed. Dan practically recoiled, as though I'd pushed a sour onion under his nose.

I said, 'I didn't mean it like that. I meant we haven't grown up together, any of us. So it's all a bit weird.'

'You're not helping.'

'I don't know how to help. I don't know what you went through, or what you're thinking now. Take that Strange girl, she was separated from her father at seventeen, a terrible age. I have no idea what it must have been like for her.'

'I have.'

He said it like he was pushing a knife in my side, with a little twist at the end for the extra pain it would cause.

I said, 'I can't change that. I'm sorry for what you went through, of course I am. But I can't go back in time and change my life and your mother's life so it all ends happily.'

'Tell me shit happens.'

'I'd best go.'

I stood up, putting my tea cup on a low table first.

Dan said, 'You didn't answer the question. Why haven't you taken me to see my grandmother?'

'I don't know. I've got no excuse.'

He'd remained sitting on his chair but he'd grown pink in the face and wasn't looking at me. It was a situation I hated, especially as I'd come with the best of intentions.

He said, 'I've got to go out.'

'I'll leave.'

'No, stay. Watch the television. Do what you want.'

Now I felt trapped. If I left he'd take it as a snub. But I didn't really need to stay there and watch television. I could go home and sleep.

I said, 'I'll perhaps watch something, have a drink.'

'Good.'

I sat down as he stood up and left the room.

Moments later he came back wearing a denim jacket I'd never seen before. He seemed more conciliatory.

He said, 'Don't worry about it. Don't drink too much. There's cheese in the fridge if you want something to eat.'

'Cheese is good.'

He nodded, then walked to the front door and left. He didn't have a car so I assumed he was heading somewhere in walking distance or he was being picked up. I wondered distantly what he was up to but then cut off that train of thought immediately. I wouldn't have wanted my parents to think about what I was doing at that age.

I leaned back on the sofa and stared at the blank television screen. I told myself to remember that Dan was a complete adult, someone who was of my flesh and had some of my genes and DNA flowing in his blood.

But I had no idea who he was.

It occurred to me out of nowhere that perhaps this was how Anjelica Strange felt about her own father.

THIRTY MINUTES LATER it was half-time in the match and I was thinking about opening one of the cans of beer. My phone rang, irrepressibly chirpy, and I pressed the button to reply.

Belinda said, 'There you are.' Her voice had an echo and there was a distant whooshing sound behind the signal. 'I'm in the car, heading your way. You weren't at home. Can I meet you? Where are you, incidentally?'

I told her I was at Dan's house. She knew where it was. She said she'd be with me in twenty minutes and we hung up.

Eighteen minutes later she turned into Dan's drive. She was in a dark blue Peugeot 206, a small and quiet car compared to her pink Volvo.

I opened the door for her. She'd recovered some of her colour and had a new bandage around her damaged left hand. In fact it wasn't just a bandage, it was a cast that wrapped around her palm and left her two small fingers protruding upright, also splinted and held rigid.

She pushed inside, grinning and looking around.

'Dan not here?'

'With a friend. I was watching football.'

'I swapped cars. A mate of mine in Burnage.'

'Why did you do that?'

'Still on the job, me, assuming you're still paying. I've just come from Hanley, thought I'd see if you were available.'

'Seems I am.'

By now we were in Dan's pale sitting room. She sat in one of his comfortable seats, placing her hands on the arms like the chairman of the board and crossing her legs.

'Guess what I saw this morning?'

'You weren't there again … '

'That fat bastard's not going to put me off just with a bit of physical argy-bargy. So guess what I saw.'

'Jenkins ascending to heaven on a white cloud.'

'Would be nice, but no. He had a visitor. Guess who.'

'Come on, Belinda.'

'Billy Passmore. Large as life and twice as smooth.'

'Are you sure?'

I'd never seen Passmore and had no concept of his appearance.

'I had Dan send me some photos he'd got online. Got my own, too.'

She pulled her hand from the leather jacket she was wearing and produced a compact Panasonic camera. She looked at the back and switched it on, then moved a knob so it was in Playback mode. She handed the camera to me.

Billy Passmore had apparently just climbed out of his car, which was parked by the side of the casino, and was looking directly at the camera.

Belinda said, 'Press to go right.'

I manipulated the large button on the back of the camera and the next image came up. He was walking into the casino, his stride long and his demeanour purposeful.

'He was in there twenty minutes then came out. I followed him back to Nantwich, where he stopped outside a house and a girl who I guess was his daughter came out. They went to church together. Isn't that sweet?'

I gave the camera back to her and she switched it off. The lens retracted into the body as if going to sleep after its long hard day.

She said, 'Thoughts, boss-man? Is this good or what?'

'Presumably he was visiting Jenkins.'

'I saw him arrive at seven-thirty. Passmore turned up at eight. Early morning worm catching. Important conversation, I suppose. Things in the offing. What shall I do?'

I had to admit it was interesting. Jenkins and Passmore meeting probably meant Passmore still had some involvement in Lorenzo Strano's life. But what? Why such an early meeting? I presumed JJ had contacted Passmore because of my and Belinda's presence. If Strano's position at The Lucky Strike meant anything, then Passmore would be the one to know and the one with the power in this situation. Whatever his current or future role in investigating corruption, he was involved in this particular state of affairs. So what did Strano know that was so important?

I said, 'Give up on Jenkins for the time being. Let's find out how Passmore and Strano are involved with each other.'

'Got it.'

'So perhaps the first thing is to find out where Strano lives.'

'Your contacts not good enough?'

'I'm guessing he's in a flat or house somewhere but not under his own name. Not yet, anyway. He's probably in a place found for him by Jenkins, or by Passmore operating through Jenkins. Let's find it, then we'll have a better idea where we stand.'

She stood and zipped up her jacket tentatively, using her left hand with care.

I said, 'How's the hand? Sorry I didn't call to check in.'

'Itches like a bastard under the cast. I'm getting used to it.'

I walked her to the front door and opened it. The air was much colder now and we both shivered.

I said, 'Is there someone local who can check on you from time to time? Where's your dad now?'

'Stop it, Sam. I'm fine. Pissed off, but fine. I don't need babying, and I certainly don't need my dad to come over and nurse me. Not that he would.'

'Have you told him what happened?'

'Not yet. I'll call him, let him know.'

'You should go see him.'

She looked at me oddly. 'What's got into you? Are you going through the Change or something?'

I tried to laugh it off. 'I'm a dad. I'm developing dad genes.'

'Well you're not my dad, so give it a rest.'

'Understood.'

She climbed into the small Peugeot and switched on the lights. As she reversed out and drove away, I saw her face looking at me through the driver's window. She still looked confused.

BY EIGHT O'CLOCK Dan still hadn't returned home so I turned out the lights and left. I hoped he had a key with him but I happened to know he also had one buried in the front garden if necessary.

I made myself a quick curry with some chicken and a jar of Sharwood's Tikka Masala sauce, then sat and listened to a replay of Bob Harris' country music radio show from Thursday night while I read Lawrence Wright's *The Looming Tower*. A strange juxtaposition if ever there was one.

It slowly grew darker outside and I realised I wasn't concentrating on Wright's description of the home life of Osama bin Laden, but on my own. I'd started a family when barely twenty years old and had reaped none of its benefits. My wife had run off to London saying her pregnancy had been terminated by a miscarriage. I didn't see her again for eighteen years, by which time she had remarried. Shortly afterwards she died at the hands of an arrogant murderer and I learned of the existence of my son, who she'd given away for adoption.

To say my thoughts were confused would not offer a full explanation of the back and forth going on in my head: I had grown used to being single and childless. But I actually quite enjoyed being a father. I liked my own space and the ability to distance myself from others when I wanted. But I liked it when Dan came around or asked for my advice. I didn't like being responsible for anyone except myself. But I felt responsible for Dan and his future progress in the world.

I closed the book and stared out of the full-length windows at the sunset. After a moment I stood up and fetched the house phone, finding Dan's number on speed dial.

He answered. 'Where were you? I brought chips.'

'I thought you might be pulling an all-nighter somewhere. Did you have a key?'

'Always.'

'Okay.'

There was silence while I thought through what I wanted to say.

But he got in first: 'Was there anything else?'

I hesitated briefly. I don't know why. Then I said, 'When I've finished with these Strano people I'll take you to see your grandmother. She'd like to meet you.'

'Cool. Shall I get a hair-cut?'

'Don't be facetious or it's off. And when we go, don't wear a hoodie.'

CHAPTER SIXTEEN

DRIVING INTO MANCHESTER on a Monday morning is someone's version of hell. Snaking lines of cars racing and braking, swerving and squealing, looking for this week's rat-run that will get them into the town centre a minute faster than the next man.

I finally managed to park near Whitworth Street and walked up to St Peter's Square and onwards, eventually halting before one of the new tall glass monoliths that have sprung up in the last ten years. The man on reception gave me a badge and directions and I took a lift to the tenth floor. The lift doors opened almost silently and I stepped on to lush carpet. A few feet to my left the office opened out and a young woman with a bright face and shiny hair was already beaming at me.

I put on my official smile and walked up to her.

'Sam Dyke for Anjelica Strange.'

'Certainly. Is she expecting you?'

'I'm afraid not. I was in the area and thought I'd drop in.'

Her face fell. 'I'm so sorry, she's booked up this morning.'

'I'll wait. Tell her it's important.'

'She's in a meeting that's just started. She could be an hour.'

'I'll sit over there. I'm a patient kind of guy.'

I'd already started walking so she had little choice but watch me commandeer a chair that looked as though it had never been used but was positioned there for its aesthetic contribution to the look of the space.

I crossed my legs and closed my eyes.

For about ten seconds.

I couldn't relax in the chair, not with the hum of office life around me. It brought back memories of my own office time in Customs and Excise, though admittedly I preferred to be out in the field than doing the paperwork.

I looked around the office. Anjelica Strange had done well for herself. This was a pricey place and she seemed to have a few people working for her, judging by the shadows I could see moving around in the smoked-glass-windowed offices. The far end of the open-plan was a floor-to-ceiling unbreakable window, through which I could see other tall offices. Manchester was turning into Manhattan, in its dreams.

As I was looking around, trying to read the name-plates on the doors, one of them opened and Anjelica Strange stepped out. She was breathtaking in a knee-length black skirt, a grey silk blouse under a black tailored jacket and high heels. Her deep black hair was like a glossy Niagara falling from her head onto her shoulders.

She had come out of an office and started striding towards Reception when she saw me. She stopped dead, then turned and looked behind her, perhaps to see whether the visiting client had seen me in all my drab leather-jacketed glory.

She strode the three paces to me and stood with her hands on her hips.

'What are you doing here? This is my office.'

'Very nice, too. I have some information you might find
interesting.'

'Couldn't it have waited?'

'I was in the area.'

'What area was that—the north of England?'

'Can we talk in private?'

'I'm in the middle of a meeting. Give me ten minutes.'

She walked away dramatically, had a word with the
receptionist, then went back to the first office she'd come from.

Ten minutes later the door opened again and she came out,
closing it carefully behind her. She beckoned to me and we
crossed the floor in front of the full-height window and entered
her own office, indicated by her name on the door.

She closed it behind me and went behind her desk, collapsing
into a black leather swivel chair. I took one of the chairs facing
her.

She said, 'I've given them half an hour to talk over my
proposals.'

'Corporate life in action. Dynamic.'

'It's how I make my living. And pay your bill. What did you
want to tell me?'

I explained I'd had someone watching Jack Jenkins for a
while, and yesterday morning he was seen to have a meeting
with Billy Passmore. I explained Jenkins was a bad man and I
could think of no legitimate reason for him to be meeting
Passmore, clandestinely, in his casino at eight o'clock on a
Sunday morning. Could she?

'What do you expect me to say to that? How would I have any
possible idea? I'm beginning to think you've got a screw loose.'

'You wouldn't be the first to think that.'

She looked down at the laptop on her desk and closed its lid.
For all the power-dressing and corporate fancy-dancing around

me, I remembered she was still a twenty-five-year old woman who'd been without a parent for a number of years and was probably struggling to feel in control of her life.

She said, 'I'm sorry I shouted at you and Dad the other day.'

'It wasn't shouting. It was forceful talking.'

'Whatever. I thought both of you had deceived me, were playing games behind my back.'

'We hadn't planned anything. I was there to watch the casino when he turned up.'

'You'll forgive me if I don't abandon my paranoia just yet.'

I shrugged. 'We're not out to get you. But what about Passmore? Why would he be meeting a low-life like Jenkins?'

'This persistence you bragged about is really a pain in the arse, isn't it?'

'Part of my job description.'

She pointed out of the window, which showed a parallel view of the Manchester skyline to the one provided by the high window in the lobby outside.

She said, 'Look out there. Fantastic view, isn't it? I pay an extortionate rent to use this office, but I can afford it. I have great clients. Names you'd recognise. And I'm only here because Billy Passmore put some business my way. Handed my name around to people he knew. Got me a start so I was up and running within six months. Four years out of university and I've got this office and ten people working for me. I owe that to Billy Passmore. Nothing you can say will convince me he's not one of the good guys.'

'You're very persuasive.'

'There's something else you probably don't know.'

'Almost certainly.'

'Billy was able to sympathize with my dad because his own progress hadn't been smooth as silk, despite what you might think.'

'I don't think anything when it comes to him.'

'It wasn't common knowledge, but Billy had his own demons. Things he had to overcome to move on.'

'He told you this?'

'When Dad was sent to prison, Billy came back to the house with us to make sure we were okay. He didn't have to do that. He had people he could have asked, social-worker types. I remember him saying that whatever trouble Dad was in, he could get past it. He'd been in difficult situations himself, he said, and it turned out all right for him.'

'Did he mention specifics?'

'It was eight years ago, for God's sake. If he did, I don't remember them.'

'Well that's not particularly useful, is it? He might have been a bed-wetter or stalked his neighbour.'

'All I know is that Billy Passmore showed me and my mother more sensitivity and care than anyone else. I know he couldn't say anything in court to support Dad because it would have come across as special pleading and might have made things worse for both of them.'

'Is that what he told you?'

'We knew. His hands were tied. Otherwise he would have helped, wouldn't he?'

'That depends.'

'On what?

'Whether he knew what your dad was up to beforehand.'

She laughed. 'And what? Let him do it, watch him get caught, sit back and let him go to prison without saying a word in his defence? What kind of friend is that?'

'The sort that isn't a friend at all. The sort who's up to his neck in it and is letting someone else take the fall.'

'That's ridiculous, and so's this conversation. I have to get back to my meeting. Anything else you wanted to tell me? I hope you're not carrying on with this now. I won't pay you any more after Saturday's disaster.'

'I won't charge you any more.'

'That's not exactly what I asked, is it? If you're telling me my dad works at that casino then I know where to go if I want to talk to him. As long as he's alive and well, that's all I wanted to know.'

'Aren't you worried about his working for a mental-case like Jack Jenkins?'

'I don't know anything about him, and besides, Dad's a grown-up. He doesn't need my help to lead his life.'

'I hope you're right.'

'Can I go now?'

'Sure, go sell some public relations.'

She gave me a sour look and brushed past me.

I HANDED BACK my badge to the man on the security desk and went out into the chill Manchester air. I walked a hundred yards and found a coffee-shop, ordered a latte and took a high chair in the furthest corner I could find. I took out my phone and speed-dialled Dan.

His voice was blurry.

'What time is it?'

'Time a healthy young lad like you was up and doing.'

He groaned. 'Now what? You know this is the middle of the night for me?'

'Billy Passmore. I need more.'

'That policeman? What now?'

'You accused me of having a suspicious mind about him.'

'It was the other way around, actually.'

'Was it? Anyway, can you dig deeper? See if there was any trouble for him when he was younger.'

'You think there was?'

'Proof would be good.'

'I'll talk to you later. I'm going back to sleep.'

IN THE END I stayed in Manchester, visited a couple of bookshops. Bought a pair of shoes at a fancy shoe-shop. Had lunch in the Royal Exchange café, where I'd had an entertaining conversation with a crazy scientist a few months ago, just before he planned to expose thousands of people at Piccadilly Station to a lethal airborne gas.

I drove back to Crewe in the middle of the afternoon and went to the office to pick up post and look at the messages on the answering machine. There was no post and the answerphone call-count read zero. I was superfluous to requirements at the moment. Time to count the Bitcoins again.

I spent some time making out an invoice for Anjelica Strange, put it in an envelope and posted it. Then I drove home and tried to think good thoughts and get Jack Jenkins, Billy Passmore and the giant bouncers out of my mind.

It didn't last long. As I opened my front door the phone was ringing and I picked it up.

'Dad—I've got something.'

He was right. He had.

CHAPTER SEVENTEEN

THE NEXT MORNING I drove into Hanley again, but this time past the junction which led to the casino. I took the flyover and went up on the Leek road, turning left at the Mercedes garage into Cobridge.

I turned right down a long road of small dark terraced houses and found the number I was looking for. It had a low brick wall and no gate, but as the path was only two strides long, a gate wasn't necessary. There was a bay window to the left with heavy curtains visible inside it. The door was a new uPVC model—it was likely in this area that a wooden one would be broken into if there were signs of life inside, and the prospect of a sound system or television to steal and sell. There was a smell in the air of petrol fumes and industrial chemicals.

I hoped Belinda was right about the address and I wasn't about to interrupt a drug deal …

I pressed the bell and heard it ring inside. A moment later the door opened and Lorenzo Strano peered out hesitantly, as though he wasn't used to being visited at home. His face hardened when he saw me, but he pulled the door open further and stepped back.

'Come in. Don't hang about.'

I stepped through and was in the front room. The carpet was thin and worn away completely in places. A lounge chair with wooden arms and a mis-matched sofa were turned towards a small flat-screen TV in the corner, and an ancient gas fire on the hearth glowed but didn't seem to be warming the room. Through another door I could see the staircase up to what I knew would be two small bedrooms and a bathroom. At the back downstairs would be another room to act as a dining room, plus a tiny galley kitchen. I'd been in too many houses like this not to recognise the layout.

Strano knew what I was thinking as I glanced around at his digs.

He said, 'I'm an ex-con. What do you expect, the Ritz?'

'I've seen worse. Don't feel sorry for yourself.'

'I don't. What do you want, apart from gawking at my furniture?'

'I went to see Anjelica yesterday.'

'Good for you. Is that it?'

'Can we sit down?'

'No, not really. Say what you've got to say and then go. I don't know what you're up to, Dyke, but it's getting on my nerves.'

'She's sorry for how she spoke to you on Saturday. It was my fault, she thought I'd lied to her, or at least not told her what she expected to be told. Don't take it out on her. She's doing her best.'

He turned away. He was wearing jeans and a baggy green jumper. I'd have bet it was Versace not River Island.

With his back to me, he said, 'I'm making tea.'

'Milk, no sugar.'

Everywhere I went, people were drinking.

He left the room for a couple of minutes and came back with two mugs. I took mine and sat on the chair. It was the most uncomfortable piece of furniture I'd ever experienced. The atmosphere had not exactly thawed but there was less naked aggression in the air. He sat on the sofa and stared at the fire.

He said, 'I nearly didn't recognise her. She's grown her hair long. Lost some puppy fat.'

'You should be proud of her, she's a very pretty girl.'

He looked sharply at me. 'Fancy your chances, do you?'

'She's a client. And anyway, I'm too old for her.'

'You think? But if you weren't, you'd make a play for her?'

I was on shaky ground because I had in fact enjoyed a brief affair with my last client … before she'd been murdered.

I said, 'Do you think she's still friendly with Billy Passmore?'

'Passmore? Why him?'

He had dark skin and pale eyes that usually stood in contrast to it, but now his eyes darkened as they stared at me.

I said, 'She told me Passmore took care of her and her mother when you went away.'

'Maria didn't want anything to do with me. I suppose I can't blame her. Nothing worse than a crooked cop, is there?'

'Is that what you were?'

'You can finish your tea and go when you like.'

'I still haven't told you what I came to say.'

'Spit it out, then.'

I looked around again at the badly-decorated and rank-smelling room. I couldn't work out Strano's attitude. I understood any bitterness he might have had towards Passmore, who appeared to have left him out to dry, but he seemed completely uninterested in his daughter and his late wife. Perhaps it was a defence mechanism. Perhaps the feelings were too raw to be admitted—he'd let them down, abandoned his daughter, was absent when his wife had died. Perhaps it was all too much to think about, especially with a stranger like me sitting there.

Finally I said, 'I've been looking into Passmore. I couldn't understand why he didn't come to your defence when you were on trial.'

'Yeah, I noticed that.'

'Did you know he'd been investigated himself? Something called the Criminal Cases Review Commission.'

'I know it. If you think you've suffered a miscarriage of justice you go to them and spill your guts.'

'Exactly. And Passmore was involved in a case in the nineties where someone called Derek Leary claimed he was set up with rigged evidence. Passmore had just made detective and it was one of his first cases. Leary appealed but was knocked back, so he went to this Commission.'

'What happened?'

'They talked to Passmore but didn't push the case up the line. They must have believed whatever he told them. Leary got out of prison a few years later and then he vanished.'

For the first time, Strano seemed interested.

'There was always talk about him, even when he was my boss. He was like butter, you couldn't pin him down.'

'And there's something else.'

'Go on.'

'We've been watching JJ at the casino. Did you know he's friendly with Passmore?'

His eyes flickered briefly before he got his response under control. He hadn't known.

'So what? Senior cops have all sorts of odd friends.'

'This wasn't a chance meeting at the golf club. It was an early-morning appointment, at The Lucky Strike. You've never seen him there?'

Strano shook his head. 'Never.'

'Weird, isn't it?'

'I don't know why you're telling me these things. What am I supposed to do? Look at this shit-heap. It's all I can afford. Every night I have to shoo the tarts away from the front door or they'd be having it away against the windows. Cars drive down the road at ten miles an hour, you can see the men's tongues hanging out from the end of the street. Do you think I like it?'

'Get away from Jenkins. There's something going on that's not going to be good. If I were you I'd be looking at why he gave you this job knowing you were a mate of Passmore's, his own buddy.'

'I'm no mate of Billy Passmore's. I can't stand him.'

'After what he did for you in court, I'm not surprised. So quit the casino, leave them behind.' I paused. 'Anjelica's doing well for herself. Maybe—'

'No, I'm not going cap in hand to her. Definitely not.'

'All right, but do yourself a favour and leave Jenkins' employ. You shouldn't be working as a bouncer, there's more to you than that.'

'What am I supposed to do, retrain as a librarian?'

I could see he was anguished but I could also see his mind was made up. He'd set his jaw and now wouldn't meet my eyes.

I stood up and handed him my empty mug. He rose to his feet and I thought he looked smaller, somehow, diminished. I'd brought up a lot of things he probably didn't want to discuss and had managed to avoid thinking about.

I said, 'Seems to me you made a mistake eight years ago. Maybe it wasn't of your own making, I wouldn't know. But you don't want to get caught out twice, carrying water for someone else's benefit.'

'What does that mean?'

'I think you're in danger of being used. Passmore and Jenkins are up to something. Get yourself on the Saturday morning shift and see who comes in.'

'I tried to do that so I could have Saturday afternoon off. They wouldn't let me do it.'

'Did they give you a reason?'

'Nothing that made sense. I didn't push it because I don't want to antagonise them.'

I moved past him and headed to the door.

'Pretty soon that's going to be the least of your worries.'

CHAPTER EIGHTEEN

I SPENT THE following day on the telephone with the Staffordshire police. There was a press office. There was a liaison officer. There was the administrative office of the inspector himself, secretaries, aide-de-camps, major-domos and butlers.

Well, not butlers.

But I certainly felt like I was ascending a hierarchy. Eventually they fitted me in and I had an appointment the following morning at eleven o'clock. I felt as if I was about to meet the Queen, or at least a very close relative.

THE NEXT MORNING I presented myself in the foyer of the shiny office block that had been designated as the new HQ for the PTIU - the Police Transparency Investigation Unit. The police force had never been very good with acronyms and generally picked titles that described exactly what the department did. In the case of a 'Transparency' unit I suppose that was even more important.

I was asked to sit on a bench for a while, then an older policeman in shirt-sleeves came along and asked if I was Mr Dyke. I agreed I was and he asked me to follow him.

We went along a carpeted corridor lined with empty cork notice boards and into a lift, then up three floors to a suite of offices, not all of which were yet furnished. My guide walked ahead of me slowly, rolling slightly from side to side with the stateliness of someone who knew the place really well and was monumentally bored by passing through the same corridors all day every week.

Over his shoulder, he said, 'Inspector Passmore doesn't officially start till next month. You're lucky he's in, getting a feel for the place.'

'What's his role going to be, exactly?'

He looked over his shoulder again and frowned at me, as though I'd made an indecent suggestion.

'I think you'd better take that up with him. It's not my place.'

I suppose when you're the boss of a department whose job is to investigate your colleagues, you inspire a certain amount of apprehension. I didn't blame him for being reluctant to give me any ammunition.

We were walking down another corridor, past more empty glass-walled offices, and finally he stopped at a grey door and knocked. I expected a voice from inside, but instead the door was yanked open and Billy Passmore stood there, looking inquisitively at the pair of us.

He said, 'That's okay, Craig,' and opened the door further.

Craig peeled away from my side and Passmore stood back. He was a fraction shorter than me and in his early fifties. His greying hair was combed into so rigid an angle across his forehead I felt he could have turned cartwheels without dislodging it. His skin was institutional grey, too, with only a hint of colour, and his eyes were of that peculiar type that I'd only met a couple of times before—the pupil was like a pinhead, meaning almost the whole of the iris was a deep blue. Looking at him was disconcerting because his eyes gave no hint of his emotion and you were drawn into their depthlessness, like staring into a void. I'd known people whose eyes took on this form as a result of certain drugs, but I guessed that wouldn't be true of a senior police officer.

He'd seated himself behind his desk and was gesturing me towards the chair facing him. The office was not really furnished and besides his desk and our two chairs contained only a laptop, a set of grey metal filing cabinets and a telephone. The view outside of his window showed a grey sky and some tall commercial buildings reflecting grey clouds. In fact his blue eyes were the only hint of colour in our entire environment.

He said, 'I'll tell you now I only agreed to this interview under pressure. I'm too busy to be concerned about people who are no longer part of this police force. Do you understand that, Mr Dyke?'

'I understand. I shouldn't take up too much of your day. Then you can get back to fighting crime.'

He seemed to be on the point of responding to my attitude, but then perhaps he remembered where he was and that he was in a new job and he should watch his words. He bit his tongue and leaned back.

He said, 'Explain to me what this is about.'

'I was hired by someone to find Lorenzo Strano after he was released from prison. I don't know whether you were aware he seemed to have disappeared. People were worried about him.'

'You used the past tense. I take it you found him.'

'Fortunately, yes.'

'Then why are we having this conversation? Your case is closed. Strano served out his debt to society. All's well and a choir of angels sing.'

'I'm sure you're aware there's more to it than that.'

'Am I? What should I be aware of? I'm only a humble policeman, Mr Dyke, please enlighten me.'

'There's the whole question of the trial and his demeanour during it.'

'What on earth do you mean?' He leaned forward. He seemed almost to be enjoying playing innocent. 'I hadn't realised his "demeanour" was a central plank of the prosecution's case. All these years I've thought it was the fact that Lorenzo Strano was witnessed selling steroids and was found to have many samples thereof in a suitcase in his bedroom. I hadn't realised he was in fact tried and found guilty on the inappropriateness of his demeanour. My understanding of the British legal system is obviously sorely lacking.'

'I can tell you've had media training. The way you react calmly to direct questioning is a model all junior policemen should follow.'

'When I'm dealing with the media and not a private investigator my "demeanour" will be appropriate enough.'

Stand-off. We stared at each other for a moment, then he seemed to relax. He breathed out and wiggled a finger between his collar and his neck to loosen his tie.

'You caught me on a bad day. I'm getting grief from the Commissioner because it's all taking longer than it should to set up the Unit. Plus he's got an Ethics committee he's trying to run, as well as meeting the punters on the street. You know, my first day on the job, thirty years ago now, I had to get a cat down from a tree. That was as exciting as it got. I thought I'd done something really helpful and useful. Joe Public could be proud of me. The higher you go up the bureaucracy the harder it is to join the dots between what you do on a daily basis and the sense anyone might actually be benefitting from it.'

'I worked for the government. The day we started calling the public "customers" was when it all started going downhill."

He laughed rather jovially and pointed to his empty wire in-tray basket.

'Two weeks' time that thing will be overflowing and I'll look back on this period as if it was a golden age. At the moment my head's spinning.'

'I get that. I'm not trying to be difficult.'

'You're trying to satisfy your customer. I know. Let me guess—it's Anjelica, isn't it?'

'You know I can't tell you anything.'

'Well you could, but you don't have to. Did you know I knew her and her mother?'

'She told me. She won't hear anything said against you.'

'Really? Well that's rather nice. I haven't seen her in a couple of years, since she started her company. I put some business her way.'

'She's grateful.'

'Is she? Would have been nice if she mentioned it … Anyway, never mind that. What's her problem, exactly? Didn't Larry get in touch when he came out? Is she worried about him?'

Although his eyes never lost their innocent blankness, there was a playfulness in his tone I didn't like. It felt as though I was being played, as though he was dangling bait in front of me to see whether I'd snap at it.

'I'm not here to discuss my client, Inspector Passmore.'

He raised his hands. 'No, of course not. You're here to dig up an old case and beat me over the head with it. In fact I still don't know why you're here. What can I possibly tell you now, after all this time?'

I put some steel in my voice. 'People have been telling me you didn't exactly support Strano in court. Your evidence, such as it was, didn't help him. You said you were disappointed in his actions but had no idea why he was selling steroids.'

'That's true.'

'True you said it or true you had no idea why he was doing it?'

'Don't be pedantic, Dyke. As a matter of fact it was true on both counts. And as far as backing him in court was concerned, I should imagine he was grateful I did as much as I did.'

'What do you mean?'

He rotated his chair sideways and laid his left arm over the keyboard of his computer.

'Have you talked to him since you found him?'

'Yes.'

'I don't suppose he told you he'd been caught at it before.'

The look on my face amused him.

'No, I didn't think so. Kept that to himself, didn't he?'

'You have proof?'

'Of course not. It was a conversation between me and him. One of my juniors saw him in a club one night, talking to a couple of known dealers. They asked around, quietly, and found out there was no ongoing investigation, no reason at that time for Strano to even be involved in narcotics' patch. So they told me about it and he and I had a conversation. Within four walls. He told me he'd been having some financial problems and saw selling steroids as a quick fix. I put him right in no uncertain terms and gave him a warning. But I didn't commit it to paper because I liked him and his family. I thought it was an uncharacteristic error of judgement and it shouldn't go any further. Do you understand me?'

He was letting me know I shouldn't spread it around either.

I said, 'If you didn't write it down there's no proof one way or the other.'

'You ever worked in uniform?'

'Not this one. Government.'

'Judging by the size of you it wasn't behind a desk. Well this job is different. Sometimes you get to know criminals better than you'd like. Often they're from the same background as you, maybe even went to the same school. You have to mingle and mix and sometimes—I've seen it—your values get screwed up. You make a poor decision because you've lost your footing. It happens more than you'd think.'

'This is coming from the new chief of the Transparency Unit? Forgiveness and understanding?'

'Worldly wisdom. Judge not lest ye be judged. Matthew 7:1.'

'Won't that make it hard for you to do your job? Passing judgement on your colleagues' behaviour?'

He leaned forward now and seemed to warm to his theme.

'You've got it wrong, like most people do. Jesus wasn't saying you should never judge other people in case you're judged by them. What he meant was that if you pass judgement on others, then you have to be prepared to be held to the same standard. It was a guard against hypocrisy, not an injunction against having standards in the first place. I gave Larry Strano a chance to put his house in order and he failed. The second time around I couldn't help him. I didn't tell anyone what I knew of his previous actions, and I suppose you could say that was weak of me. But what I couldn't do was stand up in court and go overboard in praising the man.'

I thought about this for a while and watched him glance at his computer screen and move his mouse around its mat.

I said, 'You know he's now working for Jack Jenkins. What's your connection to him?'

His eyes turned to focus on me again, if the blank-eyed stare could be called a focus.

'What do you mean?'

'I know you've been talking to Jack Jenkins. Surely it's not a secret. You were seen walking into his casino in broad daylight. Though admittedly a little early on a Sunday morning.'

He took his time in replying and I wondered if for the first time I detected surprise or maybe apprehension in his smooth carapace.

He said, 'I won't legitimise that statement with a reply. I told you earlier, sometimes you have to deal with people you rather wish you didn't have to.'

'Jenkins has no record and seems to be a perfectly acceptable member of society. Why would you refuse to explain your relationship to him?'

'Because I don't have to and because this is now very tiresome. I agreed to see you because when I heard what you wanted to discuss I thought it might have something to do with Anjelica, whom I still hold in very high regard. Now you seem to be wandering off-piste and I don't have to justify myself or my actions to you.'

He had started to rise from his chair in an attempt to usher me from the room.

I said, 'What happened to Derek Leary?'

He stopped. 'Who?'

'You were investigated by the Criminal Cases Review Commission when Leary appealed his sentence. He said you'd planted evidence to get the conviction. Lucky for you they believed your side of the story instead of his. When he finally got out, he disappeared. I was wondering if you knew what happened to him.'

Now he stood to his full height and I felt compelled to stand too so that he couldn't lean over me.

'That man was a thug who we caught practically reeking of drugs. They were in him, on him and up his backside. The thought we planted anything on him was ludicrous. I can get you the Commission's report on my evidence if you want to read it.'

'I've read it. They were very complimentary about you. It's just odd he went missing within a few months of getting out of prison.'

'Perhaps he fancied a life in the sun. Went back to Jamaica. Opened a bar on a beach. How the fuck should I know what happened to him? I wasn't even in the same city by the time he got out. Now, if you'll excuse me. I have important police work to catch up on. Work that's taking place in the present.'

There must have been a signal or a button or something, because the door opened and I saw Craig was there again, ready to escort me out. He looked at his boss from under heavy eyebrows and nodded.

When I turned back, Passmore was engrossed in his computer screen again and didn't look up or say a word as I left. The important police work was already occupying his full attention.

Or so he wanted me to believe.

CHAPTER NINETEEN

I DON'T NEED this shit right now, he thought, locking his car and walking up the short drive to his front door. The plans were laid for the biggest job ever pulled in this part of the world, and to have this scuzzy private investigator sniffing around Strano was bad timing. At first he'd thought it was a clever idea to get Strano back into the fold, through Jenkins and the casino, but if it caused a problem he might have to think again and tweak the plan.

He let himself in and laid his briefcase down in the living room. Since his split from Sara he'd only been able to afford to rent a small cottage but it was enough for him in truth. He went upstairs and changed into Lee Cooper jeans and a Gap shirt, both of which he'd ironed the night before. Then he went downstairs, washed a potato under the tap, spiked it with a fork and put it in the microwave, pressing the Jacket Potato option. While it started to cook he took a brick of cheddar cheese from the fridge and started to grate it. He'd never been a big eater and lately he'd found his appetite waning further. He'd vaguely wondered whether he was coming down with something but then realised it was probably stress.

He sometimes felt as though his head would burst with everything it carried and tried to organise. He liked being ordered and neat and knowing where he was. But at the moment there was too much going on—his new job, the divorce, keeping Phar at bay and monitoring Jenkins, making sure the Event would go according to plan ... Dyke was one wrinkle too far.

In a way it was right what he'd said to him—when he'd rescued that cat from that old woman's tree thirty years ago it was the highlight of his policing career. Ever since then he'd been a politician and a front man and, face it, a fraud. Sara had been the first to see it. At first she'd been dazzled by his status and career prospects, but she soon saw that his personality excluded her and viewed her as a nuisance, a distraction. It had taken over twenty years for her to make her move but it was no real surprise to him she'd found someone to go off with, even a funeral director ... he was probably more in touch with the living than he was, Passmore thought grimly.

If he could have changed, he would have. But in the end his own agenda had always been more important to him than placating someone else. When that agenda involved satisfying his own desire to take risks, to gamble, to experience the momentary high of winning, then at that precise instant he didn't care about Sara or anybody else. He was validated, his judgement had been authenticated by Fate or God, and he felt whole, if only for a brief second.

How could he explain that to anyone? How could he go sit in a dank church hall full of anonymous gamblers and confess to the sin of pride? Someone in his position? He'd thought about it often, especially as the debts had mounted, but he couldn't bring himself to submit himself to that level of scrutiny. And if the amount of his indebtedness ever leaked he would be ruined.

It was better to keep it under wraps and keep it in his control, even though that meant doing occasional favours for Phar and his consortium. It had grown harder over the years to act independently even with his elevated status in the force, but he could command enough obedience that so far he'd been able to get away with it.

Now he had his escape route planned. His documents were in order. His finances organised.

But he worried about Dyke.

Dyke had nothing to lose as far as he could see, and Passmore could tell from their conversation that he wasn't the type to let things go. He'd shown no respect for Passmore or his office and was blatantly impertinent when it came to his relationship with Strano.

Strano.

It always came back to him, and their complicated relationship. At one time he'd thought he might be able to take Strano under his wing, bring him up the ranks with him as he progressed.

But Strano had a wife and a daughter who had held him back, lent him a sense of right and wrong that Passmore had paid lip service to but in reality ignored. Of course he believed in God but He was Someone who knew the Passmore unseen by anyone else: the striver, the victim, the man hamstrung by desires he couldn't evade. Passmore had thought Strano might be someone to share this side of him with, but it wasn't to be. In the end he'd had to tip him overboard and use some fancy footwork to ensure Strano didn't squeal. That's when the wife and daughter had come in useful, thankfully. Strano didn't want them involved and hadn't wanted anything to happen to them, naturally. So he'd kept his trap shut and done the time. Even seemed grateful when Jenkins' man had tapped him up in jail and offered him protection and a job. Lucky that Jenkins owed him some favours too, Passmore thought.

As for Dyke … there were options. He was working with this woman McFee. She was probably out of the picture if she was operating with a couple of broken fingers. It would take her a while to get back in the frame.

And there was Dyke's son, bit of a layabout by all accounts. Not seen around much these days, though he was involved in one of Dyke's cases a couple of years ago—he'd read the report from Howard on the sly. Passmore didn't know how far Dyke was involved with his son's life, whether that relationship could be leveraged in any way …

And there was, of course, Dyke's mother, living alone in Yorkshire. Small village. Big house. Possibilities there …

He sat and ate his baked potato and cheese on a tray in front of the television, watching the news but not really seeing it. When he'd finished he washed his plate and cutlery and poured himself a half glass of Pinot Grigio, then sat on his sofa looking out at the dying light beyond his windows.

He didn't really have a choice, did he?

He reached out a hand to the phone.

CHAPTER TWENTY

SHE'D DRIVEN AROUND the back of the casino, into a section of the retail park that was yet to open. Another cavernous hangar stood ready to be converted into a mattress warehouse or a furniture showroom, but at the moment it was shuttered and locked up. A single lamp on a tall pole illuminated the empty car park with a harsh white light.

She reached into the back seat of the Peugeot, having to twist so she could use her right hand, and drew out a plastic case about a foot square. Opening it on the passenger seat, she took out the contact microphone and connected it to a small cassette recorder, then took the folding Sony earphones that came with the unit and plugged its connector into the small square control box. The unit had cost her nearly £300 from a distributor in Kansas and this was the first time she'd used it, apart from practice runs. It was compatible with audio spectrum analysis software and had an internal gain control … whatever that meant. She hoped it was as good in real life as it had been when pretending.

It was dark outside now so she opened the door and ran quietly in the shadows to the back of the casino. There were no windows here except a couple very high up, under the eaves of the roof.

The first place she attached the microphone's pick-ups to yielded no sound after ten minutes. She moved fifteen yards to her left and after a few moments heard the flush of a toilet.

On her third attempt she heard voices immediately. Lots of voices, apparently all talking at once. The sound was extremely faint and she couldn't tell how many people were speaking or what they were saying. She moved the contacts slightly and settled in again, leaning her back against the roughly-textured wall.

The voices had been quiet for a few minutes, and she was considering moving again, when they started up once more. She thought there were probably only three or four, talking very quickly. She was certain one of them was Jack Jenkins' light, almost feminine voice. There was something in the cadence and the way his speech was listened to by the others that led her to believe this person was more important than the others.

There was also another distinctive voice—but one she hadn't heard before. This was male but also high-pitched, and spoke very quickly. The words were just too faint to make out but she knew the recorder would yield sufficient data for her to be able to boost the sound and identify what was being said, even if she couldn't put a face to the speaker. What occurred to her was that the voice seemed Asian, speaking very quickly and abruptly. Given the number of small men with black hair she'd seen moving in and out of the casino, she wasn't surprised. She'd assumed they were gamblers but maybe they had a role to play in the casino itself.

Car headlights raked across the casino's wall and she froze. She had no valid reason to be lurking around the back of the building and if any kind of security group were on the case she'd have a hard time explaining her presence.

The headlights had moved past her position as the vehicle turned in the car park. The vehicle circled her Peugeot completely but didn't stop, heading immediately back for the exit. She thought it was probably someone using the empty car park to turn around.

The vehicle accelerated away and she breathed out, forcing her heartbeat to stabilise.

Putting the contacts on the wall again, she heard the temperature of the conversation had risen. The two voices she'd picked out were now talking even more rapidly and loudly and it sounded like a full-blown argument was in progress. She crouched down to present less of a shadow if anyone should come around the back, then found a comfortable position from which she could rest the recorder's contacts against the wall.

It might be a long night.

CHAPTER TWENTY-ONE

IT WAS TYPICAL of Phar not to appear himself but to send one of his lieutenants. The man came into the pub wearing a lightweight cream suit and followed by two broad men in loose jackets and black jeans whose eyes roamed over the lounge as they walked. The trio knew Passmore immediately and came across to his table. The leader pushed out his hand.

'I'm David. You call me David, okay?'

Passmore shook the hand. 'Phar too busy?'

'That's right, Mr Phar is a very busy man. He sends me for the important work, okay?'

Passmore glanced around at the other people in the room. He'd chosen a place for the meeting on the outskirts of Newcastle-under-Lyme where it was unlikely he'd come across anyone he knew. He hadn't wanted Phar to roll up outside his own house in one of his stretch limousines, sending the neighbours into a curtain-twitching frenzy, but neither did he want to meet him in a completely isolated environment. With Phar you never knew what he might do. That was his reputation.

Passmore didn't expect this 'David' to be any more pliable, however.

He said, 'Sit down and try to look less serious. And no kung-fu, please.'

David pulled out a chair and sat and his two colleagues took their place either side of the table. Their faces were narrow and sculpted with sharp cheek-bones, their eyelashes long and feminine.

Passmore pulled a plasticated menu from a wooden block and scanned it. The Asians watched but didn't follow his lead. He felt himself becoming unnerved.

David said, 'I have a degree from MIT and an MBA from Princeton. I've never practised kung-fu or any other comic martial art, okay? Now, why did you want to talk to Mr Phar?'

'If I speak to you am I speaking to him?'

'Directly. I even know how to use a telephone if necessary.'

'All right.' Passmore hesitated. He found it hard to talk about this business to people he didn't know well. 'This concerns our project. I want you to tell Mr Phar that everything is going according to plan but there is a threat. There is a man who is interested in learning information about one of our colleagues, and therefore possibly about the project.'

'You're talking in riddles, old man. Speak plainly or I cannot guarantee Mr Phar will understand.'

Passmore found himself being irritated by the man's smooth skin, by the brightness in his eyes and his faint air of superiority. He even spoke in an accent that suggested a high-class education. Was he from Singapore? Taiwan? Kuala Lumpur? Phar seemed to recruit men from the entire region, with a range of skills.

He said, 'The man is called Dyke, Sam Dyke. He's a private investigator and he's beginning to find out more about the casino and its operation than I think is healthy. We need to do something about him.'

'You want us to remove his balls? We can do that.'

'They teach you that at Princeton?'

David's eyes widened and Passmore wondered whether he'd gone too far.

But then David spoke rapidly to his colleagues and they all laughed, and when he turned back, David was smiling.

'That was a good joke, okay? The idea that an institution of higher learning like Princeton would teach me the fine arts of torture and persuasion is very amusing. For a while. So, what do you want us to do with Dyke if removal of his balls is not appropriate?'

'I need to send him a message, something to warn him to stay away.'

'Why can we not dispose of him?'

'It's too obvious. Nothing must happen to him because he's been seen talking to me. He came to my office. He's talked to people around me. If anything were to happen to him then the investigations would come back to me.'

David stroked his chin in a way that suggested to Passmore that it was something he'd seen in movies or read about in books. It was inauthentic as a means of suggesting what he actually thought.

David said, 'Do you have any other ideas?'

Passmore knew this was the moment of commitment. He was about to step over a line he couldn't retreat from. He felt himself go calm at his centre even as he said the words.

'There is a girl. Removing her will send a message that Dyke will understand.'

David's eyes lit up. 'You surprise me, okay? I thought people like you never took this step. I'm impressed.'

'The advantage is that it can be done without my involvement. You're unknown over here, without any connection to her. She can go missing and no one will know anything.'

'But if she simply goes missing, the message to Mr Dyke will not be heard.'

'True. So she has to be found, but in a way that's completely unconnected to the casino or Jenkins.'

'Or Mr Phar.'

'Of course.'

'And do you think we are capable of such an act?'

'I do.'

'Good. We appreciate your support, my colleagues and I.'

He stopped talking but continued looking directly at Passmore for a moment.

Then he said, 'Your eyes are very unusual. There are people where I come from who would be scared of you. They would say you were related to the devil, or you had no soul. Is that true?'

'That's not for me to say. I believe I have a soul.'

Passmore felt uncomfortable though he didn't know why. David continued to stare at him as if weighing him up.

Then he bounced the palm of his hands lightly, once, off the table-top.

'It seems the waitress is not going to arrive and offer us food. Therefore we're going to leave. I will talk to Mr Phar about your proposal. We will be in touch if we need the name and description of this person. Perhaps you should wait a decent period of time before following us outside, okay?'

'Okay.'

CHAPTER TWENTY-TWO

FRIDAY LUNCHTIME I had a call from Hannah Hall, the cub reporter and part-time barkeep.

'You up for a meet tonight?'

'Let me just check my social calendar … yes, that appears to be in order.'

'Funny guy. Where do you want to do it?'

'Can you get to Sandbach?'

'I can.'

'There's an olde-worlde pub on the right of the hill as you go down to the traffic lights.'

'I know it. Eight o'clock?'

'Can you tell me what it's about?'

'Saving it up for later. Gotta go. See you then.'

I hadn't given much thought to her since our last meeting and I wondered what she wanted this time. As a reporter she was no doubt hoping to get something in return for whatever she offered, and would probably offer very little. There was no reason for her to tell me anything when she could save it up for her world-beating article.

Since my meeting with Passmore the day before I hadn't made much progress. There were routine things to do around the office, and I'd had two exciting phone calls: one asking me for a job and another trying to sell me electronic gear valuable to someone in my line of work. Most of the time my job was as mundane as the next man's. I lived closer to the threat of violence than the average worker, but day-to-day life was spent completing paper-work, organising my timetable and thinking of ways to do the job more effectively.

When people like Hannah Hall pushed themselves into my life I found myself dealing with them using a mixture of irritation and impatience. I'd tried to master a Zen approach and let events wash over me, but I had some kind of internal driver that continually wanted to move on to the next task. Sitting back patiently while someone else played out their own personality constructs on my time was not something I managed easily.

INSULT TO INJURY, she was fifteen minutes late. I'd arrived early and had found a seat in a corner away from a large group of people who looked as though they'd just arrived from a gym. They glowed with health and energy burst from them in shouts and laughter and squalls of riotousness.

When Hannah arrived she looked absurdly young and fragile, carrying the same bag that held her tablet and wearing a shiny black mackintosh like a girl from the sixties. She wore a serious face and glanced around before sitting next to me with her back to the wall, looking out. She placed her bag on the heavy wooden table in front of us and sought out her tablet but didn't switch it on. It was as though she was checking it was still there.

I asked if she wanted a drink and she said no and I felt guilty immediately about the pint of Guinness that stood like a rebuke before me.

She said, 'It's getting worse.'

'A clue would help me out.'

'At the casino. I'm not racist but it's getting hard to work when you're constantly being stared at or chatted up by men who look at you as though you're an alien life-form.'

'Maybe a casino isn't the place to expect fans of equal opportunities legislation.'

'I know that and anyway, it's besides the point. The point is, the number of Asians has doubled since I spoke to you last week.'

'You still don't know what they're doing?'

'Funnily enough, Jumbo Jack doesn't confide in me as much as I'd like.'

I turned away and tried to think Zen thoughts. And failed.

I said, 'You wanted this meeting. Was that it? There are more sexist Asians in the club, please help?'

She had undone her shiny mackintosh and slipped her hands into the pockets of a rainbow-coloured waistcoat. I noticed she was rocking back and forth ever so slightly and I began to worry for her and her stress levels. Her hair was unkempt and her skin was coarse, as though she'd applied a day's make-up over a previous layer without scrubbing first. Unlike the previous times I'd met her, she wore a ring in her left eye-brow and a stud in her nose.

She said, 'They're gearing up for something. There's a room we're not allowed into, near the back. I think that's where they go on a Saturday afternoon, when the private party arrives. I've seen a couple of men going in with tool-boxes and carrying cables. I think it's a wire-room. Do you know what that is?'

'A place where people can gamble online. Usually from a location that's acting as a cover. Having a wire-room in a casino seems a bit of a redundancy.'

'What if it's not straightforward gambling?'

'Such as?'

'What if they're gambling on fixed games—football, cricket, whatever?'

'Then they're being very naughty. Do you have proof that's what's going on?'

She sat back, taking her hands from her waistcoat pockets and folding her arms. I knew I was about to be told off.

'Do you know how much money is involved in illegal betting?'

'Tell me what Google says.'

'Up to a trillion dollars a year—that's over half a billion pounds. A big incentive to cheat. In some places in the far east it's illegal to bet online. Singapore, for example. But it doesn't stop people doing it, and there are gangsters who've made fortunes through manipulating syndicates.'

I saw where she was going with this.

'So you think these Asians are over here to take advantage of our lenient gambling regulations.'

'No, actually, I don't.'

I was surprised. 'Then what?'

'It's not just illegal gambling, it's match fixing that's the problem. If syndicates can fix matches and persuade enough people to bet on them, there are huge profits. But in those circumstances there are two potential victims.'

'The players who don't do as they're told to throw the games, and the gamblers who don't pay up when they lose.'

She nodded. She seemed unsurprised by my ready grasp of the issues.

'Exactly. I think all these Asian men are here as enforcers. I've been doing my research and the FBI has been catching up on these guys, the big players. Some of the bosses of the Triads like to gamble themselves. They go to Las Vegas and play in the poker competitions. They spend their money on the American life-style. They been known to take over whole floors in hotels, put in their own electronic equipment and run their scams from there rather than Singapore. So they can walk down the road and play poker afterwards. But it's been made too hot for them now.'

'So they head for Stoke, Mecca of the North?'

She nearly smiled but managed to put a brake on it.

'They're less than an hour away from City Airport by private jet. That's quicker than commuting into town from a mansion in Wimbledon. And they have less of a profile up here.'

The taste of my Guinness was beginning to sour on my tongue.

I said, 'It's all a bit of a stretch, isn't it? Why not go forty miles further north to Manchester or Liverpool where they at least pretend to have a high-life? You do know the Hilton in Stoke closed down for lack of interest?'

'How do *I* know why they're here? Maybe I'm wrong. Maybe they're all on holiday, taking a City Break because they're bored with white sandy beaches and blue skies. Maybe Stoke is an adventure for them.'

We were silent for a while. I hadn't dismissed her ideas completely but I was a long way down that road. She was like a patient using the Internet to research her disease and finding a worst-case-scenario that fit her symptoms exactly. The absolutism of youth.

I said, 'It sounds like you're having a tough time there. Why don't you just quit, research your article about online gambling and submit that to your editor? You don't have to be Woodward and Bernstein all rolled into one.'

She stood up and pulled the flaps of her mackintosh together, then tied the belt tightly around her waist. She didn't look me in the eye. When she spoke her voice was harsh and loud, as though she was trying to embolden herself with invented anger.

'I told you once before I don't need advice from you. I just thought you should know. It was a gift, because I hoped you might be a useful contact somewhere down the line. I admit it, all right?'

'I know you don't like advice but I think you should be very careful around these men. Whether you're right or not, you shouldn't go antagonising them. Just watch what you say, and do, all right?'

Now she looked at me with her almond-shaped eyes and they were tearful.

She said, 'I thought you might believe me. Unlike everyone else.'

Then she turned and stomped away, leaving me feeling like the dregs of my Guinness floating in the bottom of the empty glass.

CHAPTER TWENTY-THREE

SATURDAY MORNING DAWNED bright and I rose early to run. I have a route that drops down from the back of my house, along the side of the field that runs down to the road, then across and back in a loop that takes about forty minutes. At eight o'clock on a Saturday morning the traffic is quieter than usual and I swear I heard a bird call.

The sun had just risen like a ripe orange as I unlocked my back door and took off my trainers. On cue, the phone rang.

I answered and a voice said, 'I didn't expect to find you in the Yellow Pages.'

I pictured a sour-faced ex-policeman waiting outside a pub for opening time, moving from foot to foot expectantly as his thirst grew.

'Leatherby? What do you want?'

He said, 'Thought you should know—I'm not happy.'

'You're right, I needed to know that. It's made my day. What have I done now?'

'Not you. JJ and his gang. Passmore, the whole lot of them.'

'You're not being very specific and I've got a shower waiting for me.'

'You haven't heard, have you?'

'Heard what?'

'Body of a girl found in the car park of Waitrose.'

Although I'd worked up a nice sweat, I went cold instantly.

'Where? What girl?'

'Sandbach. Girl who used to work at The Lucky Strike. Hannah Hall.'

'Jesus.'

'You know her?'

I'd already started thinking over what Hannah and I had discussed the night before.

I said, 'It's eight-fifteen in the morning. How come you know about it already?'

'Local news is a wonderful thing.' He paused and when he spoke again his voice was leaden with disgust. 'How did you know her?'

'Did they say how she died?'

'Too early for that. Let's say natural causes are not suspected.'

I'd found a seat in my kitchen by now and dropped into it like a sack of bones. I hate being close to people who die young and it had happened too often lately.

I said, 'What did you tell Jenkins about me?'

He barked a short laugh. 'Oh you guessed that, did you? I confess, caught bang to rights. He tapped me up months ago to keep him on the same page as, you know, the boys in blue. I still have friends there. A quick drink and a chat. Fifty quid in my pocket from Jumbo. Who's hurt?'

'Hannah Hall.'

His voice turned hard. 'Don't put that on me. It was me got her in the door in the first place.'

'Say that again.'

'She's the niece of a friend of mine. She knew I used to be a cop and was looking for something to write about, something to get her brownie points with her boss at the paper.'

'So you suggested she get involved with a bunch of thugs and villains at the casino? I knew you had the morals of a snake when I met you, but you've surpassed yourself.'

'Go fuck yourself. She was a grown-up. I told her to watch herself and just listen. She wasn't supposed to snoop.'

'Did you tell Jenkins what she was?'

'Don't be stupid.'

'So you played one off against the other. Told tales to Jenkins for money but put a mole in his organisation. That make you feel good?'

'After I finish this phone call I don't want to talk to you again.' His voice was becoming thick—perhaps Hannah's death had got to him after all, despite his bravado. 'Passmore is the one you want. Rumour is, he's up to his arse in debt. Ask yourself why he's friendly with a casino owner who invites Asian gangsters to his place on a regular basis.'

'Perhaps it's to use his wire-room.'

Leatherby paused and I sensed him reconfiguring his ideas about what I knew.

He said, 'But what does Passmore get out of that? Jack shit. He lets it happen on his watch, turns a blind eye, but he gets nothing. He still owes money. He's bought some time but the debt needs to be paid.'

'Where are you getting this from?'

'Not the good old local news.'

'What do you know? What's going to happen?'

'I'm on a plane to Sweden later today. I don't know anything. Just think about the irony of the local chief of 'transparency in policing' heading up a crime syndicate stretching to Indonesia. That'll make you choke on your cornflakes.'

The line went dead.

I was beginning to consider what I should do when I was reminded again that we're not always in control of our own destinies, especially when criminal matters are involved. The reminder came in the form of a knock on my front door.

I knew before I got there who it was. The silhouettes were unmistakable.

THEY PUT ME in the back of a car without hand-cuffing me, though they did leave another car in my drive with a couple of cops lounging around inside.

The man who'd arrived to talk to me was someone I didn't know — he'd given his name as Greene and said he'd come from Stoke and they wanted me to go back with them for a conversation. He wasn't arresting me but he didn't mention a lawyer. As soon as he arrested me, the PACE clock would start and he'd have twenty-four hours before having to let me go. The Police and Criminal Evidence Act had made it much harder for the police to bully suspects, but they still found ways around it if you weren't alert.

I had a very good lawyer but I didn't call her. I had nothing to hide and I'd been through this routine before. They were going to press me and push me and see if there was enough there to arrest me. As long as they didn't arrest me, and I didn't ask for a lawyer, we could have a conversation for as long as we liked.

I thought they'd got to me pretty quickly, but then remembered Hannah and I had parted on less than good terms and we were in sight of any number of people in the pub. Someone might have reported our disagreement, the police might have looked at surveillance cameras from the pub, found my car, read its number plate … it would all have been achieved pretty quickly.

Greene was a man in his mid-thirties with short black hair and a face just running to paunch, the jowls dropping, the eyelids drooping. He'd been respectful enough while at the same time acting as though he wasn't going to take any back-chat from the likes of me. I watched the A500 reel past as we headed to his station. I was struck again by the bleakness and desolation that surrounded Stoke like a noose that was tightening daily.

I said, 'Are you going to tell me what it's about? Or shall we play twenty questions?'

He turned to me, his eyes sagging with weariness.

'You know what I'm going to say, don't you? You've done this before.'

'I like the excitement, though. Seeing whether I can catch you out or trip you up so you say something in front of these chaps here.'

There were two other policemen in the car—a driver and a passenger. They were studiously impartial and didn't look at me once. I felt they were on my side, however, unlike Greene.

At the station—another nondescript office block similar to the one in which I'd met Passmore—I was taken straight through to an interview room and seated at a table. There were no windows and no distractions except for a coffee-making machine, which everyone seemed to ignore. A couple of fluorescent strips overhead threw an unflattering light over everything. The usual plastic chairs sagged in the middle and a waste bin in the corner was overflowing with cellophane sandwich wrappers.

Greene came in with a colleague and in no time they got down to it. They didn't have to record me and we were just there to have a chat. They were low-key, almost apathetic, as though cynicism had worn down every spark of life they might once have had. Greene's new colleague was older than him but seemed to be junior, to judge by his attitude. He did everything but pull back Greene's chair so that he could seat himself more comfortably.

The first session of an interview is always very factual and laid back. There are certain details the police need to clarify, to lay down their base line from which they can start to dig away, like prisoners of war excavating a tunnel with spoons, one prod at a time. Although I wasn't being interviewed under caution, they still followed the prescribed routine. Every policeman who interviews suspects has been through a training course which outlines a process that makes the interview sessions extremely detailed and boring. They're trained to ask 'open' questions and probe for more information if the interviewee doesn't answer directly. Every question they asked, they already knew the answer to. In that way they could test my veracity by finding out where I was lying—if I was. At this point they'd be trying to treat me like a witness, not a suspect. They were establishing details, not accusing me of any wrong-doing.

We were there two hours while they asked me where I was the night before, what I'd done, who I'd seen, asking for more detail every time I was vague. After a while they asked me to write it down as a witness statement, which took me about fifteen minutes.

I was honest with them. I told them I'd met Hannah in the pub but she left before me.

I had nothing to hide … except the fact I'd been told by Leatherby what had happened to her. I thought it would be bad for me if I admitted I already knew Hannah was dead, and certainly bad for Leatherby. I had no reason to protect him, but likewise I had no cause to drop him into a cauldron of hot water.

Eventually I said, 'You're asking me what I did last night. Care to let me know where I was supposed to be and what I might have done?'

'Have you done something?'

'Don't twist my words. Better men than you have tried. I'll cooperate but you need to tell me what's going on.'

Greene laid down his pen as if he were making a point. 'I don't think you understand the power structure in this room. As it happens, we're the ones who are required to ask you questions. We're not required to tell you anything. The sooner you understand that, the easier this interview will go.'

'I thought it was going quite well. You've asked questions, I've answered them. What more can you expect of an interview? It could be a bit pacier and I suppose my answers could be a bit more exciting, but that's where we are.'

Greene glanced at his colleague and leaned forward. He was wearing a blue suit and a brown tie. The elbows of the suit jacket were shiny and one of its buttons was working its way loose. Lorenzo Strano would have turned away in disgust.

He said, 'You can stop running off at the mouth, Dyke. You know as well as we do what this is about.'

'Do I? News to me.'

'The young lady you were seen with last night was found dead early this morning just around the corner from where you met her. It seems she'd parked her car there but was intercepted before she reached it.'

I said nothing and stared at Greene. I felt like a sham pretending not to have known and I wondered how I'd got myself into this position. I couldn't pretend grief because I'd barely known the girl, but I knew it was a waste of her young life, and I suppose I felt in some small part I was responsible. I should have told her editor or done something to have her removed from The Lucky Strike.

Whatever the police investigation came up with, I had no doubt her murder was linked to the casino. And probably linked to the fact that she'd spoken to me twice. After Jack Jenkins saw her talking to me—with me asking a series of questions—she was always likely to be under suspicion.

But I couldn't let any of this show on my face. I couldn't admit to any emotional relationship with this girl that might suggest there was more of a connection than existed in fact. And even playing it deadpan brought its own problems: how could I be so apparently callous and unfeeling in the face of a young girl's death? Didn't that fact in itself suggest a pathology that might have led me to murder her … ?

I said, 'How did she die?'

Greene said, 'I don't need to tell you that.'

'I'll find out eventually.'

'Probably. Tell me again why you were meeting her. What did you want to talk about?'

'I didn't. She called me. She got my number from the Yellow Pages and asked to talk to me about crimes and criminals in the area. She was just starting out as a reporter and decided to specialise in crime and she wanted to get a handle on what was going on, crime-wise. I was reluctant to get her involved, to be honest. And that upset her.'

'Upset her so much she ran from the room, according to witnesses.'

'Don't be silly, Greene. There isn't a single witness who told you that. And if there were, you wouldn't tell me.'

'You seem to know a lot about what I know.'

'I've been in your chair. I recognise the games.'

'Oh yes, the Excise Investigator who left under a cloud. I've read about you. You were just a jumped-up taxman, weren't you?'

'That's how we saw ourselves. Have abacus, will travel. Tracking down tax avoiders for a better world.'

'Oh yeah, the inappropriate humour, too. I'm sure Miss Hall's parents will be thrilled by that.'

'Are we done here? If I'm not under arrest I can go, can't I?'

The policemen looked at each other, then Greene said, 'I think there's more we can do. Wait here.'

And they left without even looking backwards at me.

IF I'D BEEN under arrest they would have had to give me a fifteen minutes break after two hours of questioning anyway, as well as offering me refreshments when appropriate. As it was, this was a friendly conversation and they owed me nothing. I had no idea what they were thinking because it must have been plain from my dealings with them in the past that I wasn't a murderer and I'd had next to no contact with Hannah Hall before she was murdered.

But twenty minutes later they came back in and we went through it all again before lunch. At that point they gave me a couple of chicken salad sandwiches and coffee and left me to contemplate my future.

After lunch it was the same procedure. They must have had a conversation between them and found a couple of incomplete answers because they went back and probed exactly what Hannah had said to me and how I'd replied to her questions. They asked for more details of how soon after she left the pub did I leave, where was my car, what route I took to get home, did I see anyone, what did I do when I got home, when did I get to bed.

And so on.

We took a tea-break at four-thirty and then started on the evening session. Greene's young and eager companion was replaced by a fierce-looking woman with short blonde hair and cheek-bones that could carve a hunk of beef. The cheek-bones seemed to force her small mouth and lips into a purse of permanent disapproval and I felt she was making mental notes on what she'd like to do to me if she ever found me in a dark alley and she had her taser to hand …

During the day Greene had become more rumpled and seemed even chunkier than he had in the morning, as though he couldn't keep up the effort of holding himself together for a whole day.

At about eight o'clock that night he said, 'So you've got nothing to add to your story?'

'It's not a story. And no, nothing's changed since eight o'clock this morning. Tough day's work for you but you've got nothing, so can I go now?'

Greene didn't like it—and the female officer with the cheek-bones certainly didn't approve—but they glanced at each other and stood up at the same time as if choreographed and Greene picked up his file from the table. He walked to the door and opened it.

He said, 'We'll be in touch. Now bugger off.'

I stood up and stretched my back and my arms. It felt like a wasted day and I thought the police officers knew it too. It was almost as though we'd gone through a charade for the sake of form, so they couldn't be accused of neglecting lines of inquiry or passing up a suitable witness for interrogation. My media profile from a few months ago must have planted seeds of doubt in Greene and his colleagues, though, because what happened at that time had painted me in such a good light. I was almost a saint, after all.

He didn't move as I squeezed past him in the doorway.

I said, 'Nice doing business with you. If you need me again, you know where I live.'

Now I wish I hadn't said that.

A UNIFORM WAS waiting outside the interview room to take me out. He nodded at me and indicated with his eyes which direction I should take. We were walking towards the end of the corridor when Billy Passmore came around the corner. He halted when he saw me and let us walk up to him, then raised a hand to stop us. He turned to the officer.

'Chris, give me a second with Mr Dyke, will you?'

'I'll be just around the corner.'

The uniform went ahead and I was left looking at Passmore's depthless eyes. He stared back at me, then indicated a door to the side — another interview room, presently unused.

'Step in here, Dyke.'

I did as I was told and he closed the door behind us. He raised a hand and smoothed down his hair, in which there wasn't any sign of a ruffle. Then without any preamble he said, 'What was your connection to this poor girl?'

'I've answered all the questions I'm going to answer today. Talk to Greene. Listen to what he says. Get off my case.'

'You don't care who you piss off, do you? I know you think you're the big hero because of what happened at Piccadilly, but one swallow doesn't make a summer. You might still be a bad boy for all we know. You're on the radar now, not under it.'

'What the hell is that supposed to mean? Speak straight or get out of my way.'

'You can't go around playing fast and loose with people's lives. I understand you've been released for the moment, but it wouldn't take much to have you arrested and back inside for questioning.'

'What's all this got to do with you? Murder isn't your area now.'

'I'm still a policeman. I don't like dead people turning up in my patch.'

'You've got a hell of a big patch.'

He pulled down the bottom of his buttoned uniform jacket and made sure his shirt cuffs were showing beneath the edge of the sleeves, winkling them out with his fingers and checking that the same amount of cuff was showing on each arm.

He said, 'Just remember, you're playing with fire, Dyke. Playing with fire.'

Then he turned, opened the door and walked out.

NO ONE OFFERED to drive me home and I hadn't called Dan or Belinda to tell them where I was. I hadn't wanted to get them involved—or even in the close neighbourhood of a police station.

So I found a taxi around the corner from the station and gave the driver instructions. It was dark and it had apparently been raining during the day, judging by the gleam on the roads and the sparkle of the cars parked on the streets.

I sat back in the rear of the Toyota mini-cab and thought about the day I'd had. As soon as I was greeted on my doorstep this morning by Greene I'd known what was in store for me. I'd been through similar days before, sitting on both sides of the table. The trick was to remain calm and not be riled by the apparent senselessness and repetition of the questioning. The officers went through a routine that was intended to help them prove a case should it become possible. They covered all the angles by asking as many questions as occurred to them and by allowing me to talk at my own pace, without interruption. You could fall asleep while listening to one of these interviews on tape.

I thought again about Hannah. Why had she parked in the Waitrose car park in the first place? What was wrong with the car park at the pub? How had her killer got close to her without her screaming or putting up a struggle? That part of Sandbach was reasonably busy on a Friday night. The supermarket stayed open till the middle of the evening and then there were usually groups of youths going to the various pubs and clubs on the square.

I could only imagine that whoever had done it had taken her and finished the job quickly, before she'd had time to scream or struggle. I hoped for her sake it had been painless.

I wondered briefly whether I should contact her newspaper and get them involved, and also whether I should contact Anjelica Strange. But I wasn't officially working for her, now, so I decided it was best to leave her out of it.

The more I knew, the more I was certain it wasn't a random murder and Hannah had been the unfortunate victim of a crazed killer. To my shame, the message her murder sent was aimed at me. I just had to prove who had composed and dispatched it.

It was close to nine o'clock by now and Crewe was brightly lit. My driver turned left past the station and we headed out past the high gates of the football ground, soon moving away from the terraced houses and industrial parks that edged the main road and heading into the semi-rural plots beyond.

Looking through the window I saw the dull urban glow that hovers over every city at night, the street-lamps polluting the darkness with their orange haze.

We were heading away from the centre of town and into an area where the lighting was sparser and there were fewer houses or industrial zones casting their light upwards. But the glow became brighter and more distinct as we approached the turn-off to the track that led down to my house.

The driver slowed and half-turned towards me.

'Down there, mate? Don't think I can get in.'

I followed his view through the windscreen and saw men in yellow hazard jackets, one of them walking towards us with his hand held in front of him.

I threw a twenty at the driver and climbed out of the car, which started to reverse immediately. The man with the yellow jacket was still walking towards me, shaking his head. There was a smell in the air that I didn't recognise but didn't like.

The man said, 'Can't go down there, sir. Keep back.'

'I live down there, what's going on?'

I didn't need to be told what was going on. While the policeman started talking into his shoulder-mic I dodged around him and ran down the track. I heard him shout behind me. Fifty yards on I rounded the corner and saw my house, flames bursting from its roof and billowing out of the windows. Thick smoke roiled upwards into the skies and there was a sizzling, snapping roar coming from the centre of the house.

Without thinking, I ran towards the house and as if from nowhere two other men appeared and grabbed me.

'Can't do that, mate, too dangerous.'

'It's my house!'

'Leave it to them.'

Now I saw there was a fire engine to one side throwing a plume of water over the roof and a couple of men at ground-level pointing hoses through the two windows. The heat from thirty yards was extraordinary, the flames building on themselves, retreating briefly then coming on with more force, while above the roof the rolling curl of thick black smoke rose upwards. The fire roared and there was an insistent crackling sound of the wood in the floorboards and roof-beams burning. I imagined my furniture, my electronic equipment, my rare CDs, my books … all devoured by an obscene level of heat.

I'd stopped struggling and the men let me go. I saw they were policemen too and were taking no part in the fire-fighting. We stood and watched as the fire continued despite the efforts of the fire-fighters to dampen it.

The policeman who had tried to stop me at the entrance walked up to one of the fire-fighters who was standing by the appliance and pointed me out. The other man nodded and then headed towards me, his face red and sweating under his helmet.

He said, 'Anyone else in there? Any pets?'

I shook my head. 'No one lives there, just me.'

He looked at me carefully for a moment as if assessing my state of mind.

I said, 'It's not slowing, is it?'

'I can't say anything official.' He glanced at the two officers at my side. 'Personally I reckon someone's had this go up. It went too quick too soon. By the time we got here it was well set in. Best we can do is contain it to the house, but I don't think we'll save it.'

'My car?'

'Round the side? Black when we got here. Sorry. You must have really pissed somebody off.'

He walked away almost casually, watching his men work with a professional eye, calling out instructions to someone, straightening a piece of cable, climbing into the cab of the fire-appliance and probably, for all I know, about to eat a sandwich.

I watched until I was certain the house was going to collapse, then I walked away. No one tried to stop me, which was probably a good job. The way I was feeling I might not have been able to act polite.

IT WAS PROBABLY midnight by the time I arrived at Dan's house, having walked for the best part of an hour to get there. My feet ached, my house was cinders, I'd lost nearly all of my possessions and I didn't have a job. I was a single man with a lonely old age in prospect and no pension to speak of.

Life was good.

I rang Dan's bell and he arrived promptly, awake because he was online, making money.

He stared at me. I knew I'd be covered in soot and would be looking ragged at the edges. There'd also been a slight drizzle for the last ten minutes, so I was wet. He took in the vision and raised his eyebrows slightly.

'You better come in and wash.'

'You know that spare room you've got upstairs?'

'Yes …'

'Does it have a bed in it?'

CHAPTER TWENTY-FOUR

THANKFULLY, INSURANCE COMPANIES work on Sundays. It was relatively straightforward to tell my insurers that all my worldly goods had gone up in smoke. I expected a tough battle but they promised to have someone around by the end of the week to inspect the damage and start the estimation process. My car insurers also gave me the go ahead to hire a replacement until I could fund one of my own.

Despite being easy, it still took time and ate up most of the day. On Monday morning I took a taxi up to the house to have a look at its condition. There was still police tape around the site and even thirty-six hours later there was smoke issuing from the burnt and blackened timberwork of the roof and cross-beams. The walls had collapsed inwards and the entire upper floor had crashed through so the remains of my old iron bed lay in the sitting room and the Victorian bath with its claw feet was in the kitchen. My Mondeo sat desolately to one side, a black husk, its tyres melted. I stood and looked at the space where my house had stood, then turned and got back in the taxi.

The driver said, 'Yours?'

'It was. Belongs to the insurance company now.'

'You all right?'

'I'll let you know.'

When the police came to call just after lunch I was in no mood for politeness.

I'd given Dan's address to one of the officers at the scene of the fire and two plainclothes detectives came in wearing looks of serious formality. We sat in Dan's front room while he went up to his bedroom to do more work on his laptop.

From the beginning, the policemen seemed more inclined to believe I'd set fire to the house myself. It was probably too difficult to deal with if it involved foul play from someone else. Much easier to believe I was in financial difficulties and I needed the money to pay off debts.

I said, 'I don't have any debts. You can look at my accounts.' I hesitated, wondering where my next statement would take me. But I said it anyway. 'The fire chief at the site suggested it *was* arson. But I'm telling you it wasn't me.'

The lead officer was a worried-looking man in his late twenties with thinning hair and a short moustache he seemed to be growing for a bet.

He said, 'Why would anyone burn down your house? Have you upset someone?'

'Not lately.'

I could hardly point them in the direction of Billy Passmore. And I wasn't going to share my knowledge of him and Jumbo Jack Jenkins with anyone else. Not now. Or not yet.

The other policeman said, 'So this is just a hypothetical then? For insurance purposes? You want to blame someone else so you don't feel guilty or something?'

'I don't feel guilty.'

'You know the owner is the first person we look at if it's a case of arson.'

'I do.'

'So where were you Saturday before the fire?'

This is going to be fun, I thought.

'I was in a police station in Stoke.'

They both appeared to sit up, mentally.

'Oh yeah? What were you doing there?'

'I was being questioned about the murder of someone I'd met on Friday night. She was found dead just before midnight. Your colleagues thought I might be able to help them out. As a witness.'

'And could you?'

'I'm here, aren't I? Not banged up in a cell. That should mean something.'

They looked at each other as if doing mathematics in their heads.

Then they turned back to me and the conversation took a strange direction.

Moustache-man said, 'Who was in charge?'

'A D.I. called Greene. With an e.'

They glanced at each other again. Then at me.

Moustache-man said, 'We'll have to look into it. Don't go anywhere without letting us know.'

'What's this about?'

They'd already risen from the sofa and had started gathering their things—coats, briefcases, papers. The lead officer gave me his card. Then they headed towards the front door as if in convoy.

The second man, who I suddenly realised had a strong resemblance to Al Pacino, if taller, stopped and leaned back towards me.

'You didn't hear this from us, but Derek Greene doesn't work out of Stoke. We're going to do some checking to find out why he's involved, and why we weren't told about you.'

'And you're telling me this because ... ?'

They glanced at each other again and the one with the moustache nodded shortly.

His colleague said, 'He had a bit of bother some while ago. He works out of a different unit now, all about Transparency. Quis custodiet ipsos custodes, eh? That's Latin, that. Look it up.'

I didn't need to look it up. He was telling me Detective Greene was operating a little out of his legal sphere of operations. So it had been no surprise when Billy Passmore had shown up in the station—he'd set me up for the 'conversation' all along, maybe to get me out of the house while another of his minions set fire to my house.

He was taking risks on so many fronts it could only mean one thing—he was scared, and probably on the point of doing something that was unbelievably stupid.

LATER THAT AFTERNOON Belinda arrived. I'd called her that morning to tell her about Hannah Hall's murder and that my house was now a smoking ruin, and after the usual expressions of horror she said she might have something to put us back on track.

Dan let her in and organised tea while Belinda set up a small playback device and plugged it into a loudspeaker via its headphone socket.

When we were all seated and had drinks, she pressed a button and playback began.

It was almost incomprehensible.

I looked at her and she waggled her head from side to side.

'I know. But it gets better. I cleaned it up.'

After a couple of minutes it did get better. I recognised Jack Jenkins' voice talking to someone else with an accent that was probably Asian. It was staccato and rapid and harder to follow than Jenkins' fluty tenor.

We listened for ten minutes and then Belinda turned it off. Although it was clearer it was still undecipherable to me.

I said, 'I appreciate the effort, but I still couldn't understand most of it.'

She said, 'Took me all day Friday and most of Saturday to get it that clear, believe it or not. Could you make any of it out? I've heard it so many times I could practically recite it.'

'When did you tape it?'

'Thursday night.'

'You were supposed to be resting.'

'Was I? Oh, that slipped my mind. So, what do you think?'

'I don't think anything. Tell me what you hear.'

'Jenkins is talking to someone about some unspecified deal. He mentions transport and he mentions manpower, but he doesn't say what it is and when it's going to happen.'

'So something is definitely happening but we don't know what.'

'Correct. I get the feeling it's all been organised and they're just waiting for the right time to do whatever they're going to do. It was like they were going over it again but didn't need to work out the details—who goes where and when, that kind of thing.'

'What about the argument at the beginning?'

'Took me an hour to tune that in. And it iurned out to be nothing. A difference of opinion about tea.'

She grinned at us.

I pointed to the playback machine. 'Does it get us any further?'

'Well there's a rather important point in there.'

I knew what she meant. I'd heard the name 'Strano' mentioned but it was maddeningly vague.

'What do they say about Strano?'

'Jenkins says Strano has to be in position by ten thirty but he doesn't specify where. Then there's an argument about which men are to be used in which location, but again they're not specific. It's as if they knew I was listening.'

We thought about that for a while. It occurred to me to wonder whether Strano knew he was involved in this or not? And if he did, and he was, should I talk to him or to Anjelica about it?

Dan said, 'What's with all these Asian men? Where do they fit in?'

I said, 'Hannah Hall had a theory they were here as strong-arm thugs. She thought there was a big-time Triad member holed up in the area and using The Lucky Strike for match-fixing. Players who don't stick to their promises are punished. And anyone who doesn't pay their gambling debts gets roughed up.'

Belinda was stowing her gear. She glanced at me.

'You sound as though you didn't believe her. I bet that cheered her up.'

'We didn't part on the best of terms, no. I'm sorry about that now. I liked her, though I thought she was playing a dangerous game.'

'So have you got any better ideas?'

'Come on, this is Stoke. Why would Triad members come here when there are bigger attractions in Manchester and … hold on.' A thought had occurred to me. 'Dan, you can help me out here.'

'I live to serve.'

'Check out what's going on in the area—big events, festivals, celebrity appearances, sporting matches, anything like that. And see if you can find out when banks move money around. Is there a calendar, or do they change it all the time so crooks don't know when and where they are?'

'I can do that. Are you all set up now?'

He was looking towards an old Lenovo laptop he'd given me earlier in the day. It sat waiting balefully on a side table, as though it knew in advance what terrors I was going to inflict on it. Thankfully Dan had organised me months ago so that all my files and important data, including passwords and favourites for my web-browser, had been backed-up to the cloud on a regular basis. Today he'd downloaded it all on to the old laptop and set it up so it was hardly different to the one I'd used in the office and at home. Kids can be useful after all.

'I'm fine, thanks. If you can just replace two thousand CDs now it would be perfect.'

He took me seriously. 'I'll see what I can do.'

I said to Belinda, 'There's something else.'

'There always is. Life's never boring around you, is it?'

'The cops who came today to talk to me about my house fire were very weird when I mentioned I'd been questioned by Greene. They didn't say anything … well, actually they did, which is also weird. They implied Greene was acting outside of his remit.'

'What do you mean?'

'I don't know what I mean. He came with a bunch of other cops and we went to a proper police station and I was interviewed in the presence of two different detectives. But it didn't hang right with the men I saw today. And then after I'd been interviewed on Saturday I ran into Billy Passmore in the hall, as though he was just on his way to something important. At eight o'clock at night.'

'So you think he's used some influence in how Hannah's murder is being investigated?'

'Who knows? I'm sure there are processes and procedures so everything's done according to the book. But maybe Passmore has got more weight than we thought around here. And when he assumes his new post he'll have even more, because ordinary coppers will be scared of him.'

'I thought we'd put all that behind us. Corruption and what not.'

'Don't you believe it. They're only people. It's a job. And they get to meet some pretty horrible crooks who thrive and make lots of money. It must be tempting.'

'Don't defend him, Sam. Wanna bet he went to church again yesterday morning and prayed to the Lord? I can't stand hypocrisy like that. I might not always play by the rules, but I don't stand up and pretend to live by them, either.'

'I'm not defending him. But I understand the temptations. When you've seen how some of these crooks live it must be galling.'

She put on her leather jacket and zipped it up, then slung her bag of equipment over her shoulder. Her broken fingers seemed to be giving her less pain than before.

'Sounds to me like he's up to his eyeballs in some bad shit. Whatever's going to happen will be soon because he won't want all these Asian gamblers on his patch for long—they're too obvious. So why don't we concentrate on nailing them, and nailing Passmore, and leave the hearts and flowers in the bin?'

'I'm all for that. I'm going to push things a little and we'll see where we get to. I'll be in touch. Thanks for your work on the recording.'

'Let's hope it was worth it.'

CHAPTER TWENTY-FIVE

FIRST THING ON Tuesday morning my loaner car was delivered. I signed for a Volkswagen Polo and the man who brought it went off with one of his colleagues in a nice Audi. I'd rather hoped it was going to be the other way around when they turned up outside Dan's house in both cars.

So I familiarised myself with the controls and drove to my office, armed with my new laptop and a sense of righteous anger.

The office was still intact and hadn't burned to the ground, which was good news. I thought even Billy Passmore couldn't set fire to half of Crewe's shopping centre just to send me another message.

Though I was beginning to see he was getting pretty desperate.

I looked at and binned the post, then sat and stared at the phone for a while. I had some information but nowhere to take it and at the moment there seemed to be nothing I could do with it. With Passmore being so prominent in the local police force hierarchy I felt I had to watch my step—for two reasons: first, I might be laughed at by his fellow officers who wouldn't believe he could be guilty of such devilry; second, whoever I spoke to might be one of Passmore's crew. I felt that was unlikely because I didn't believe he could have enrolled so many coppers into his little gang, especially in these days of 'transparency' and 'ethics committees'. Having said that, it was only a couple of years since the West Midlands force had sacked twenty-one officers for corruption and breaches of professional standards. So some policemen were still finding it difficult to resist the lure of the Dark Side.

Eventually I picked up the phone and dialled Anjelica's office number.

The woman at the reception desk must have had new instructions about me because she found Anjelica quickly. I could see the frown on her face as she came to the phone.

'I thought we were done. I'm still waiting for your invoice.'

'It's in the post. I have new information about the people your dad's working for. And about Billy Passmore.'

I heard her sigh. 'Not that again.'

'He burned down my house on Saturday night.'

This time there was a pause but no sigh.

'What do you mean?'

'A girl I knew was murdered on Friday night and I was asked in for questioning on Saturday. When I got home that night my house was on fire and couldn't be saved. They think it was arson.'

'That doesn't mean—'

'I saw Passmore at the police station. He told me I was playing with fire. What other message do you think I should take from that?'

'You're insane if you think he had anything to do with this.'

'Can we go talk to your father?'

'Why would I do that?'

'Because you still have feelings for him and I think he'll talk to you but not to me if I turn up alone.'

'So you want me to trick him into talking to you.'

'I think in business you'd call it facilitating a meeting. See it in those terms and it won't seem so hard.'

HALF AN HOUR later she called me back. She'd phoned The Lucky Strike and asked to speak to her father but he wasn't at work that day. However, the receptionist was happy enough to give her Strano's mobile phone number and she'd contacted him at home. He was willing to speak to her that afternoon and given her directions.

I said, 'Be prepared. It's not the Ritz.'

'I don't even know why I'm doing this.'

'Because you don't want your father to come to harm.'

'I'll see you there at three o'clock. Just before.'

WHEN I TURNED into Strano's street at 2:50 she was already there, parked a little down the road and leaning with her back to her Porsche. She looked like a butterfly in a dung heap, completely out of place.

I parked behind and went to stand next to her.

She glanced at the Polo and said, 'Changed your car?'

'The old one went up in smoke with the house. I'm using this till I sort out another.'

'I recommend trading up. That Mondeo was bad for the image.'

'Can we talk about your father? Why does he think you asked to see him?'

She shifted her weight. 'Making peace. Talking. That kind of thing. I don't think he wants to do it, and seeing this place I'm not surprised he didn't get in touch.'

'Don't judge him. He's finding his feet.'

'He's my father, I'll take whatever attitude I like.'

I shrugged. I thought I understood. She was still angry and hadn't yet worked it out of her system. Maybe this meeting would turn out to be another of my bad ideas …

She said, 'Can we go in now? I can't stay long. I've got a conference call in an hour.'

'It's that door there.'

She followed my pointing arm and walked towards the door. I moved a little further down the street and closer to the houses, out of the direct sight-line of Strano's front door.

I watched as Anjelica approached the door, hesitated, then knocked. The door was opened quickly and she talked to her father without stepping inside. Then she glanced down the road at me and he stepped forward so he could see me too.

He went back inside and Anjelica waved me forwards.

When I arrived at the door they were standing in the middle of the living room as though they didn't know each other. Seeing them close together again I recognised the similarities in their colouring, their features, their bearing. They were a good-looking family with pride and a certain amount of style. I felt like an intruder into their world.

Strano said, 'Don't expect a cup of tea this time. What do you want?'

'First, don't blame Anjelica for this. I convinced her it was in your own best interests to talk to me.'

'Big of you.'

'Second, I really think you two should talk anyway. Neither of you seems to know it, but take it from an observer looking in, you both care for each other.'

Anjelica swung her handbag from her shoulder and laid it on the armchair.

'Thanks, Doctor Phil. Any more advice?'

'Can we sit down?'

I could tell Strano hated doing it, but he fetched another chair from the back room and eventually we all sat down. He was wearing a black tee-shirt that showed his muscles and a pair of black jeans that had been carefully ironed, including the pockets. He couldn't help himself.

Anjelica took off her short jacket and revealed her own bare, tanned arms poking out of a purple short-sleeved blouse that was cut low at the front. She wore a gold necklace that rested just at the top of her breasts. Not like any office-wear I remembered.

I started to tell Strano what I'd learned about the casino, Jack Jenkins and Billy Passmore. I told him what I'd discovered about the Asian men and the setting up of the wire-room, about Hannah Hall's death and the burning of my house. From the look on his face I guessed I was having the same effect as the last time I'd talked to him about Jenkins and Passmore. Precisely none. I wondered why I was here again—what was I trying to prove by getting him away from the casino? Even as I spoke I felt the urgency leave my voice. It was his life to ruin, if that's what he wanted.

Then he surprised me.

He said, 'Even if I wanted to I couldn't get out.'

'What do you mean?'

He sat back and spread his arms.

'Jenkins knows I owe him. The job. The advance he gave me to buy my car. Helped me find this place, dump though it is. If I even hinted I wanted to leave he'd want it all back, every penny. And he'd send his boys to get it. Is that what you want? For me to get beaten to a pulp?'

Now Anjelica leaned forward and glanced at me before looking at her father.

'Do you believe him? Is he right? Even about Billy Passmore?'

He turned a blank gaze towards her.

'I couldn't say, could I?'

This response seemed to anger her but she kept herself in check.

She said, 'Dad, I don't understand what happened to you.'

'It's all very complicated.'

'Then explain it to me. I'm a big girl now.'

He looked away, seeming to find the fireplace terrifically interesting. I watched from the sidelines as they played out something that had damaged both their lives without either of them fully understanding it.

Strano said, 'There's such a thing as loyalty. Doing your job.'

'And do you think Billy was loyal to you?'

'He did what he had to.'

'What, even after he left you to hang in court? Didn't you even feel angry, or bitter? Why didn't you say something? If you were on a project for him, why didn't you bring it up? Why did you leave mum and me in the lurch for all that time?'

Her voice had grown louder in the small room and Strano glanced at the neighbouring wall. She saw the look and it inflamed her further.

'No I won't keep my voice down. I hated the way you just took it, day after day in that court, staring ahead as though nothing could get to you, nothing mattered, ignoring me, ignoring your friends, just shut away in that little world of yours, that secret little world.'

'Anjelica—'

'No, I've said what I came here to say. I can't take this any more.' She stood up and grabbed her jacket and handbag. 'I've got to go. I don't understand you. I don't understand why you did it. You were just a … just a … coward. You didn't stand up for yourself. Well you won't catch me doing that.'

She turned and walked in two strides to the door, pulling it open with enough force to have brought down the wall if it resisted. The cold grey street life outside was visible for a moment, then she slammed the door shut and was gone.

There was liquid in Strano's eyes but he didn't cry. His strong, straight features seemed oddly vulnerable, though, and I realised something in a sudden rush.

I said, 'You couldn't say anything could you? You were being threatened.'

He used his hands to wipe down his face and when he looked at me again there was a new openness there.

'Clever man. I wondered if you'd ever get to it. Took your bloody time.'

'Don't let me guess. Tell me about it.'

'Like I said to Anjelica, it's complicated. You'll have heard it all before.'

'I've got time. You have to tell someone eventually or you'll explode.'

His whole face had become strained, as though he were forcibly holding something back through force of will.

But then he leaned back in his chair and raised his face to stare at the ceiling, and all the fight went out of him. He began to tell me the story.

He'd been born to English parents in Princes Risborough in Buckinghamshire, a small town north west of London. His paternal grandfather had been Italian and captured during the fighting in Sicily at the beginning of the Italian campaign in the Second World War. He was then brought back to the internment camp established at Peterley Wood. After the war dozens of the prisoners stayed in the area, including Arturo Strano. Many of the people in the town still spoke with Italian accents because of the close family ties that bonded them together and kept their culture alive.

But Lorenzo Strano had lost his accent early because he was always good at fitting in, and he'd fitted in with the English population more comfortably than with his extended family.

When he'd joined the police force he'd moved north into the Midlands, even further away from his family, and had got to know Billy Passmore, who was a few years older and was already rising in the local force's pecking order.

'He lived a charmed life, that man. Nice house, good at his job, lovely wife. Took me under his wing and said we'd go places together. Well I went to prison and I guess he's going to hell.'

'Tell me what happened.'

'As I said, I was good at fitting in. I could blend in to most groups of people pretty easy. So he used to send me on jobs, undercover stuff. Get to know the villains in a particular gang, have a pint, learn what was going on, then let him know. He'd set things up and we'd bust them and they never knew it was me, so I could move on to the next gang.'

'So what went wrong? Why did you end up in jail?'

Strano stared ahead for so long without speaking it was as though he'd forgotten me. Then he frowned and began speaking again.

'It was so fucked up. He sent me on another job. I was to find out who was selling steroids in this gym. There were lots of coppers used it but it was out of our area, so no one knew me. I joined up and hung around, made myself popular in the bar by buying drinks. Usual stuff. Told some jokes, you know what men are like. Didn't take me long to work out what was going on. The owner of the gym was this chubby bloke I'd known at school.'

'Jenkins?'

'Him. I worked out it was him selling the drugs on the side as a way of keeping the gym going. It was cheap to join but had way too many special extras—massages, fitness classes, tanning. So he was slowly going broke. Didn't take Einstein to realise he was the one that wound up funding it with his extra-curricular retail activities.'

'So you told Passmore and what happened?'

'Nothing. Sod all. I put in reports every week and he said thank you and nothing happened. Next thing I knew, I was hauled out of bed one morning, put on gardening leave and eventually charged with selling steroids to other customers. A handy suitcase full of the things was found in my bedroom by his mate Craig and I was a goner.'

'What did Passmore say?'

'He told me not to worry. Everything would be all right when it came to court.'

'But it changed.'

'Understatement of the year.'

I leaned back. What he said didn't make sense in terms of police protocol.

'Weren't the reports you gave to Passmore filed and recorded? Couldn't your lawyers get them submitted in court?'

'Good idea, why didn't we think of that? Oh, we did. Trouble was, they didn't exist. Passmore never recorded them. They weren't in the records and not in the files where they should have been. All he was doing was getting dirt on Jenkins to use against him, and I was the gardener.'

'But he was taking a huge risk you'd shop him. At the least there'd be an investigation or something. He'd be in the firing line.'

'Well he took care of that, didn't he?'

He stared at me with red eyes, waiting for me to understand. Eventually I did.

I said, 'That was the threat. He threatened you … or your family.'

'Bingo. He threatened Anjelica. Him and Jenkins. She was seventeen. Threatened her with some awful stuff. I can't talk about it. Couldn't tell them, her and her mum … '

He glanced away again, his eyes moistening. Then he wiped them once more with the palms of his hands and carried on, his voice softer.

'Seems Passmore was already in debt and somehow Jenkins owned part of it. It was in both their interests to keep me quiet. So they threatened my family if I didn't take the hit. I've lived with that for eight years.'

'What was that story you told about being recruited in jail by one of Jenkins' men? Why didn't you run a mile?'

'You find yourself in my position, see what you'd do. No job, no pension, no prospects. I thought I'd just stand in a doorway and act tough towards drunken gamblers till I could get my own thing going. I didn't know Passmore was going to be involved again. I thought he'd learned his lesson and if he'd had any sense he'd have split from Jenkins as soon as he could. But he was an addict, a gambler. He takes risks for the adrenaline high.'

I realised my throat was dry and I swallowed to put some moisture on my tongue. Eventually I said, 'That's why Jenkins was able to get the casino license even though he's a scumbag.'

'Exactly. Passmore greased the wheels. I think that probably erased his debt to Jenkins. Now they're in hock to each other, each of them up to their eyeballs in shit. And both of them in hock to this Malaysian gangster, Phar.'

I took a moment to digest this new information.

I said, 'I thought you didn't know anything about that.'

'I didn't. I've done some digging of my own in the last couple of days. Kept my eyes and ears open. You forget I used to be a cop. I don't know anything about Phar personally because everyone's tight-lipped. But he's not a saint. You should Google him.'

I eased my shoulders, realising I'd been sitting as tense as an over-wound clock. I looked around at the drab room and understood what Strano had been going through in order to keep his family safe. And they had been estranged from him for all of that time—and even now.

I said, 'Do you know what's going to happen? We know something's being planned and your name came up in the planning.'

'What do you mean?'

I explained quickly what Belinda and I had learned from the tape she'd made of the conversation at the casino.

Strano said, 'Well I'm at the casino all this week, afternoons only. So 10:30 doesn't make any sense for me. But next week I'm on company business, according to the rota.'

'What company business?'

'Working for the security firm that Jenkins runs. Starts next Sunday, at the Museum.'

'What do you intend to do?'

'Go to work, of course. What else can I do? Don't you understand, they're bigger than me and you. More men, more power, more influence. Look what happened to me. I fought the law and the law won.'

'But you didn't have me on your side. Things are different now.'

Though not that different, as I was shortly to find out.

CHAPTER TWENTY-SIX

DESPITE WHAT YOU see in films and read in books, my job description doesn't involve a lot of violence. Mostly the work is measured, careful, passive and observant. Of course the fact you're often involved in people's private lives arouses passions, which in turn can lead to anger and the expression of that emotion through violent words and actions.

But most of the time I'm able to talk to people and they see reason, usually because there's some kind of legal authority behind what I do. And besides, I keep myself fit, I hit the bag in my home-gym and I generally watch my diet. So I'm not exactly a pushover.

As a result, when violence does arrive without warning—as it typically does—I might be taken a little by surprise but I'm generally up to the job of defending myself. And that makes it doubly annoying when I'm not.

After talking to Strano I drove back to my office. I needed to sit and think my way around the situation to find a course of action that was manageable and kept everyone safe. It was approaching five o'clock when I unlocked my office door and took a step inside.

Which was when they hit me.

Not a hit to begin with, but a shove. The door was still swinging open when a pair of hands pushed me in the back and I stumbled inside the room. I'd been vaguely aware of a noise at my back but hadn't had the time to react before I was propelled forward.

I was finding my balance, half bent over, my hands outstretched, when a leg hooked itself around my ankles and yanked them from under me. I fell face forwards, trying to roll to avoid anyone landing on my back.

But there were too many of them.

I sensed three sets of running feet coming through the doorway, the door itself slamming shut behind them.

I felt a foot kick me in the small of my back, even as I was rolling, and my breath was forced from my lungs. I'd brought my hands up to my face, which just gave another of the men the chance to kick me in the stomach, causing me to double over.

I heard myself shouting, 'Wait! Wait!'

But it made no difference. They were standing in a circle now, each one taking turns to aim a kick—one in my back, one in my stomach, one to the back of my legs. They were grunting too because it takes effort to kick while you're standing still, constantly revising your balance and adjusting your legs.

Not that I had any sympathy for them.

I was beginning to get their rhythm and was able to cover my front and relax my back and calves when I sensed the kicks coming, though they weren't exactly keeping a four-four time. They seemed to be treating it more like a chore than something they were enjoying, which was some comfort.

I rolled to my knees and pulled everything in as though submitting. Then as the next kick came I whipped out an arm and took the man's legs from beneath him so that he crashed to the carpet and, I think, banged his head on the back of my desk.

I sprang towards him, my hands reaching for his throat … but the other two men were quick and grabbed me by my upper arms and pulled me up and backwards, flinging me on to the floor, face up.

Now I was looking at them directly. All three were Asian, with short black hair, very slender body types and angular features. I had no doubt where they'd come from. The one I'd brought down had scrambled to his feet and now came close to me, bent down, his face red, his hair dishevelled. He looked to be in his mid-twenties.

'My name is David, okay?' He stood upright again and kicked me in the ribs. 'I have a degree from MIT and an MBA from Princeton. You do not push me to the floor, okay?'

'You started it.'

He said something rapidly to his colleagues and I thought they were going to carry on with the kicking, but instead they reached down and picked me up. David fetched an office chair and they pushed me into it. They didn't want me standing because I was nearly a foot taller than all of them.

David had been adjusting his clothing and brushing down his hair.

'You are a big man but there are three of us. Your office is rubbish. This is how you say it, okay?'

'It's rubbish, I agree.'

'Good. This is a message for you. We beat you up and you learn a lesson. We could do you more harm.'

He looked at the man to my right and the next thing I knew he'd punched me in the jaw. I felt the skin on my upper cheek tear and knew it would bleed any second. I'm prone to migraines occasionally and I guessed a big one was coming when they left. So I did what someone had advised me to do when a migraine was on its way—I focused on my breathing, concentrating on the movement of air in and out of my nostrils. Admittedly, this was a little difficult when surrounded by Asian hard-cases, but I gave it my best shot.

David said, 'Do you want to know what the warning is?'

'Let me guess—'

'No! I must give you the warning. This is a warning to stay out of the business of Jack Jenkins.'

'Was it you who burned down my house?'

I thought he'd deny it, but a slow smile spread across his face, as though he were pleased his achievement had been recognised.

'That was phase two, okay? This is phase three.'

'And the murder of Hannah Hall was phase one?'

He waved a hand dismissively. 'We discussed that it wouldn't be enough for a tough cookie like you. So we had a three-phase plan, okay? All good communications come in threes. I learned that on my MBA at Princeton. Presentation skills. Tell them what you're going to do. Do it. Tell them what you did. So, have you learned?'

'I've heard the message, if that's what you mean.'

He frowned. 'You suggest you haven't learned.'

'I've learned that you're a poor student who has no understanding of western psychology. Or human values. I've learned that you're a very bad human being who doesn't deserve to live. *Okay*?'

He looked at me as though trying to understand the words. Then he got them. Then he spoke rapidly to his two colleagues again.

And then they finished what they'd come to do.

CHAPTER TWENTY-SEVEN

DAN MUST HAVE wondered which version of his father he was going to see every time he opened his front door.

This time it was the one with the bleeding face, the ragged clothing and the winded appearance of a scarecrow left too long in the rain.

'Jesus, what happened to you?'

'His name was David. He has a degree from MIT and an MBA from Princeton.'

'You couldn't handle one man?'

'He had his less-educated friends with him to help.'

He stood back and I stumbled inside, heading for the sofa. Dan went to the kitchen and came back with a bowl of warm water and some towels. He left them on the floor as if he wasn't quite sure what to do next. I doubt he'd had much experience of nursing in his short life. I leaned forward and began to wash myself down.

Fifteen minutes later he'd made tea, ordered a curry for delivery and found me a tee-shirt to wear. I still hadn't replaced my wardrobe except for a grab-bag of underpants and socks I'd managed to get from a supermarket. I needed shirts and trousers and jackets … the list made my head throb again, though I had passed through the migraine stage by now.

Dan sat opposite me while I lay back on the sofa, staring at the ceiling.

'So who were they?'

'Lightweight thugs sent from Jack Jenkins. It was another warning—Hannah Hall, my house, now this.'

'So is it time to call in reinforcements? Talk to someone, even the press?'

'Sure, if you want to see your old man locked up and the key thrown away. What have we actually got in terms of proof? It's just guesswork and speculation and hearsay.'

'Isn't it what they call circumstantial evidence?'

I shook my head. 'I wouldn't glorify it with that name. We've got a shaky conversation from the casino, obtained illegally. Then we've got a lot of join-the-dots theories about the connections between Jenkins and Passmore and these Asian gangsters. Even if they raided the wire-room at the casino—on what pretext, I don't know—I'm not sure it would hold up in court. They're just watching television after all.'

Dan raised his eyebrows. 'Does this pessimism run in our family? Is my Gran going to be as miserable as you?'

'I doubt it.'

He sensed something in my voice and after a moment moved away quietly. I ached all over and couldn't really get comfortable. I'd tried my best against David and his co-thugs, and got in a couple of good punches, but they were too quick for me and three against one is never good odds.

I touched the cheek where the first man had punched me and drawn blood. Before I'd left the office I'd staunched it with paper towels from the bathroom but I needed to put a plaster or something on it, otherwise it was going to bleed all over Dan's carpet. If I could get myself from the sofa ...

I woke with a start and nearly fell off the sofa. There had been a knock at the front door and Dan was taking delivery of the curry.

I obviously needed the sleep.

We ate ravenously and I felt some of my energy returning. I'd only been asleep for thirty minutes but it seemed to have re-set my attitude.

Dan said, 'I phoned Belinda and told her what happened. I thought she should be warned to watch out for herself.'

'Thanks. You're right, but somehow I don't think they're worried about her. They probably think they've scared her off with the finger-breaking.'

'They don't know her.'

'Exactly. And I might be able to use that.'

He forked a mouthful of chicken jalfrezi between his lips, chewed and swallowed. He ate like a starving animal most of the time.

He said, 'You're getting her involved again?'

'I don't know, but probably. Otherwise she might just go off like a loaded gun. Better to direct the blast than wait to see where the explosion takes place.'

We ate in silence for a while, then Dan said, 'You asked me to look out for things happening in the area. Events and so on.'

'Nothing doing? Quiet week now summer's over, I suppose.'

'If you call Bon Jovi playing again at the Britannia Stadium quiet.'

'Really?'

'Saturday night. All booked up if you wanted tickets.'

I thought about that for a while and wondered what there would be in it for Jenkins or Passmore. There would surely be a lot of money … but then again, people bought their tickets online these days, so perhaps the physical box office takings on the night wouldn't be so great. Besides, the Britannia Stadium was a modern football stadium with a lot of security. Difficult to break into.

'Anything else?'

'Nothing much. I couldn't find out the bank timetables for moving cash, which is probably just as well. If I could have found them, so could others. There are a couple of rock concerts, a celebrity darts match, a new exhibition at the Museum … '

I put down my fork. I'd remembered where Lorenzo Strano had said he was going to be working next week.

'What kind of exhibition?'

'Oh, boring. They're putting all the bits of the Staffordshire Hoard together for the first time.'

'That's not boring, that's your history.'

'It's still old bits of pots, isn't it?'

I didn't know much about the Staffordshire Hoard except it wasn't pots. It was nearly all gold and silver military artifacts that had been found in a field and dated from the Anglo-Saxon period. I remembered reading that when the man who found it started digging it up, the first lot filled nearly two hundred and fifty bags. It was bought for over three million pounds and if I remembered correctly was shared between two museums in Birmingham and Stoke-on-Trent.

I said, 'So what's happening, exactly?'

'There was an article saying they're going to bring the two collections together. First they're going to bring the Birmingham half up here and show it for a couple of months, then they're going to take the whole lot back down to Birmingham.'

'And when's it going to start?'

'The exhibition opens in a couple of weeks, but they're bringing it up this weekend. In convoy. That's local news for you—museum transportation makes the front page.'

It was statements like that which reminded me that Dan was still a youngster. But he didn't know what I did.

I said, 'Can you call Belinda and see if she can come down tonight? We've got some planning to do.'

CHAPTER TWENTY-EIGHT

SHE SAT IN the car and breathed deeply. The day outside was calm, the sky blue, the temperature moderate for late autumn. She knew this had been her idea and she didn't regret it.

But.

Having the idea and carrying it out were two separate functions. She knew she couldn't change her mind because Sam was depending on her doing what she'd suggested ... albeit over his objections. Nevertheless, it was going to be risky and hard and probably dangerous.

She looked at her left hand. She'd had Dan build up the cast on her wrist and hand with Modroc, the plaster bandages used in hospitals to hold broken bones in place, and easily sourced from Amazon. The lengths of material had been briefly soaked in water then laid in successive strips over her wrist, wrapped around and smoothed down, then left for several hours to dry. Her broken fingers were well-protected inside with splints and the cut-off fingers of a pair of climbing gloves. The hand was now a monstrous, heavy club surrounded entirely by thick, hard plaster. Fortunately the Peugeot 206 she'd borrowed again from Josie in Burnage was an automatic and she could just about manage to move the stick from Park to Drive.

Taking one final breath, she climbed from the car, used her right hand to zip up her jacket, and walked towards The Lucky Strike Casino.

It was just after Friday lunchtime and there were a few punters coming in and out. Because little trouble was anticipated at this time of day there were no bouncers on the doors. She walked towards the steps leading to the large glass entrance doors, then turned at the last moment to go around the side of the dull grey oblong towards the delivery entrance.

She'd timed her arrival to match the departure of a bread truck she'd watched earlier. She'd seen them carrying in flat wire trays of continental breads for the restaurants and had given the delivery-man enough time to have worked his way through the contents of his van.

As she approached on the narrow tarmacked path, she saw him slamming shut the rear doors and climbing in the cab. He started the engine and headed towards the bottom of the track so that he could turn around and come back the same way. He drove past her and she waved casually. She heard the side door of the casino slam shut just before she got there, the person inside not having seen her approach.

She gave it a minute, then pounded on the metal door, painted grey like the rest of the building. She hoped whoever was inside would think it was the delivery-man having forgotten something.

It seemed to work, because the door opened wide and a young man wearing a white apron and with flour on his arms peered out at her.

She took no notice of him and pushed straight past. He said something to her back but she was already on her way.

As she'd thought, this was the place she'd been brought to when Jenkins' men had kidnapped and blindfolded her. They'd tried to fool her by taking her on a mystery trip around Stoke and Hanley, but in fact there was only one place it could be: The Lucky Strike Casino.

Once through the small lobby, created by two pairs of swing-doors with a six foot gap between them, she was in the large arena her senses told her was the place she'd been brought when blindfolded. It had the same antiseptic smell and the same acoustics. Looking around she saw it mostly contained cardboard boxes piled two or three deep and labelled with the names of various foodstuffs—tuna, tomatoes, peas, pasta, rice—as well as crates and crates of bottled beers, ciders and wines. High overhead the bare skin of the building was visible above the metal beams and plumbing conduits that were part of its construction. A dozen conical lampshades hung down from other cross beams and cast an even light over the floor. The antiseptic odour came from a stack of cleaning materials and bleaches set apart in a far corner so they didn't infect the foodstuffs through direct contact with their smell. It was basically a store room but on a grand scale for a large operation.

She thought back to the night she'd been taken and oriented herself, then turned half-left towards a heavy door with a round glass window positioned in the far corner of the room. As she crossed the floor, the feel of the place began to make her heart pound, her body unable to forget what had happened in Jenkins' office. She'd tried not to relive what he'd done to her but it was hard, and she'd had a couple of nights when she'd woken in a sweat and with her broken fingers aching. But at least it made it hard to forget the look on his face when he'd abused her. And she didn't want to forget that.

Before she reached the windowed door, it opened, and the large man with big features who'd held her when Jenkins broke her fingers came through. He'd pushed the door open with one hand while looking down at the phone he held in the other, so didn't see her immediately.

Belinda didn't break stride but began to wind up with her left arm. He was probably eighteen inches taller than her, but as his gaze broke from his phone and he glanced upwards, his mouth opening with surprise, Belinda's armoured left hand caught him flush on the side of his face, staggering him sideways. The shock ran up her arm but was painless. She took another step and kicked him hard where his legs joined. He continued to fall, his phone clattering to the floor. He grunted with pain when he hit the floor, then folded in on himself and nursed his private parts.

Belinda moved on.

Now she recognised the corridor she'd been taken down prior to being forced into JJ's office. There had been six steps and then they'd turned right. She counted them off and there was a door with 'Jack Jenkins' written on it. Bingo. She walked in without knocking.

Jenkins was behind his desk and was alone in the room. His phone was to his ear and at first he held out a hand to Belinda, quieting her, before he realised who it was.

Then the recognition came and he lowered the phone.

Belinda walked up to his desk, raised her arm-club and brought it down hard on the desk. His laptop jumped an inch in the air and a pen rolled to the floor.

Before he could speak she brushed his table lamp and wire letter basket to the floor with her good hand.

'We've got you, Jenkins, you bastard. We know what you're up to, you and Passmore. Thought you could get away with torturing me and burning down Dyke's house? Think again.'

Jenkins had raised his hands placatingly, his round body drawn back against the wall, his demeanour not exactly scared but unwilling to raise the temperature in the room. Without his men around, Belinda thought, he was actually a physical coward.

As she stood there glaring at him, waiting for the door behind to burst open, she found she was enjoying herself. Her fear had evaporated and she felt in charge, ready for whatever came next.

Jenkins seemed to have been on the balls of his feet because he slowly settled to the ground.

'I can understand you feel upset but you realise there's no easy way out for you now, don't you?'

She slammed her bound fist on the desk again.

'Do you think I give a shit, you ball of pus? We know you're using Strano, and he knows, and your plan is busted. Think again.'

She saw his eyes flicker over her head and knew the game was up. She turned quickly but was immediately bound by two sets of arms that pinioned her. One was the man called Terry and the other was an Asian wearing a pale suit who had a couple of bruises on either side of his face. He must have been one of the men Dyke had fought in his office.

She didn't struggle and let them hold her still.

Terry said, 'What do we do with her, JJ? She gave Gonzo a good whack on the head.'

Jenkins came away from the wall and sat in his chair. She could see thoughts pass across his face like shadows as he worked through the implications of what she'd told him. If what she said was true, who else knew what she knew? Dyke, obviously. But maybe the police, too? What could he do to her? Maybe this was a set-up, maybe she was wired in some way. Maybe they were trying to get him to punish her again so they could raid The Strike on a pretence. And he couldn't just put her in a back room somewhere for the same reasons.

It was all too risky just now. He had little choice.

He said, 'Throw her out. She just wanted to antagonise me, I understand that.'

'But—'

'Throw her out!'

Belinda noticed he was trembling and knew she'd frightened him, but she didn't know whether it was what she'd said or what she'd done that had caused the fear.

The men frog-marched her from the room, down the corridor and across the storage hangar. The big man she'd hit had vanished and there was a group of kitchen staff and waiters standing around watching.

She raised her clubbed arm and said, 'Power to the people!'

Then they pushed her out of the side door and closed it behind her.

The air was clean and bright after the artificial environment inside and she took deep breaths as she walked quickly back to her car. Inside, she picked up her phone and speed-dialled Dyke, who answered immediately.

She said, 'Done. The trap's baited.'

'Are you all right?'

'Worked like a dream. He's too frightened to try anything else. He realised we knew too much.'

'Okay, find somewhere else to park and keep a watch. Let me know what happens. Hopefully it won't be long.'

They hung up and Belinda reached into the well of the passenger seat and picked up a pair of gardening shears. She began to cut at the edge of the plaster where it went around her lower arm.

CHAPTER TWENTY-NINE

I PUT THE phone down and looked out of the window. There was a car in Passmore's drive but I hadn't seen any movement since I'd arrived half an hour ago. I didn't know whether he was in or not. Just as I was thinking of climbing out of my car and knocking on his door to check, his front door opened and he came out, walking quickly. In a moment he'd reversed his Citroen from the drive and accelerated away, heading into town. I waited another five minutes, then got out of my Polo and crossed the road.

I went up to the front door and knocked for the sake of appearances, then looked around, walked quickly past his quarter-paned front window and slid down the side of the house. There was a wooden fence between him and his neighbour and two wheely-bins in black and grey standing to one side. A white cat walked along the top of the fence ahead of me, as if ushering me in, then leaped off at the end and ran forwards through his garden, which was a small square of lawn bordered with flower beds.

Despite being a senior policeman, his sense of security was terrible. It was easy to bump open his back door and slip inside.

I paused for a moment to get a sense of the house. It was a small detached cottage built in the seventies, probably with two bedrooms and a bathroom upstairs, two rooms and a kitchen downstairs. It looked as though it had been constructed as part of some estate expansion scheme to house workers for local industry when things were going better for the economy. It had no frills and was certainly not a luxury home for someone of Passmore's elevated rank.

I walked into the front room and looked through the windows at his tiny front garden and the road beyond – there was no sign of him returning. We'd hoped Jenkins would call Passmore to tell him what we knew—or what we wanted him to think we knew—and they'd call a panic meeting. I'd discovered when trying to make my appointment with Passmore that he worked from home on Fridays. Therefore we had to get him out of the house. Belinda had suggested the plan and while I wasn't altogether happy with it, she'd been insistent. I knew it gave her the opportunity to have a measure of revenge on Jenkins and his crew so I didn't argue too much. It seemed to have had the right effect. As I stood in Passmore's sitting room, I wondered how much damage Belinda had done and whether she felt better for it. My guess was that she did.

Now the question I had to answer was where to begin. As usual in these circumstances I didn't know what I was looking for. Passmore had separated from his wife and it was possible he'd left documents at his former house. On the other hand, why would he do that? It could have been creating a hostage to fortune if his wife found something he didn't want her to.

Of course he had an office at the headquarters where he was stationed, but he was unlikely to leave incriminating evidence there either. It made sense, then, for him to have brought material home. That was my guess, anyway, and I'm very partial to my guesses.

I went back into the kitchen. Fairly standard. Fitted cabinets on the walls and beneath the counters, plastic sink with single draining board, Whirlpool washing machine, marbled grey preparation surfaces. I pulled open some of the doors and glanced inside—cups, saucers, plates. Kelloggs Cornflakes. Some Knorr packet soups and other tins of ready-made foodstuffs. It was all neat and tidy. I'd had the impression when I met him at his office that he was well-organised, And White had told me at the golf club that he had a reputation for OCD in his personal habits. If that was the case, then it was likely that whatever material he brought home with him would also be filed neatly.

I went back into the sitting-room. Sofa, armchair, television. A table pushed against the wall with a lamp on it, one drawer. I went through it quickly, found some interesting stuff. Then I went upstairs and pushed open the doors to the bedrooms. They smelled fresh, as though he'd cleaned recently. Everything was modern and new, and I suspected Passmore didn't really care much about the actual quality of his home surroundings so long as they were clean and well-ordered.

I went upstairs—as I'd thought: two bedrooms and one bathroom. Both bedrooms had single beds. One bedroom seemed to be in use. Although the bedclothes were tidy there were two pairs of black shoes lined up under the window and three ties draped over the back of a chair. I opened the wardrobe door and looked inside. As you might expect, there were suits, shirts, dress uniforms. More shoes laid at the bottom of the wardrobe.

I rummaged around amongst the clothes for a while but there was obviously nothing else to see. This was turning into a bust and I was getting anxious. I didn't usually stay this long inside houses I'd broken into.

I looked around the room again. It was without personality and colour, rather like the man himself. There wasn't even a book on the bedside table. I checked my watch and told myself to get a move on.

I went through to the second bedroom. This was even blander than the first. There was a bed, a small chest of drawers, and a single upright chair. No bedside table, no rug on the floor, not even any curtains. I suspected he had few guests to stay.

That was when the front door opened downstairs. I stopped dead for a moment, my hands frozen on the drawer of the bedside table.

I closed the drawer silently then I crossed to the window and looked outside—no car in the drive, so it wasn't Passmore.

I had no idea who it might be. Especially as it was somebody who had a key. I was certain he wouldn't allow any of his colleagues to enter the house without him being there.

Then the mystery was solved. A girl's voice called out, 'Dad, are you in? Dad?'

I carefully closed the door to the second bedroom and moved further inside until I was on the far side of the bed. I could hear the girl walking through to the kitchen and doing something with crockery, opening and closing the cabinet doors.

This was my fault. I hadn't done enough research on Passmore's daughter. Why was she not at school? Was her school local to here? Did she spend Friday afternoon with her father through some arrangement?

I didn't know. All I could do was stay still and hope she didn't come upstairs. This bedroom was so bare there seemed to be no reason for her to come in. At least I hoped so.

After about five minutes, the noise died down. I guessed that if she'd been preparing herself a sandwich or something then now she was eating it. I hadn't really thought about Passmore's relationship to his daughter. Why would I? I'd been more interested in Strano's relationship to Anjelica. The thought Passmore might have a relationship to his own daughter that he also needed to massage hadn't occurred to me. I suppose even villains have families, though it rarely helped me to think about things like that. The criminals I dealt with had to take responsibility for their own actions.

The consequences for their families were their own fault, after all.

Ten minutes later there was another clattering of crockery and then, worryingly, the pounding of feet on the stairs, coming up. I lowered myself quickly to the carpet, concealing myself from the door by lying behind the bed.

As I heard the door to the bathroom next door being closed, my eyes glanced beneath the bedstead.

It was an old iron construction with high sides and a spring box to support the mattress. As an old-fashioned design, it had plenty of space beneath. Staring me in the face were two cardboard boxes.

Bingo, I thought to myself.

The toilet chain pulled, the feet pounded down the stairs again, and moments later the front door slammed shut. I was alone in the house.

I stood up.

Then I reached under the bed and pulled out each box in turn. They were the height of standard manila folders, about eighteen inches long and maybe twelve inches wide.

I took the cover off the first box and was confronted by rows of brown folders, each of them containing A4 writing paper. It didn't take me long to find the reports Strano had submitted to Passmore, but Passmore hadn't officially recorded.

This was turning out to be a very interesting burglary.

CHAPTER THIRTY

I PHONED STRANO from the car and told him I was coming to see him. He didn't sound enthusiastic about my visit but I didn't care. This was my last throw of the dice with him. I understood he was scared of what Passmore and Jenkins might do to Anjelica, but they couldn't be allowed to continue frightening people. *I* wouldn't allow it.

There was also the matter of the Staffordshire Hoard. All I could do with Strano was hope to persuade him to get away from Jenkins. But that didn't mean Passmore and Jenkins would be given a free pass. I had some ideas, but I needed to know what Strano would do first.

There was heavy traffic around Stoke before I arrived at Strano's house. I sat for ten minutes in a queue waiting to turn off for the road that led to his street. It gave me the opportunity to think about what was going to happen on Sunday. Dan had learned the Hoard would be brought to the museum in Hanley in two secure vans. What happened after that was impossible for us to know. It seemed Jenkins' security company would be responsible for security inside the museum, while a larger, national company like Group 4 would be in charge of the transportation. In other words there would be a period of handover during which, presumably, there'd be a gap in authority. During that small time period would be the perfect moment for Jenkins to make his move.

When I arrived at Strano's house, he was standing on his doorstep, smoking. For once he was dressed down in a vest and a pair of dirty jeans. He looked like a character from a British film of the early sixties—beaten down but defiant, waiting for Julie Christie to take him away to the bright lights of London. He flicked his cigarette into the street when he saw me arrive, then turned and went back inside. I followed him in.

'What you want now?'

'These are for you.'

I threw the reports I'd taken from Passmore's cardboard box onto the sofa. Two of them fell onto the floor and he bent to pick them up. He opened the top one and I saw the recognition flicker in his eyes. He looked at me.

'Where did you get these from?'

'It doesn't matter where they came from. This is the evidence you needed. What are you going to do about it?'

'What do you *want* me to do about it?'

'That's not my job.'

'I've been wondering what your job is. I can't seem to get rid of you. Answer the question—what do you expect me to do?'

'I want you to accept your responsibilities. I want you to stop mooching around feeling sorry for yourself and looking like a dog who trapped his tail in a door. I want you to stand up and be counted against these jokers.'

'That's easy for you to say. You know the position I was in. I didn't have any choice.'

'You always have a choice. Sometimes we don't want to take it.'

'Take your bloody philosophising elsewhere. You don't know me. You have no idea what it's been like to be me for the last eight years. I don't care if you have photos of Passmore and Jenkins having it off over his desk in police headquarters. I can't take the risk. Do you even understand what that means?'

'I've got a kid too. I know what Anjelica means to you. But she's a grown-up now and she'd expect you to make the right decision. You can't hide behind her any longer. Now's your chance to make it right with her and to get Passmore for everything he's done to you.'

He flung the two folders onto the sofa with the others and turned to face the wall. He leaned forward and placed his hands flat on the chimney breast above his fire. There was quiet in the room for a moment, and then I realised Strano was crying.

I didn't say anything. I sensed there'd been a lot of pressure building up in him since his release from prison. I hadn't helped with that at all.

I said, 'When's your next shift?'

He didn't reply for a minute. Then he stood up and wiped his face with his hands – a gesture that was becoming familiar to me – and turned towards me again.

'Tomorrow night. At The Strike. Then Sunday morning I'm to wear my uniform and turn up at the Museum for ten o'clock.'

'Has anyone told you what your duties are?'

'No one's said anything to me about what's happening on Sunday. It's just on the rota. Usually Gonzo or one of the other men is there first and gives us instructions.'

'Then the choice is yours. I can't tell you what to do. I suggest you talk to Anjelica and then have a long, hard think about your future.'

He'd regained his composure now and the hard look in his eyes had returned.

He said, 'Don't think you can come in here and catch me off-guard, then start telling me what to do. You're not living my life.'

'The point is, are you?'

TEN MINUTES LATER I closed his front door behind me and walked the few yards to my rental car.

I climbed inside and sank into the seat. I realised I was bone-weary. Nothing I'd done seemed to work. Strano was still in the same mind-set as he was before he went to jail. It seemed impossible to budge him from his position. It was now Friday evening and the Hoard was being delivered on Sunday morning. There was very little time left.

I found my phone in my coat jacket and dialled. After two rings it was answered.

Inspector Howard said, 'What do you want, Dyke?'

CHAPTER THIRTY-ONE

THE BASEMENT OF the museum was spacious and quiet. There were wooden packing crates piled in one corner that, I guessed, held exhibits from previous exhibitions. There were five glass cabinets along one wall, three fire extinguishers and four large wooden tables with scratched tops and strong legs that had been pushed over to one side to make room for the new delivery. The light came from low-grade fluorescent strips and cast deep shadows. Spotlights were available but hadn't been switched on as their intensity wasn't needed to unpack a few crates.

Outside it was Sunday morning in Hanley — a little traffic and some pedestrians, but most of the activity was taking place in the retail park just beyond the link roads or in the Potteries Centre mall. The museum itself was actually still open to customers but was doing little business as yet.

I had arrived at 9:30 and talked my way in under the pretence of being one of JJ's security men who'd got the time wrong. The fact I was wearing the right uniform and Strano's name was on his list persuaded the man in charge to let me in and direct me downstairs via one of the two industrial lifts. Although the

Staffordshire Hoard was worth over £3 million to the right buyer, I guess they thought it would be difficult to sell and its market would be limited anyway, so a big heist was probably out of the question. After all, who wanted to fill their mansion in Malaga with Anglo-Saxon belt-buckles and assorted metalwork? So while the security was well-organised, I didn't expect it to be top-notch and vigilant.

I'd introduced myself to a security man downstairs who seemed to be more senior, apologising for being early. He had a pock-marked face and thinning hair and regarded me dubiously, but as his partner upstairs had let me in there was nothing much he could do about it. He asked me if I wanted a cup of tea and I politely said no.

Then I faded into the background. I muttered brief hellos to the other men, and one woman, and went and stood with my back to a wall, pretending to be reading texts on my phone. I slowly moved so that I was out of sight of the security detail, most of whom had placed plastic seats in a circle and were talking quietly amongst themselves. I wasn't in their group so I pretended to a shyness I rarely felt. If they thought anything, I hoped they'd think I'd gone to the toilet or outside for a cigarette, waiting for my mates to turn up.

At about 10:15, JJ's men arrived. Ready for this, I'd worked my way further to the back of the basement space where I could hide in the shadows.

The man called Gonzo strode into the basement with a dozen men behind him, all in uniform and with official-looking peaked caps, just like mine. He shook the hand of the chief of security and they talked for a minute or two, Gonzo apparently explaining why he had a massive bruise on the side of his face. I daresay he didn't mention he'd been clobbered by a woman barely five feet six inches in height. The museum's man laughed at whatever Gonzo told him, then stepped back and Gonzo started giving instructions to both groups, official and fake. In no time the museum's official security men had been relieved of their responsibilities in the basement and had gone, possibly to service upstairs.

Gonzo took off his cap and addressed his men.

'Right boys, look lively. The convoy will be here in ten minutes. Try to look as if you know what you're doing. That means no smoking, no farting, no playing with your winkles.'

The men laughed and relaxed. I had expected to see the fair-haired Terry amongst them. He wasn't there but I recognised a couple of the others who'd been acting as bouncers at the casino.

By this time I'd retreated into the furthest corner of the basement, where earlier I'd noticed a Fire Exit door. When Gonzo arrived I'd cracked open the door and stepped behind it, leaving a small gap through which I could watch what they did. I ran a finger around my collar and took Strano's cap from my head, laying it on the floor behind me. He'd finally called me the night before and said he couldn't carry on. He said he'd been arguing with himself for several days before making the call. I'd quickly amended our plan and then driven over to his house to pick up his uniform. It was loose on me but not too bad.

While I was there I'd asked what made him change his mind.

'That bastard Passmore. Doing it to me again. If you can stop him, do it. I'm walking away from them.'

'What about Anjelica—the threats?'

'I'll look after Anjelica. Besides, if you can stitch them up on Sunday I won't need to worry, will I?'

That seemed easier said than done right now.

The stairwell in which I was standing led upstairs to the ground floor, and I guessed there was another Fire Door to the outside. Through it I heard the sounds of two large vehicles arriving in low gear and then stopping. I realised it must have been the convoy arriving. As if to prove me right there was a commotion in the basement and Gonzo looked at his phone, maybe reading a text from a lookout in the street. 'Okay boys, here we go.'

I still had no idea what was going to happen. I assumed Gonzo and his men would take delivery of the Hoard and then some kind of fake robbery would be allowed to proceed. The uniformed men in the basement could hardly take delivery themselves and then load it all into a different set of vans. That would give the game away that they'd been involved in some fashion. Also, I expected there would be administrators in the building somewhere who would oversee paperwork and make sure the transfer from the Birmingham collection went smoothly. They would have to be convinced the robbery was real and not staged by JJ's security company. Not to mention the fact that there were actual visitors upstairs in the main part of the museum who couldn't be involved or endangered, or the theft would take on a whole new dimension and bring down a shitstorm on JJ's head.

I glanced at my watch. It was 10:30. I'd phoned Howard last night after Strano had contacted me. As I expected, he wasn't happy, didn't really believe me, and wasn't hopeful anything could be done in time anyway.

'Couldn't you have rung me a bit later? Given me a chance to wake up some really senior coppers and ruin my reputation?'

'I thought I should give you twelve hours notice at least. I don't think even you could screw this up.'

'You sure about this?'

'Bet on it. No jokes intended. These are likely to be dangerous people with nothing to lose, so come mob-handed.'

'No promises.'

He'd hung up. And here I was, just me and a dozen big men, with another crew outside ready to commit one of the biggest robberies since the Brinks-Mat theft.

As it stood, I was It.

The basement was now quiet as half of Gonzo's men had gone upstairs. After a few minutes the large lifts in the basement began to ping open. As they did, JJ's men and the security guards who'd brought the material from Birmingham wheeled out several large wooden crates and began to put them in position. The transportation guys wore heavy blue outfits and helmets with visors and truncheons on their belts. They made Gonzo's men look like amateurs, for all their size. The basement was suddenly full of activity, with instructions being given and some tense laughter. A man in a neat grey suit arrived from upstairs and began to check off identification numbers on the sides of the boxes, marking them in a little notebook.

I watched Gonzo carefully.

Like me, he'd moved further away from the main action and also like me was checking his watch from time to time. Something was going to happen soon.

It didn't take long to bring the dozen or so packing crates downstairs and organise them in neat rows. After twenty minutes, the man in the grey suit shook Gonzo's hand and then left, and after another moment the head of the transport security group also shook his hand and pushed up his visor and stood talking to him while they all got their breath back.

At first I didn't realise what I'd heard. But when a dozen armed Asian men came flooding down the stairs, I realised there'd been the crash of breaking glass upstairs. Maybe it was a sign to Gonzo that it was about to happen and he shouldn't over-react. At any rate, the Asian man who entered first, who I recognised as David, started shouting at both sets of security men, who seemed to have frozen, their hands half-way to their truncheons. He used a language nobody else in the basement recognised, but that was probably his intention.

Along with most of the other invaders he held a Shooters S.A.M X9 Tactical machine gun with a folding stock in one hand. This was a lightweight semi-automatic made in the Philippines and I had no doubt the weapons had been smuggled in alongside the men themselves. They sometimes jammed but shouldn't be argued with.

David walked up to Gonzo and poked him in the chest with the barrel of his gun, speaking rapidly. The other security man had gone pale and had taken a step back. The Asian men, who all wore lightweight cream suits and bandanas across the lower half of their faces, surrounded both security teams and pointed their weapons menacingly.

It was all show, of course, performed to convince the witnesses there was no collusion between the Asians and the Museum security staff.

I wondered what Strano's role in this little play was supposed to have been. Somehow he was to have been shown as the guilty man – the one who'd let in the thieves or given them access. Without him, JJ's men must have been improvising this morning, much as I was.

But now David's men were beginning to spread around the basement. They had started shouting at the uniformed men and pointing their weapons. I recognised the two who had been with David in my office, and especially the one who had punched me in the face. It was easy to recognise him because he was walking straight towards me.

CHAPTER THIRTY-TWO

SHE HAD DRIVEN around the centre of Hanley for twenty minutes before she spotted the van. It was white and plain and its licence plates were smudged with mud. She had an idea it was the one she'd been thrown in the night she was kidnapped.

JJ was sitting in the driving seat but nobody else was visible. The van was illegally parked on a back street and was the only vehicle on a double yellow line. Just like JJ to ignore the rules that didn't suit him.

She circled the block again and when she came round for the second time she angled in front of the van, blocking it off from the road. It's only way to move was to reverse first. She was driving her pink Volvo today and Jenkins would know who it was immediately.

She sprang open the door and stepped out in one movement. Already Jenkins had opened his own door and was climbing carefully to the ground, holding on to the door stanchions for support.

He was talking almost before he turned to face her.

'Well, well, well. I must say I admire your stamina, even though it irritates the hell out of me.'

She stood facing him square on.

'What are you doing here, you sack of guts?'

'You don't have to be impolite.'

'After what you did to me I think I can say what the hell I like.'

Today he was wearing black jeans and a massive fleece. His round face looked pinched and worried. Being this close to the robbery in the flesh was obviously something he didn't relish.

He said, 'Well, this is a bit of a stand-off, isn't it? What do you intend to do? Remain there until someone comes to your rescue?'

'I don't need rescuing. You're the one who's in trouble, not me.'

'Why am *I* in trouble? I'm just parking here perfectly innocently. Whereas you're the one who seems intent on making a scene.'

She shook her head in disbelief. 'Do you go through life believing your own publicity? The game's over. We know what you're up to. You won't get away with it.'

'I find your confidence charming, if misplaced. You and I are going to have a nice conversation and then you'll stay out of my hair. I don't think you quite know the people you're dealing with here.'

'You mean Phar? That shrunken Asian Godfather who likes a flutter on the cricket now and then? We know all about him. I think you overestimate your importance. If there's the slightest sign of a problem he'll be in his private jet and up and away to Singapore.'

Though his smile barely wavered she knew she'd got through to him. He was still walking towards her, but she wasn't worried about his physical threat. She'd trained in Krav Maga, an Israeli self-defence martial art, while serving in Germany. She'd had to train against men much more agile than Jack

Jenkins, though perhaps not as weighty. As long as she could prevent him from falling on top of her she thought she'd be safe.

A car passed them on the street and she wondered briefly what this must look like to a passer-by—a twenty-stone man six feet in height walking towards a slender woman who was barely five feet six. It was a bright day though the surroundings were bleak: closed-down shops, brownstone office blocks, a scrubby parking lot served by a ticket machine. No humans in sight. This was an event happening off-stage, in a parallel world, and she'd never be able to explain to anyone else what it felt like.

Except Dyke.

Perhaps he would understand.

She said, 'What's it going to be then, eh? Are you going to wrestle me to the ground? Think you can do it without your farmyard animals to back you up?'

'I see you're not wearing your cast any more, just a little bitty thing around your fingers. Doesn't that make you more vulnerable and less able to inflict damage? My poor desk still hasn't recovered from the beating you gave it.'

'I don't need a weapon to take you down, fat man.'

He stopped six feet from her and pushed his hands into the pockets of his fleece. Out in the air he was less at ease than in the artificial atmosphere of the casino. A fish out of water. Or a whale, she thought, grinning.

'What's so funny?'

She said, 'You wouldn't understand. So are you going to come peacefully or am I going to have to kick you in the nuts?'

'I'm not coming anywhere with you, young lady. Rather the opposite, I think.'

He stood aside now and from behind the white van came two tall figures. One was the man called Terry, the other was the half-wit with the lopsided grin who'd been eager to work her over at The Lucky Strike. They were both over six feet tall and were lean and fit.

Jenkins said to them over his shoulder, 'What kept you? I only asked for a packet of fags, not Cuban cigars.'

Terry said, 'We had to find a newsagent. It's Sunday, boss.'

'Never mind. Take care of Miss McFee again, would you? Stick her in the back of the van. I'm sure Phar will find something for her to do in a sweatshop in Singapore.'

Terry elbowed his grinning colleague. 'Fancy a bit of that, Lefty?'

Lefty, who Belinda noticed had a slight squint in his left eye, giggled like a child.

'Juicy. Very fit, Terry. Juicy.'

Jenkins had backed away as the two men had advanced towards her. He looked both ways along the road then crossed to the other side. He turned and shouted across to his men.

'Hurry up about it. I'm bloody freezing. They'll be calling for the van soon.'

He took his left fist out of his fleece and now it contained a phone. He glanced at the screen.

'That's them. Get this over with so we can get round to the Museum. It's on.'

Belinda stood her ground, wondering which of the two men would step forward first.

CHAPTER THIRTY-THREE

THE ASIAN CONTINUED to walk towards me but his eyes weren't looking in my direction. He had turned his head so he could see what was happening behind him, in the basement.

He came to a halt just in front of the Fire Door, which I'd pushed to within two inches of fully closed. Now with his back to me, he was less than two feet distant. Arm's length.

Meanwhile, David had lined up the two security crews—one real, one fake—against a wall. He told them to be still while he took out his phone and texted someone—possibly the driver of the van that was to take the Hoard away, or someone whose job was to warn him. There was no sound from upstairs and I couldn't hear the wail of approaching police cars, so I guessed there was also a crew in the main gallery above us, keeping the administrators and visitors quiet.

There was nothing for it, I had to act. I had no guarantee Howard would arrive in time with an armed tactical squad. While I didn't want to get shot by this bunch, I thought it was more likely they were thieves than murderers. After all, David had a degree from MIT and an MBA from Princeton.

I had the advantage of speed, surprise and shadows. I opened the Fire Door quickly, wrapped my hand around the Asian mobster's head, and yanked him backwards into the stairwell with me, pushing the door shut with my free hand.

He fell backwards, clattering to the floor. Fortunately for me, he let go of his weapon as he fell. I stepped around him sharply and picked it up, then pointed at him. It was light and well balanced and had black tape wrapped around its handle. I'd seen the model before though I'd never fired one, but I found the trigger and pointed the barrel at him and that frightened him enough. He probably remembered the kicking he gave me in my office and thought I was about to extract revenge. Well I remembered too, but I wasn't going to hurt him. Unless it was necessary.

We stared at each other for a moment, waiting for a commotion to come from the other side of the door.

Nothing happened. It had been too quick and David and his colleagues had other things on their mind.

I said, 'Take off your belt. Put your wrist through a loop and pull tight.'

He waited a moment until I encouraged him by waving the barrel at him. Then he slid out his belt and made a loop and placed his left wrist through it, pulling it tight and leaving a trailing tongue of leather. I backed him up to the bottom of the iron stairs and passed the tongue through one of the rails and then back. He struggled but only half-heartedly and I thumped him on the back of the neck to keep him quiet.

I laid the machine-gun down behind me, still holding on to the belt, and wrapped it around his other hand. It was a thin belt but strong. When he was secure I took the bandana from around his neck. I opened my mouth to show him what to do and reluctantly he did so. I stuffed the cloth between his small white teeth and into the cavity of his mouth. He wouldn't be able to use his tongue to expel it but he could breathe through his nose. I watched him for a few seconds to check his breathing was okay.

Then I pulled his lightweight jacket off his shoulders and down over his arms, wrapping the bottom around his wrists and tying it roughly. I thought I wouldn't need to incapacitate him for more than fifteen minutes.

He'd turned himself around to face me, his eyes flashing with hatred. I patted him on the cheek.

'Just think, I could do a lot worse and no one would know. So be good.'

Picking up the machine-gun, I went back to the door and slowly pushed down on the horizontal bar. The Asian crew had started manoeuvring the crates on to wheeled furniture trolleys, but there were only two of them so most of the crew stood around pointing their weapons at the two groups of security men. I counted ten Asians in all and probably another three or four upstairs.

I thought what a crazy idea this was to allow the crates to be brought down to the basement before having to take them back up again. The point, I suppose, was to keep Jenkins' security company in the clear. He'd bid for the project, presumably, and won on a low bid. Once his men—Gonzo's crew—were in place, they would make sure the theft went smoothly. There'd be no heroics from genuine security officers. Carrying out the theft while the transportation men were there acted as a witnessed validation of the robbery. And if the job had been done upstairs in the main museum, or in the road outside, there would have been no way to lay the blame off on Strano, the robbers' 'inside man'.

I guessed that at some point in the handover this morning, Gonzo would have told Strano to go and open a door or watch the entrance. He would have been overwhelmed by the superior numbers of the Asian crew but would have been blamed for the lapse anyway, especially with his prison record.

I wondered how they'd explain the robbery now. It put more pressure on Jenkins to avoid blame because he couldn't pass it on to Strano.

All this thinking was my way of putting off the inevitable.

I glanced over my shoulder at the man strapped to the balustrade, then eased the door open further, inch by inch. There was so much clatter at the far end of the basement that any noise I might have made was drowned. The Asians' attention was naturally focused on the loading of the crates, and both sets of security men were facing the wall.

Except for the chief of the transportation crew.

He happened to look over his shoulder as I ran from the doorway to the wall opposite. He saw me but made no sign. I pressed my back to the wall and when I looked around the corner he glanced back at me again.

Essentially the basement was a gigantic L-shape, with the two lifts placed next to each other at what would be the top of the upright stroke. Each stroke, upright and horizontal, was in fact about twenty yards in width. I had been in a stairwell in the bottom right-hand corner of the L and I'd run from this position, which was shadowed and populated by old exhibition crates, across the twenty yards to the other side of the space. As I inched along I would start coming into view of the men on the left-hand side of the upright, who were clustered close to the lifts and had their backs to the security men facing that wall.

I'd switched my phone off earlier and I didn't want to switch it on now and attract attention. Otherwise I would have texted

Howard to tell him what was happening. If he was coming, where was he?

Then above the noise of the crates being loaded, I heard footsteps walking towards me, around the corner. A voice called something in an Asian language I didn't understand and I guessed someone had noticed the man I held captive had gone missing.

I edged back and flattened myself to the wall.

A young man with red streaks in his black hair sauntered around the corner, his weapon hanging loosely at his side. He saw me as I stepped into him and caught him flush on the jaw with a sucker punch. He went down and all hell was let loose.

As I was bending down to pick up his weapon there were shouts from the other end of the basement. I rounded the corner and two Asians were running towards me, their weapons held in both hands across their chest. I caught one in the throat with the butt of my own weapon, then swung it around and caught the other man crushingly on his nose. They both dropped to the floor and I continued walking.

I saw the chief of the transport security turn and realise what was happening. He continued his turn and shouted towards David, whose attention had been drawn to me. He turned back to find the security man charging towards him, arms spread wide. They fell backwards to the floor. The other security men had turned now and started shouting. We had five of the Asians down and two still holding on to the wheeled trolleys they were guiding towards the lifts.

That left three Asians, who started to back away and raise their guns.

Gonzo and his team had also begun to turn. They didn't know what to do. They should have been attacking the Asians but that would ruin the plan. On the other hand, if they went for the transport security crew it would give the game away.

So they stood there, hands in the air, staring at each other.

David and the transport chief were still rolling on the ground. The three other Asians continued to back away, pointing their weapons at the men advancing towards them. Everyone was shouting, the sounds echoing from the stone walls of the basement.

Then David stood up. He'd managed to land a heavy blow on the other man's cheek and he stayed down. David's bandana had been torn from his face and hung around his neck. He hurriedly pulled it back into place.

Then he saw me.

His eyes widened. He looked around and found his weapon on the floor, taking a stride and snatching it up.

It had gone completely quiet now. The transport security team had stopped advancing and the three Asians who'd been guarding them pointed them back towards the wall.

David was furious with me. Still ten yards away, he raised his gun.

He said, 'You have done all this, okay? It's your fault. You can blame yourself.'

I think he was really about to shoot me when a stain of red bloomed in his left side. He uttered a yelp and looked down. He put his hand to his side and looked up at me.

Then his legs began to falter and he fell to his knees.

I looked towards the stairs to my right.

A team of bulky men in heavy assault gear, wearing helmets and carrying SIG SG 550 assault rifles, ran down the stairs shouting at the Asians to put down their weapons. They did so and backed away, raising their hands.

I went up to David and knelt down. He was breathing heavily. I took the bandana from around his neck and put it in his hand.

'Press that to your side. Ambulance will be here shortly.'

He nodded but said nothing, all the fight gone from him now.

The Tactical Response Unit had spread out and rounded up the Asians, who had given up meekly when they saw the superior numbers of armed men thumping into the basement. There was a heavy new smell of testosterone and machine oil in the air.

Howard appeared last at the top of the stairs. He wore a thick blue jacket but wasn't armed. I waved at him and he came down the stairs swiftly.

I pointed to Gonzo and his men, who'd lowered their arms and were trying to sidle away out of the basement and head towards the lifts.

'Those are Jack Jenkins' men. Don't let them go. They're in on it.'

Howard turned and called to one of the Response Unit's men, who came over at a trot.

Howard said, 'That mob sneaking out over there. Pull 'em in. Keep them apart from the others.'

'Okay. Same with the ones upstairs?'

Howard glanced at me.

I said, 'Museum staff are good to go. Any wearing this uniform you need to hold on to.'

The man nodded curtly and ran off, pulling a couple of men with him and heading towards the lifts and cutting off Gonzo.

I said, 'You might have let me know. I would have waited.'

'Check your phone. I texted twenty minutes ago. Thought you might not appreciate a ringing call.'

We stood there for a minute watching the Response Unit herd the various men together and handcuff them. The Asians were arguing furiously amongst themselves. Someone must have called above to a waiting ambulance outside because two paramedics carrying a lightweight stretcher and medical kits came down the stairs. They looked around for the wounded person and one of the policemen pointed towards David, who was sitting up with his hand pressed tight to his side.

Howard said, 'We haven't found Jenkins yet. And there's more good news. Passmore's gone. Apparently cleared out his bank account on Friday. We checked and he's booked a flight to Singapore. Irony, eh?'

'Let me guess—no extradition treaty.'

'He did his research.'

'He won't be going far.'

'Why?'

'You can't go anywhere without a passport, can you?'

Howard stared at me.

'It's best if I don't ask, isn't it?'

I'd found the passport in the drawer in Passmore's house. I took it on impulse but now I could call it foresight.

And then something occurred to me.

'Is anyone with Anjelica?'

'Not as far as I know. Why?'

'Just wondering.'

I broke away from Howard and turned back to David, who by now was lying on the paramedics' stretcher while they tended his wound. They'd taken off his jacket which lay to one side. I crouched down next to them and felt through the pockets. Found his phone. I stood up and walked towards the stairs.

Howard called out, 'Where are you going? You've got a lot of paperwork to do.'

'I'll be back. I need some fresh air.'

I took the stairs three at a time. Unable to flee the country, Passmore might just take it in mind to carry out his threat to Anjelica. His OCD meant he wouldn't like to leave jobs unfinished, would he?

CHAPTER THIRTY-FOUR

BELINDA HAD ALREADY decided which of the two men she was going to take down first. Lefty probably had reduced hand-eye co-ordination and doubtless thought his size would overpower her. He was seven or eight inches taller than her, wiry and with a slightly inward-turned gait, as though one of his feet was squinting as well as his eye.

She moved sideways to present herself as a more obvious target to him. He stepped forward, eager to show Terry and JJ he was man enough for the job.

From the far side of the road, Jenkins said, 'Watch yourself, Lefty. She's bigger than she looks.'

Belinda grinned.

'Come on, Lefty. Let's see what you're made of.'

It was obvious he'd had no training in martial arts or any sort of fighting techniques. He didn't seem to know what he was going to do with Belinda when he'd got her, other than force her into the back of the white van, but he came at her quickly.

Belinda's Krav Maga instructor had instilled in her the mantra of 'hands, body, feet,' which was the order in which she was to think of her actions. She already knew what she was going to do with Lefty and had something in mind for Terry, too.

Lefty was almost on her, his hands reaching up, when she raised her own hands and pushed his groping arms downward. At the same time she stepped sharply to her left and then raised her right hand to his face, gripping his jaw and pushing. He would have seen it coming, and he tilted backwards to avoid having his nose stoved in or his eyes gouged. But his legs had continued forward while his upper body was bent back, still trying to move away from the grip of her hand. Gravity took him and with nothing behind to support him he fell backwards. In a training exercise she would have stepped behind him and cradled his head so it didn't hit the ground.

Here, she let him fall. His head hit the paving slabs and he bounced once and lay still.

As she thought, Terry had already started moving, trying to catch her off balance.

But a large part of her training was to be constantly aware of her surroundings and what might be happening in the corner of her eye.

Like many martial arts, Krav Maga billed itself as a form of self-defence. But to watch a confrontation where it was involved, she thought, would lead you to believe it was one of the most aggressive fighting techniques in use.

So when Terry moved towards her, a growl starting low in his throat, she didn't stand back or try to avoid him. Instead she moved in close and got a grip with both hands on the meaty muscle between his neck and his right shoulder. His arms started to close on her but she was moving too quickly. Although her left hand was weakened by the loss of the two damaged fingers, she pulled down with all her strength.

Psychologically, Terry knew what was coming, so drew back the centre of his body. But this simply made him duck down further. Belinda leaned in and quickly kneed him in the groin. Not once, as was usually the case in movies. But three times in quick succession. Bam, bam, bam. With each kick she levered herself upwards with her grounded foot so all her weight travelled up through her torso and found its point of impact at the end of her knee. Because she was holding Terry's shoulder, she could not only keep him in position for the landing of each blow, but actually pull him down on to it.

The fight was over in about five seconds, with two large men lying on the ground, moaning.

Jenkins had been on the move before she'd even engaged with Terry. Now he was crossing the road in a busy waddle, aiming for the safety of his van.

'Hey, fat man, you scared of me?'

He didn't reply but stared intently at the door of his vehicle as he hastened towards it. Belinda thought she could time it just right and walked slowly after him.

He had opened the door and climbed up on the first step, his arms trying to pull his weight up into the driver's seat.

Belinda seized him by the belt of his jeans and yanked hard, moving out of the way as she did. The surprise as much as her strength caused him to lose his grip and he fell backwards past her and landed softly on the road, his arms outstretched.

The opportunity was too good for her to pass up, especially after what he'd done to her and instructed Terry and Lefty to do moments before.

She fell on to his right arm with her knee, took his hand and broke three of his fingers. After each one he gave a squeal that seemed to vibrate through his entire body.

It wasn't as satisfying as she'd hoped, but it would do.

CHAPTER THIRTY-FIVE

AS SOON AS I reached my car I tried Anjelica's phone—both her home and mobile. There was no reply. I had no idea whether Passmore would have gone there, but I didn't want to take the chance. The way he'd treated Lorenzo Strano led me to believe he could be vindictive and unforgiving. And if he couldn't leave the country without his passport, and his face would shortly be all over the television news, what else could he do but go out in a blaze of glory?

The roads in Hanley were relatively quiet so I went up to Strano's house first. It was a five minute detour and I thought I should check whether Passmore had gone there.

No reply at Strano's front door and no cars out front—neither his nor Passmore's. I peered through the front windows and there was no sign of life. If Strano wasn't there and was in hiding from Jenkins, there was a good chance he'd gone to Anjelica's house too.

I climbed into my car and made a phone call on the iPhone I'd taken from David's jacket pocket. Then I turned the car in the narrow road and set off. There was traffic coming in to the shopping malls now but little going out of town so I wasn't held up. Unfortunately my small loaner car didn't have a lot of horse-power, however hard I mashed the pedal.

My phone rang. I don't normally answer while I'm driving but I saw from the screen it was Belinda.

I picked it up. 'Late morning? Leisurely breakfast?'

'Sam, people keep telling you you're not funny. Believe them.'

'So how did it go?'

'I found JJ in a white van around the corner. Good guess on your part.'

'I didn't think he'd trust anyone else with that swag.'

'He didn't want to be there, I could tell.'

'Did you beat him up?'

'And his two goons. Learned 'em a lesson. What about you? What happened? There are lots of cop cars around here now.'

'Howard showed up just as I was trying to get my head blown off. It'd been fun till then.'

'Where are you, anyway?'

'En route to Anjelica's, Blythe Bridge. Passmore emptied his bank account. He was on his way out of the country till he found I'd got his passport.'

'You reckon he might take it out on Anjelica?'

'I think Strano's there, too. Get hold of Howard for me and let him know, will you? Gotta go.'

I hung up and turned off onto the A50 towards Derby, weaving through the sparse traffic that felt it should obey the fifty-miles-an-hour limit. The Britannia football stadium flashed by on my right and soon I was in open country, squinting into a low sun and hammering the little Polo hard.

I came to the large island this side of Blythe Bridge and hurtled across it, startling a lorry driver who amazingly thought he had the right of way. In no time I came to the stretch of road where Anjelica lived and I practically did a handbrake turn into her driveway.

There were four cars in the drive. Anjelica's two sports cars in front of the double garage, her father's Japanese wreck and Passmore's maroon Citroen.

The front door of the house was open and there were voices inside.

I pushed the door further open and crept into the hall. I wished I'd kept hold of one of the weapons from the Museum's basement. The air was cool and there was the smell of roast beef coming from the kitchen. I somehow thought they'd be eating lasagne. Or spaghetti. That's stereotyping for you.

I followed the voices slowly to the same room where I'd sat and talked to Anjelica. Passmore and Lorenzo Strano were in heated conversation, but there was an underlying menace in Passmore's voice.

I had no weapon. I had no plan. I knew the layout of the room but I didn't know where the main players were standing or sitting.

In the end I knocked on the door and pushed it open. After a delicate pause, I went in.

Anjelica and her father were together on the cream sofa, legs together, hands on their knees. They were sitting upright, not at all comfortable.

Billy Passmore faced them carrying a small Glock. He looked ill, pasty-faced and nervous. I almost felt sorry for him. But not quite.

He'd lost none of his chutzpah, though.

'Ah, Dyke, now the cast is complete. I was just telling Larry here I didn't appreciate him backing out of our arrangement for this morning. Especially after everything I've done for him. What do you think?'

'I think you're not going to use that gun, you're not going anywhere, and your best course now is just to give yourself up. The theft this morning was busted and all your pals are in the clink.'

'I kind of guessed that, actually. When I went for my passport and it wasn't there. I thought something was in the wind. Was it you, or Larry here?'

I reached into my jacket pocket and pulled out his passport.

'Passmore, passport-less. Besides, your ticket to Singapore was pulled. You weren't going anywhere.'

His face tightened and I saw him clenching and unclenching his fingers on the Glock. British policemen aren't issued with pistols as standard, but when they are, the Glock 17 is often the weapon of choice. Lightweight plastic and reliable, they don't often go wrong. Having been in the police force for as long as he had, there were a number of ways he might have got hold of one.

I said, 'What were you doing with Phar? And why steal the Hoard? I don't understand the plan.'

'Ah, the Plan. Funny you should mention that. You ever been in debt? I mean, real soul-destroying, knee-deep debt?'

'Can't say I have.'

'It's a terrible feeling, Dyke. Almost literally like a big lead slab hanging over your head, waiting to crush you. And believe me, my debt was big.'

'And the Hoard would have paid it off?'

He shrugged almost casually.

'Phar went for it in a big way. Yes there was the money angle, but he liked the idea of stealing part of Britain's history and taking it back to Singapore. I don't think he would have tried to sell it, he'd have just kept it. Like cutting out a piece of

England's heart and hanging on to it like a trophy. Like something from Shakespeare.'

'It was never going to work, though, was it? You must have known.'

'I thought the ninjas would screw it up. Or Jenkins. You can't rely on anyone these days, can you?'

Now Strano spoke from the sofa.

'Pack it in, Billy. Give yourself up. I did my time, now you do yours. You'll get used to it after a couple of years.' Then he grinned. 'Just don't tell anyone you were a senior copper. You'll be all right.'

Passmore scowled and turned to me, waving his pistol to indicate I should walk over and join the others. I crossed the room but I didn't sit on the sofa. I remained standing so at least I had some options.

Passmore said, 'You think this is how it ends? I've got exciting news for you. One way or the other, I'm not going in. Do you think I'm stupid? Look what happened to you, Larry. You came out a shambles. You might think I had an ulterior motive to get Jenkins to hire you, but I genuinely thought you might do well out of it. Get on your feet again.'

I said, 'Stop preaching, Billy. You're not behind a pulpit now. Incidentally, how's Bella going to get to church this morning?'

'Don't you mention her name! Leave her out of it!'

'Why? You were willing to get Larry's daughter caught up in this, weren't you?' I turned to Anjelica. 'Did you know the reason your dad went to prison without causing a fuss was because your pal Billy here threatened you and your mother?'

'What do you mean?'

Strano looked up at me with imploring eyes but I ignored him. She needed to know sometime.

I said, 'Passmore and Jenkins told your dad if he didn't keep quiet about their arrangement, then you and your mother would come to harm. All the while he was hanging around you, pretending to be caring, he was just checking out options and building a cover story.'

Anjelica's eyes flashed at Passmore and she stood up, taking a step forward.

'Is that true? You used me to get at my dad?'

Passmore shrugged. 'You do what you have to do.'

'Why? Why did he have to go away for eight years just to keep you safe? Why are you so much better than him? You and all your Christian charity ... it was bullshit, wasn't it?'

Passmore was beginning to sweat. His self-belief was waning, and with it his strength.

He said, 'A debt is a debt. You don't understand these people. They would have cut my head off and delivered it to my daughter's birthday party.'

'So you ruined my life instead. You selfish bastard.'

Passmore seemed to have lost any sense of proportion.

He said simply, 'You had to be there,' and turned to look out of the full-length windows into the garden.

Passmore was distracted, and this was the moment Strano chose to launch himself from the sofa. He rose quickly, pushing up with his thighs and using his arms for leverage. Whether he thought Passmore wouldn't shoot or he'd be on him before Passmore could do anything, it's hard to say. Maybe he was just sick of it all.

I moved forward but his strong left arm brushed me aside.

And Passmore turned and fired.

In his panic he didn't see Anjelica had moved in front of her father to stop him rushing forward. The shot was still echoing in the room when blood began to seep from her right shoulder blade and moments later she started to fall. Strano caught her around the waist and I stepped back, out of the way. Her eyes were still open but were already glazing over from the shock.

Passmore let out a sound that was neither a cry nor a moan but something in-between. I think in that second he was truly horrified by what he'd become. He threw down the weapon, lifted a hand to his mouth, then turned and ran from the room.

Strano said, 'Get him!'

'Wait ...'

I gave Passmore five seconds to get out of the house and then moved quickly after him. I hoped I had the timing right.

Strano shouted after me, 'Run!'

By the time I reached the front door Passmore had almost reached his car.

But he wasn't going to get in it and drive away because four Asian men had surrounded him. One of them clubbed him to the ground with a heavy fist and then each man bent and took a limb and carried him struggling down the drive and around the corner of the garden hedge. One of the men had put a black bag over his head.

A moment later a long dark limousine pulled in front of the drive and a rear window slid down. A craggy Asian face wearing sunglasses stared at me, then raised a hand and waved three fingers in a small gesture of acknowledgement. Seconds later the smoked-glass window went up and the car drove away as silently as a ghost ship.

CHAPTER THIRTY-SIX

WHEN PHAR AND his associates were arrested at the airport where they were boarding his private jet, the arresting officers found Passmore in the boot of the limousine, breathing hoarsely through a sock. Both his arms and his legs were broken, the little fingers of each hand had been chopped off and his nose had been slit the way Roman Polanski slit Jack Nicholson's in *Chinatown*, with a knife shearing up from inside a nostril. Phar was a movie buff, it seemed, and he'd always wanted to do that.

I was in two minds whether to be disappointed or not that he'd been found. Passmore had brought it on his own head by submitting to his addictions, and he'd certainly got into bed with the wrong people in Jack Jenkins and Phar. But I wondered whether he was a victim, too. A victim of his own psychology, certainly, and his lack of personal restraint. And also a victim of a culture that thought it rational to not only permit gambling on an almost industrial scale, but practically to coerce it. You couldn't watch a football match on television without being hounded to bet on its outcome during the commercial break. The late-evening schedules were filled with programmes where people phoned in to test their gambling skills against the silent forces of Fate in its many guises, whether it was a roulette wheel or some so-called unbiased computer that asked random general knowledge questions. You could play poker online with people you never even saw, or buy lotto tickets cheaply and wait for another computer to turn up your numbers.

Even I was earning money through gambling on the Bitcoin market.

Passmore seemed to parcel up all this negative energy and transform it into a series of misinformed or misdirected actions, fooling himself into believing he could beat the House and wind up a winner.

But you never beat the House.

TWO WEEKS AFTER being shot Anjelica was allowed home. She'd been lucky in that the bullet had ricocheted off her shoulder blade and exited without puncturing a lung or tearing away too much muscle. It must have narrowly missed her father on its way out and was found high up in her living room wall by the forensic staff sent to investigate. Luckily her father had some first-aid training and had been able to staunch the wound and keep her awake until the ambulance came and the paramedics took over.

When she'd been home for a week, I drove out to see her. The air was heavy with the threat of rain, dark clouds massing on the horizon just waiting for the word to strike. Lorenzo Strano answered the door and let me in. Now the season had changed from autumn to winter the central heating in the house was set to stun, presumably to suit the invalid. He led me through to the same living room I knew well. So well, I was beginning to wonder whether the place contained any other rooms.

Anjelica was sitting on the sofa wrapped in a silk house-coat and with her arm in a sling, her other hand holding a phone to her ear. Her hair had lost some of its sheen but despite the time she'd spent in hospital she was still astonishingly beautiful. She signed off quickly when she saw me enter and then smiled.

'How's the homeless man doing? Is life on the streets as tough as they say?'

'I signed for the rebuild today. They reckon it will take fifteen weeks once they've cleared out the rubble of the old one.'

'Who's paying? Insurance?'

'Yes, but they're getting a hefty load back from the police. They've more or less admitted Passmore had it burned down by Asian gangsters. Once those boys started talking it was apparently hard to stop them. The one called David had a particular gripe to get off his chest.'

Strano said, 'Howard was here the other day. He said Phar's going back to the States. They've got him on operating an illegal gambling business.'

'How do you feel about that?'

'I don't give a shit about him. It's Passmore and Jenkins I want to see suffer.'

Belinda had rounded up Jenkins and his two henchmen and put them in the back of the white panel van they'd been driving. She told Howard where to find them eventually. After they'd shared the back of the van for a few hours, nursing their wounds.

Strano sat down next to his daughter. 'I don't know what happened to me. I was paralysed. I couldn't see anything but Anjie and her mum being hurt by Passmore and his crew. I couldn't trust anyone, not even you when you came to help.'

I sat in a facing chair. 'I wasn't exactly tactful myself. I should have twigged earlier you were under some kind of threat. You weren't acting rationally.'

'That's because I wasn't in a rational frame of mind.'

We fell quiet for a moment. I didn't know about them, but for my part I was going over what had happened in that room the last time I was there. When you're in the middle of a series of events that seem to be heading in one direction you have no perspective. Afterwards, you wonder how you got into that situation and what's more, how you coped. I'd been in that position more often than Strano or his daughter but it still surprised me when I contemplated what had happened with Jenkins, Passmore and Phar. It was like being in a fugue state which took over your waking life so there seemed to be no escape.

Eventually Anjelica said, 'So who's making tea?'

Strano stood up. 'My job.'

He left and Anjelica and I looked at each other. I was full of regret and anger and a kind of suppressed desire but I couldn't express any of it, and I certainly had no idea what was passing through her mind. She didn't seem any more keen to share her thoughts than I was, and I wondered how she'd cope with the new relationship with her father.

In the end I turned to banalities. I said, 'How long will it take to recover?'

'From this?' She glanced at her shoulder. 'Lots of surgery, physio. It can take two years, apparently, and even then I might not get full mobility back.'

'You don't sound too worried.'

'What can I do? If I hadn't been there he would have got Dad right in the chest. Though of course he was the stupid bugger who forced Passmore to shoot in the first place.'

'When are you going back to work?'

'When I can. I do phone calls and stuff but I get tired quickly. All the drugs in my body. I won't be going anywhere for a while. Dad's staying here now so he says he'll look after me.'

I looked around in surprise. 'Is this place big enough for two people?'

'Ha ha. He's set up his own company as well. Working as a security adviser. The cops offered him his job back when they saw the reports you found in Passmore's house, and then the rest when they raided it themselves. It was obvious what Billy had done. But Dad didn't want to work for them any more.'

'Can't say I blame him. Incidentally ...'

'Yes?'

'If you want any running around I can do it. I received a very generous cheque from you this week so I can spare some time, if you'd like.'

She smiled and looked me up and down.

'Why, Mr Dyke, I do believe you're trying to make friends.'

'It's one of the rules you learn in private detective school: if you can't prevent a client getting shot, at least make sure they don't sue.'

I LEFT THE house mid-afternoon and drove back to Dan's place. I'd given him instructions to be ready for 3:00 so we'd miss the rush-hour traffic.

He was sitting on a chair in the living room reading a book, a stuffed roll-bag lying at his feet.

'Hi, Dad.'

'You had something to eat? I don't want to stop for a burger or a tin of boiled sweets.'

'I'm done. Beans on toast. You put petrol in the car?'

I looked through the window at the new Mondeo sitting on the drive. The insurance company had come through quickly and it didn't take me long to find a replacement vehicle.

He put down his book and stared at the carpet for a moment. When he looked up there was uncertainty and hesitation in his eyes.

'I need to tell you something before we go.'

I sat down facing him. 'What's up?'

'I hope you're going to be all right with it.'

'Spit it out.'

'Well ... I'm gay.'

'All right.'

'There's someone I've been seeing. You know, when I've been going out. Like that night you were here.'

'Good for you. About time.'

'When I was going with Kelly I thought it might help, you know. Persuade me I could be straight.'

'You are what you are. It sometimes takes time to sink in and accept it.'

'So you're all right with it?'

'Look, I know I'm from Yorkshire but I'm not an ogre. If you're happy, I'm happy. Don't fret about it.'

'That's cool.'

I reached a hand across his low coffee table and we shook. I said, 'I'm ready. The trip'll only take a couple of hours. Your grandmother's cooking one of her meat-and-potato pies. You'll love it.'

'Will I?'

'Yes. Or you're no son of mine.'

Final Note

Thank you for reading this book. I'd be grateful if you could write a review on Amazon or any other site you wish.

Thanks again.
Keith Dixon

TURN THE PAGE TO READ CHAPTER ONE OF THE NEXT EXCITING BOOK IN THIS SERIES, *THE SECRET SHARERS*!

BONUS CHAPTER – THE SECRET SHARERS

CHAPTER ONE

THERE WAS A MAN sitting in my office at nine o'clock that morning, and there were two things wrong with this picture.

First, he was sitting in my chair. And second, I'd locked the office door the previous night.

He added a third wrong thing by lying about it: 'Hope you don't mind, the door was open.'

He was a respectable-looking geezer somewhere in his sixties with a long, serious face and wearing a country gentleman's outfit—a green Barbour jacket, a grey flat cap, and, poking out from under my desk, a pair of solid brown shoes, probably by Church. There was a thin walnut cane leaning against the desk. My desk. His eyes were steady and there was a slightly challenging air about the way he reclined in the seat and waited for my response.

I came into the room and closed the door and considered putting my hands on my hips to show how offended I was.

I said, 'If you're selling subscriptions to Country Life, I have to tell you I sold my horse and hounds pack last year.

Couldn't afford all that raw meat.'

He grinned. 'I knew you were a witty man. When I read that interview with you in the Manchester Evening News I could tell you had a sense of humour.'

A few months ago I'd been involved in preventing a frustrated ideologue carry out a plan to gas commuters in Piccadilly Station in Manchester. My punishment had been a certain amount of notoriety for a week, including the kind of media exposure that you think is going to be good for business but never is. The public have such short memories.

The man went on, 'I hope you're not upset by my being here. When I found the door open I thought it much more sensible to come inside and wait rather than clutter up the corridor.'

'You and I both know the door wasn't open. There isn't a mark on it, so it wasn't forced. And I know I locked it last night.'

'Are you certain? How can you be certain about anything?'

'Can I have my chair back, please?'

'Oh, certainly.'

He stood up and made great play of pulling the chair out and presenting it for me. Then he walked around to the other side of the desk and sat down in one of the upright client chairs. I took my seat, noticing that he'd left his walking stick on my side. I handed it to him and he accepted it with a gracious bow of his head.

He said, 'So, Mr Dyke, I suppose we should get down to business now.'

'I'm not looking for any more clients at the moment. My case load is full.'

He seemed taken aback at this and pursed his lips, which were white and thin.

'That's unfortunate. I suppose all the publicity you received as a result of your recent cases means that adulterers and fraudsters are beating a path to your door.'

'Describing my work like that isn't likely to dispose me towards taking on your case, is it?'

He raised his hands palm up in apology.

'I'm sorry, I'm lapsing into stereotype.'

'Look, what exactly is it that you want, Mr … ?'

He lowered his hands and looked at the back of them, as though surprised to find the liver spots and raised veins that confronted him. Then he lifted his eyes towards me and there was an urgency behind them that was new.

He said, 'My name is Frank Wallace. And I want you to watch me.'

AFTER MY LAST couple of big cases I didn't want anything complicated or even mildly dangerous. I'd basked a little in the respect I'd been shown in my local pub and at the garage when I'd bought petrol for my new car … but work-wise, I'd wanted tranquillity. For one thing, I'd had to organise the rebuilding of my house, which had been burned to the ground by some oriental thugs, taking my clothes, furniture and—not least—my CD collection with it.

So I'd gone back to the mundane jobs that had been meat-and-drink for me in the last few years—benefit fraudsters, rent-skippers, identity checks and so on.

On the rare occasions I thought about it, I realised I'd been bunkering-down, like a tortoise who'd had too much of the outside world and preferred his own shell to the glamorous temptation of the next lettuce leaf. I hadn't been speaking much to my son, Dan, though he continued to look after my Bitcoin portfolio and do research for me; nor had I been in contact with my some-time partner, Belinda McFee. I was becoming that rare beast, the Reclusive Detective, seen only in the glare of a camera flash or in a back-alley talking to someone you'd normally cross the street to avoid.

Frank Wallace had been watching me think and must have thought I was considering taking him on as a client. He said, 'What do you need to know? How do we do this?'

'I'm sorry, Mr Wallace, but I wasn't flapping my lips for the sake of it. I'm too busy to take the case. And besides, why do you want me to watch you?'

He smiled slowly. 'See, I knew you'd be interested.'

'Call it a mild curiosity.'

He'd taken hold of his walking cane and now rapped it once against the edge of my desk, as if he were firing a starter's gun.

'I used to work as a project manager at the Toyota factory in Derby. Well, outside Derby, actually. You've probably been past it on your travels.'

'I've seen the road signs.'

'Exactly. Big place. Anyway, that's all besides the point. Except insofar as to say that towards the end of my working life there I had a … well, I suppose you'd call it an affair.' He looked at me, grinning, as though it was rather devilish for someone of an advanced age to have such an adventure. 'You must understand that my wife died years ago, but the woman I was seeing was well and truly married. The affair carried on for a couple of years and then I retired and for one reason or another we never saw each other again.'

'So what's the problem?'

'Someone's watching me. Even following me.'

'Are you certain? You're sure you're not just imagining it?'

He looked cross. 'Don't patronise me, Mr Dyke. I'm not going senile and I'm not making this up. I've seen the man in the street, in his car, down at the café. He's been there for a couple of weeks.'

'Who do you think he is?'

'Don't you see? Wendy's husband must have found out and is observing me.'

'For what reason?'

'How should I know? Perhaps he wants to bump me off.'

He put inverted commas around this phrase with his voice and his eyes danced with the perversity of the idea.

I said, 'This is all a bit far-fetched, if you don't mind me saying. How do you know this man is really watching you and not just going about his own business? You've become aware of him once or twice and now you're seeing him everywhere.'

He leaned back in the chair and glanced out of my window on to the streets of Crewe. The morning was gaining some heat and the pavements were beginning to whiten in the glare of the early sun.

He said, 'You know when the back of your neck bristles? And you turn around because you think someone's just said your name, or has come into a room when you thought you were alone? It's that feeling. Sometimes I see him and sometimes I don't but I know he's there even when I *can't* see him.'

He said all this in a melancholy tone, but he suddenly

brightened and reached inside his green jacket, pulling out a thick wallet. He opened it and extracted a fistful of notes. He rested his elbow on my desk and held the notes in the air like a prize. Thankfully he didn't wave them or I might have snatched them from his hand.

'There's three thousand, five hundred pounds here. We'll call it a down payment. Seven days at five hundred pounds a day, which I guess is about your going rate. When can you start?'

I stared at him with exasperation. I wasn't as busy as I'd led him to believe, but I couldn't see this working. He was acting like a paranoid pensioner looking for a spot of adventure to brighten his drab days.

In the end, I said, 'I don't need all that as a retainer.'

'Nonsense. And there's more where that came from.' He placed the cash on the desktop then took out a business card from the wallet and laid it next to the money. 'These are my numbers and my address. Do we have to sign a contract of some kind and identify milestones and goals and so forth?'

He really was a project manager.

Wearily, I said, 'I'll get one in the post to you.'

'If you have it in pdf format you can email it and I'll sign it electronically, if that would suffice.'

'Fine.'

I was actually thinking it might not get that far.

He said, 'Let's be clear: there are two things that I want to come out of this. First, I want to be sure I'm being followed. Secondly, I want to know by whom. Do we understand each other?'

I assured him I knew what he wanted, but even as I was telling him this I wondered when I'd actually agreed to take the job. Then I asked myself how hard it could be … watch his place for a while, follow him to his local café or bank, persuade him he's been imagining the whole thing. Perhaps it would be good for me to work for a private individual again, rather than the local government types who'd made up the majority of my clients for the last couple of months.

I didn't realise the irony of that thought for several weeks.

Wallace began to gather himself together, putting away his wallet and picking up his cane. He said, 'When will you start?'

'It's probably better if you don't know. And I have a question for you.'

'Oh, good.'

'If you believe you're being followed by this man, how do you know he didn't follow you here?'

His reply should have made me think twice about taking on the case right there.

He said, 'Because I made sure he didn't.'

Also by Keith Dixon

The Sam Dyke Series

Altered Life
The Private Lie
The Hard Swim
The Bleak
The Strange Girl
The Secret Sharers
The Innocent Dead
The Lonely Grave
The Second Guess (short story)

The Paul Storey Thriller Series

Storey
One Punch
The Song of Geneva Chance

Standalone Novels

A French Darcy – a Romance
Actress – a Contemporary novel

Essays on Writing

The Idle Writer
Crime Writing Confidential

Blog

www.cwconfidential.blogspot.com

Webpage

http://www.keithdixonnovels.com